To Mat

THE JACKASS FRIGATE

THE JACKASS FRIGATE

BY

ALARIC BOND

Fireship Press
www.FireshipPress.com

The Jackass Frigate - Copyright © 2009 by Alaric Bond

ISBN-13: 978-1-934757-73-4
ISBN-10: 1-934757-73-X

BISAC Subject Headings:
    FIC014000   FICTION / Historical
    FIC032000   FICTION / War & Military

Address all correspondence to:
Fireship Press, LLC
P.O. Box 68412
Tucson, AZ 85737
USA

Or visit our website at:
www.FireshipPress.com

1.0

CHAPTER ONE

She was fresh from the dockyard, and as King made his way along the lower deck of HMS *Pandora*, he was conscious of her strangely sweet aroma. It was the scent of tender paint mingled with fresh cut wood and new canvas; quite at odds with the normal shipboard smells of wet rot, bilges and closely packed humanity. What light there was strained through the frigate's hatches and the grating forward of the main mast, only this and his innate instinct for ship's architecture told him he was outside the starboard midshipmen's berth. He opened the screen door and stepped in.

It was a dark, narrow room with a deckhead just lower than five feet. Directly opposite, to the other side of the passageway the larboard berth would be a mirror image; together they provided a home for all the midshipmen and master's mates, as well as an eclectic assortment of other junior warrant officers. At that moment the berth was empty; *Pandora* was still working up and not yet carrying her full complement. King dropped his ditty bag next to a small table and looked about.

His last berth had been the wardroom of a sixty-four where he had carried an order as acting lieutenant for a heady and eventful few weeks. Since then, although he had passed his examination board, his commission was still to be confirmed and his sense of adventure, coloured not a little by hunger and an extreme lack of funds, had persuaded him to volunteer for *Pandora* at his former rank of midshipman. The table held a half burnt purser's dip. King fumbled with a flint and lit the wick. The fat-fed flame burned grubbily, instantly adding a dense cast to the already stuffy cockpit. There was a little consolation in the knowledge that a short distance along what was often, erroneously, called the gundeck, senior and commissioned officers would be sharing similarly uncomfortable conditions in the frigate's version of the wardroom that was equally inaccurately known as the gunroom.

The screen door opened and a marine appeared, looking oddly casual in shirtsleeves and seaman's duck trousers.

"Mr King?"

"That's right."

"Mr Fraiser sent me to see to you, sir."

"Very good. The rest of my dunnage is being taken down."

"Deep storage is for'ard, near t'surgeon's dispensary. I'll see to it after sortin' your berth, sir."

King nodded, although his head was already bent to clear the deckhead and much of the effect was lost.

"What's your name?"

"Collins, sir." Even out of uniform and in the cramped and gloomy conditions, the voice of the marine sounded firm and businesslike.

"Very good, Collins. How many other cockpit officers are aboard?"

"One master's mate berths in 'ere, sir. Then there are two other mids and a volunteer; one of them's a big bastard, but youngsters they are, none the less." He grew confidential. "Two of 'em will be first voyagers, I reckons, 'spite what it might say in their papers. They've taken the larboard berth, along with Mr Manning, who the captain's trying out as surgeon's mate; he's little more'n a squealer hi'self. T'other master's mates an' the clerk 'as yet to be appointed. An' there's no news of a chaplain." He grinned suddenly, treating King to a sight of his blackened teeth. "Might 'ave got away there."

Two young midshipmen and a lad, that didn't auger well for King, who would be in charge of training them up. He decided to leave them to their berth; they would spend enough time together without sharing the same quarters.

Where's the other master's mate?"

"Mr Lewis, sir. He's in the chart room at present."

"Lewis?"

"Yes, sir. Come down from the *Essex*, I believe."

HMS *Essex* was the nearby receiving ship, a permanently moored hulk that took in the harvest of the local press, as well as acting as an accommodation and training ship for junior officers.

"Thank you, Collins. I'll berth in here; set out my things, will you?"

"Very good, sir."

The marine turned to King's bag and began to sort the contents into the small locker that would hold all his ready use clothes as well as his razor, comb, and quadrant, and other personal equipment. There would be little space for much else, although he had once shared with a man who insisted on bringing a cockatoo into the berth. The bird had lasted three days before dying in mysterious circumstances.

Left alone King mused about the identity of the other warrant officer. A man named Lewis had been an able seaman in his last ship; in fact King was his divisional officer. He remembered him as being of roughly his own age; exceptionally bright and, more importantly, the type that men naturally respected. King had put him forward for promotion and had been pleased to learn he had been warranted after *Vigilant* paid off. If this was the same man it would be good to see him again, although King held a slight reservation about working with an officer of equivalent rank who had served under him as a lower deck hand.

There was one way of finding out; the sea chest that sat against the bulkhead would belong to Lewis. King picked up the warm dip and carried it across. The name HMS *Vigilant*, though crossed through in the naval tradition, still stood out plainly as the owner's previous ship.

"Mr King?"

With a taint of guilt King turned to see the well-remembered, though cautious smile.

"Lewis! I'd hoped it was you, I wish you joy!"

Lewis mumbled something in a shy, low voice, although his handshake was warm and firm.

"Why I haven't seen you..."

"Since *Vigilant*, sir?"

"That's right, quite a time, eh?" King gave a meaningful glance at the marine, still poring over his clothes in the corner of the berth. "There's no need for the 'sir', I've yet to be confirmed. On deck we'd better keep to the formals, but down here I'm Thomas."

"And I, William." They both smiled again, the smile of men united by past experiences.

"Might you show me the ship?" King asked.

"Aye. Now's a safe time, Mr Pigot'll be asleep, more'n like."

"Mr Pigot?"

"First lieutenant." Lewis opened his mouth to say more, then seemed to think better of it. "What say we start with the fo'c'sle?"

King followed him out of the berth, his mild confusion about the strange reference to the first lieutenant vanishing as they began to explore the frigate. He would have a bunch of adolescent reefers to knock into shape, and there was about as much chance of having his commission confirmed this side of the century as being made bishop, but it was always good to meet up with a former shipmate, and he knew in his bones that he and Lewis would work well together.

*****

"Good on yer, Josh!" Wright felt an overwhelming sense of joy flow through his body as his friends thronged about him, slapping him on the back and shaking both of his hands in their excitement. He looked across to where Jenny was being equally mobbed by shrieking females. Their eyes met and the love that had been steadily growing between them became almost tangible.

"Well, Joshua. It don't do to stand about here all day!" His father's voice was unusually gruff, hiding emotion that threatened to take him over. "We got a 'pointment at The Star; folks'll be waiting."

In fact most of those invited to the wedding reception were already with them, but Wright allowed himself to be steered out of the churchyard and on to the lane that led to their village. Jenny caught him up, and thrust her hand under his arm. They were both still smiling, as they had been for as long as each could remember. Wright stopped to brush a length of auburn hair that was trespassing across her face. Her black eyes shone lovingly at him, and there was little holding back the tears as her arm gave his an involuntary squeeze.

At half past four the dull December day was drawing to a close, but there was just light enough for them to find their way along the track. Their friends grouped about them as they went, laughing and shouting in such a way as to draw smiles from strangers that passed by. In no time The Star appeared in the gloom, lamps flickering at the small square windows. There was Jack, the landlord, waiting for them at the step, waiting to greet the happy couple and their friends, most of whom were already good customers, and all about to become a good deal better in the next few hours.

"Tables are set in the back room, Josh. Betty will be in to look after Mrs Wright shortly." The landlord smiled, a rare occasion in itself, adding his congratulations and a slap on the back for good measure.

"Take yer coat, lad, and get yon seated." His father slipped the long tailed jacket from his son's shoulders as Josh helped Jenny to her chair. The jacket had been borrowed from Mr Johnson, the apothecary who acted as doctor to the small community. Josh had been a sailor since he was fourteen, and for all of those eight years he had never owned or needed a jacket longer than the standard naval "round" design that ended just below the waist.

Jenny pushed her hair, hair that by now was becoming decidedly unruly, back beneath her veil. The two had known each other for most of their lives. For most of their lives they had fought and played together, sharing pranks, chills and the occasional fight, and living less than twenty yards from the other's home. When Josh went to sea the separation only made their friendship stronger. By the time he returned from his last voyage, a three-year Indies trip in a third rate, their wedding had been simply a matter of course; a formality that gave public acknowledgment to the love that was as natural to them as breathing.

"A glass of ale, Josh?" Ruben's voice this time, breaking through the hubbub with difficulty.

"Glass? Now there's a fancy," Wright boomed. "Since when have you known Jack to possess a glass?" The rise in laughter was stifled as the landlord reappeared carrying a small tray.

"It's glasses for yon today, Josh," he said, placing a pint of Porter in front of him. "An' for you, Mr Wright." Jack's father also accepted a drink. "Rest on you'll have pewter, same as normal, an' mind; those who dents 'em, gets to mends 'em."

Jenny had also acquired a glass of beer, although not from Jack, who never served women. She raised it in the air, tapping twice against Wright's, before they both drank to further cheers from the crowd. Food began to appear, and soon the noise subsided as the wedding guests settled themselves to the serious task of feeding. Josh's father was at his side, a place he had occupied on every practicable occasion for as long as each could remember.

"Make the most of this, Joshua, only happens once." Wright nodded. It could have happened twice for his father, whose wife had been dead some twelve years, although both knew the old man had never considered marrying again. "In a week's time yo'll be at sea, more'n like."

"More'n like," Wright agreed, although strangely the idea didn't worry him. This was the happiest day he could recall, and part of him wanted nothing more than to be with Jenny forever. But the sea held as firm a claim on him as the love for his new wife. The sea, in all its moods; life on board a man-of-war, the only vessel worth shipping in, if he was any judge, and the travel that opened up, not only new worlds, new experiences, but an extra portion of his life. "This one's a frigate," he told his father. "Reckon we might see a bit of action."

A frigate. Not the largest, but with all the dash of her class. Wright had signed, on condition he be allowed to stay ashore until the following Friday. The impressment men were reasonably happy with the arrangement; he had come as a volunteer after all.

"If it's action yon lookin' for, best keep bright," his father told him. "You've more'n one to look after now."

"Aye, an' it could be two, if him plays 'is cards right!" Ruben's voice broke through again, as common as ever. Wright grinned gamely, while Jenny pretended not to hear the comment, or the laughter that followed.

"That's as maybe, that's as maybe," said his father, to whom the idea of grandchildren was more than agreeable. "Get you back sound, an' you can think of families at your leisure."

"Come back with prize money, Josh," said Ruben, ever the realist.

"Riches beyond measure!"

"Buy up old Jack's!"

"Aye, give us'n decent pot house!"

During the laughter Jenny caught his eye.

"Just come back safe," she said, softly. "And soon."

*****

HMS *Pandora* was certainly small for her rate; armed with twenty-eight long nine-pounders as the main armament, with thirty-two-pound carronades on her forecastle and quarterdeck and a handful of popgun chasers. Her lines had been copied from a French capture, giving her a sleek hull, just under one hundred and thirty feet long, with a midships barely in excess of thirty one feet. A sixth rate, commonly known as a "Jackass," she was considered, by some, to be too small for the large jobs and too large for the small. The class had been superseded by the more powerful twelve and eighteen-pounder thirty-twos, and was decidedly inferior to the thirty-six gun frigates that were now appearing at increasingly shorter intervals. And now the French were building forty-fours; devastating ships that delivered more than twice *Pandora's* broadside weight from a hull far stronger, yet every bit as fast.

Lieutenant Pigot considered this as he swaggered confidently along the quarterdeck, and stared out over the waist. In fact the chances were very strong that any enemy worth the fight would be considerably more powerful, while there were barely enough men on board for a successful cutting out expedition. She might fare well with a sloop, but where was the prestige in that? And it was prestige that he needed; a dashing ship-to-ship action; or even a successful cruise; something that would pluck him from the mediocrity of the lieutenants' list, and on to that vital step to commander. At forty-nine, Pigot knew that he was by no means too old, although his brother, Hugh, was already a post captain. A post captain, two steps ahead of him, and with a jaunty little frigate of his own to command. However fast he made his promotion, Hugh would be ahead, while each ensuing year diminished the hope of even making it onto the captains' list. There would have to be something dramatic; something to make the rest of the world take notice of him and undergunned, undermanned and undersized as she was, *Pandora* could easily be his last chance.

He smiled grimly to himself; if it was to be a last chance, he'd make the best of it, and that began with setting the right impression on the men.

Turning back he started to pace the quarterdeck once more, hands clasped behind his back, and chin jutting forward in an attitude he had decided made him appear tough and forthright.

"Bosun!" he shouted, stopping suddenly. "The main futtock shrouds are slack." He pointed forward to the maintop. Johns, the boatswain, who was rather less than bored at that moment, looked up doubtfully.

"We've topmasts down, sir," he began, but the look of fury on Pigot's face stopped him.

"See to it."

Johns moved away, summoning up a mate and two topmen with a wave of his hand. Pigot watched them as they looked up at the futtock shrouds, and saw one shake his head.

"I'm not asking for a discussion!" he bellowed. The men moved as one, and within seconds were clambering up the main shrouds to the top.

Pigot resumed his walk, pleased with the ripples he had created. This was his second stint as a first lieutenant, although his previous ship, a tarty little sloop that showed a remarkable disinclination to hold any degree of weather helm, had carried no other commissioned officer apart from her aged commander. At least with *Pandora* he would have a bit more clout; some regular men to supervise and see that all was done properly. By the time they sailed there would be another lieutenant, as well as four mids and two master's mates; more than enough for the everyday tasks that dogged an overworked first luff.

The master appeared on deck and they exchanged nods. Pigot disliked Fraiser, although that hardly distinguished him from any other officer the first lieutenant had come across. A capable enough fellow, but too intent on his reading, and rather keen on these new theories for defining longitude. Because of this, and his whining to the captain, *Pandora* now boasted two chronometers of a very up to date design. That would have been acceptable in itself, except that Fraiser was still absorbed with lunar tables and constant sightings, testing out the various mathematical theories of determining their east-west positioning. For the past five days he and one of the master's mates had spent each afternoon watch scratching out reams of calculations, presumably attempting to work out the exact position of one of the busiest ports in England. This annoyed Pigot on several levels; first that someone should take an interest, let alone positive pleasure, in mathematical calculations, something he was prepared to encounter only when the situation absolutely demanded it. And second, because there was little he could actually do about the situation; as master, Fraiser was charged with the navigation of the ship. There was nothing in his actions that constituted a threat to discipline, or the captain's authority, and Fraiser, although not actually commissioned, was an important officer, one that he could ride heavily over only at great risk.

There was still that master's mate, however. In fact he could see him now, walking along the larboard gangway, with an unknown midshipman in tow.

"Mr Lewis!" Pigot's voice carried a deep, guttural rasp that had taken many years to perfect.

Lewis stopped, turned, and stood at attention in one fast, fluid movement that caught King by surprise.

"Sir!"

Rather than say more, Pigot merely extended his right hand in a childish beckoning motion that was intentionally demeaning to those it addressed. Lewis made his way aft at a brisk walk and King, uncertain at first if he was also required, hurriedly followed behind.

"We have a stranger aboard, Mr Lewis," Pigot informed him when both young men were on the quarterdeck.

"Yes, sir. This is Mr Midshipman King. He came aboard..."

"I am quite certain Mr King can speak for himself." The heavy eyes fell upon King, who stood uncertainly under their gaze. "Well, Mr King?"

It was an uncomfortable moment; clearly something was expected, and yet he had no idea what. It wasn't even a situation for a simple 'Yes, sir', usually the midshipman's panacea for all awkward questions.

"Mr Midshipman King, reporting for appointment to His Majesty's Ship, *Pandora*. I have my papers below, in..."

"Rather late, Mr King?" Pigot persisted.

"Sir, I was ordered to be aboard within five days of..."

"Oh, I am quite certain of it. But you did not see fit to present yourself to me on arrival?"

"Mr King reported to me, Mr Pigot." The master's low voice, that held just a hint of his native accent, cut in. Pigot fixed him with his stare, conscious that he could not continue on the same course and that a change of tack was called for.

"Mr Fraiser, I would appreciate it if you would not interfere in matters that do not concern you." That was the way to deal with meddling busybodies; there was nothing in the statement that

Fraiser could object to, and he had given what would appear to everyone as a warning shot. Satisfied, he turned back to King.

"You should present yourself to a commissioned officer upon joining a ship." Not strictly true, although he could hardly resist the further dig at Fraiser.

"Boat ahoy!" the call from the forecastle lookout broke into all their thoughts.

"Aye, Aye," came the reply; that would mean an officer coming on board, although from the larboard side, and not the captain. Pigot stiffened; this would be the other lieutenant, his junior. A lot would depend on the character of this man.

"Very well, that will do." He turned away from the two warrant officers and walked back towards the taffrail to await the newcomer.

It did not take long; Lieutenant Caulfield was on the quarterdeck facing Pigot within two minutes of the hail. He introduced himself, extending a gentle handshake that Pigot accepted reluctantly. The newcomer was young, under thirty, although premature baldness made him appear older. He was also short and almost plump, with a round, sensitive face, and a pleasant smile.

"Glad to have you aboard, Mr Caulfield," Pigot muttered, his face betraying any truth that his words may have held. "The captain's ashore, expected on the morrow, and we're to weigh as soon as we finish victualling."

"I see; any rumours as to where?"

"Rumours are for children and washerwomen, Mr Caulfield. You will be informed of everything you need to know as soon as it is necessary."

Despite the rebuke Caulfield was perceptive enough to deduce that Pigot was equally ignorant of their destination, and resented the fact. A young, but heavily built midshipman approached them, apologetically touching his hat.

"What is it?" Pigot did not know the names of most of *Pandora's* junior officers, and almost none of her people, and was in no great rush to learn.

"Beggin' your pardon, sir," the boy spoke in a faltering voice that was clearly on the very edge of breaking. "We was wonderin' what to do with Mr Caulfield's dunnage."

"Dunnage?" Pigot grunted impatiently. "Stow it in the usual manner, damn you!"

"Yes, sir. Only it was 'is instrument, sir. Mr Caulfield's man says to put it in the gunroom, but there's never the space."

Caulfield smiled. "My 'cello. It's reasonably new and the maker was worried it might come to harm. You see the timbers need to acclimatise, and the officers' store would be too cold, and probably damp; condensation, don't you know?"

"Your 'cello?" Pigot's voice could not have held more displeasure if Caulfield had just introduced an elephant into the ship.

"Yes, I play a little. Strictly for my own pleasure, of course."

Pigot turned away, and Caulfield's ready smile increased slightly as he addressed the midshipman.

"What's your name?"

"Cobb, sir."

"Very good, Mr Cobb. Place the 'cello in my cabin for the time being, I'm sure I can find a home for it." The boy touched his hat once more and disappeared from the deck.

"Do you intend to play this instrument in the ship?" Pigot still held his back to the new lieutenant, apparently addressing the horizon as he spoke.

Caulfield inclined his head slightly to the older man. "I do not intend to be a nuisance, I am sure that an occasional practice will not cause any ill feeling." He smiled to himself. "Besides, there may be others with a musical bent; perhaps a small orchestra, who knows?"

Pigot swung round to face him; Caulfield met and held his eye without flinching, and for a moment nothing was said. Then Pigot turned back, giving his entire attention to a seventy-four that was setting up topmasts, while Caulfield, smiling slightly at his back, went below to take care of his 'cello.

*****

Frigates, as a class, were relatively spacious; even the largest packed a crew less than half that of a line of battle ship into a hull almost as long, while the absence of guns on the lower deck gave a large, uncluttered area for accommodation. But what was gained in space was offset by a decrease in temperature; the absence of compact living conditions meant less of the airless fug that sailors had come to expect below, and in northern waters cold, with all its associated medical complications, could wear a body out long before the end of a commission. Decks free of guns were also far less private, there being no ridged divisions between each mess so that, on the first evening with something approaching their expected complement, and the novel ship mildly daunting to all but the most seasoned of hands, there was an atmosphere of quiet expectation on the lower deck.

Jameson and Flint shared the same mess and, being that they had been on the first draft, it was in a good spot; just aft of the foremast and almost directly beneath the galley stove. It was Friday, a Banyan day when no meat was served, and the men had just eaten through substantial portions of pease pudding with cabbage and onions, and were about to start on their duff and cheese.

"So you two have served together afore?" Wright, who had joined the ship that afternoon, asked, as he bit into a hard chunk of Warwickshire cheese.

"Aye, we were in *Vigilant*," Flint confirmed, all too aware of the effect his words would have.

"*Vigilant*, eh?" Wright had been on the other side of the world when the antiquated sixty-four had slogged it out against a far superior force, but even he was aware of the ship and what she had achieved. "You saw a touch of action then?"

"We did." For a moment Flint met Jameson's eye, but no more was said about a time that had changed both of their lives.

"An' since then?"

"Since then we took to the colliers, 'till Matthew here got a calling for change and a proper man-of-war."

Jameson accepted the responsibility with a grin, fully aware that they were both equally tired of working in under-manned and ill-equipped brigs.

"Thought it better to take the shilling and call our own berth, than to wait for the press to do it for us."

Wright nodded in appreciation. "An' it's more than a shillin' they've givin' out now." That was the truth; of late the bounty had been driven up to unheard-of heights. With the newly established Quota Act an untrained man might expect anything up to seventy pounds for making his mark, when just a few years before trained seaman, who went on to fight the country's major naval actions, had signed on for a mere five. Once enlisted, however, they could only expect their regular pay at a rate that had been set for over one hundred and fifty years.

"Aye," said Carter, an ordinary seaman from London. "Set you up proper, that do."

"Paid for my weddin' with mine," Wright reflected. "An' still enough over to leave for my wife."

"Wedding, you say?" Flint's ears had pricked up, not so much on account of Wright's marriage, as the possible excuse for celebration it might contain. "Then it's a party you'll be wanting!"

"A party?" Wright laughed. "Nay, not me!" But he picked up his leather tankard and drained it, just in case. "No, reckon I've had my fill of fiddlers, these last few days."

"Must be good to be married, though," Jameson this time. He had moved from boy to ordinary seaman by the judicial addition of a year or so to his age, although he still felt slightly awkward when joining in adult conversations. "Having someone, just for you as it were, must be a good feelin'."

"Long as it is just for you!" Carter was keen on discussions concerning sexual infidelities and would encourage them whenever possible.

"No, not my Jenny." Wright accepted a top-up from Jameson. "She's straight an' sound, she is."

"Few women you can say that about," Carter continued, hopefully.

"Say it 'bout her, I've no doubts," Wright confirmed, and for a while the others considered his situation with various degrees of doubt and envy.

"So, we know where we bound yet?" Wright broke the silence that had been of his own making. "A trip to New Holland, or scraping off some French coast on blockade?"

"Tight new ship, an' a sound captain, who can tell?" Flint's voice was low key, but there was an energy inside him he had not known since leaving *Vigilant*.

"We're working up quick," Carter added. "Quicker than any ship I been in afore."

"Aye, an' the buzz is Captain's comin' aboard permanent to-morrow."

"Do you think he'll tell us where we're going then?" Jameson asked.

"Aye," Flint assured him. "He'll tell us all we wants to know; where we're bound, what we'll do, an' how long it'll take to do it." The lad eyed him doubtfully. "Just as soon as we gets back."

*****

The first part was easy. As soon as she finished victualling, *Pandora* would be making for Gibraltar with mail, and then on to Jervis, and the Mediterranean squadron. Her captain, Sir Richard Banks, sat in the rolling carriage as it trundled towards Portsmouth. At twenty-six he was younger than either of his lieutenants and, as the product of interest, had barely enough proper sea time to be officially considered for his present rank. What time he had served had not been wasted, however. Two commissions, one based at the Leeward Islands and the other with the Jamaica squadron had proved him as an officer of exceptional ability. He had taken part in two major cutting out expeditions, commanding one, when a French schooner was taken under the very nose of shore batteries. There had also been numerous amphibious assaults around the Caribbean, raiding small fortresses and batteries. In the space of two years he earned an enviable reputation as well as substantial amounts of prize money, although, ironically, Banks had little use for either. His father's estate paid him an income in excess of most senior admirals' and as for reputation, if it had secured him command of *Pandora*, then all very well; if not, he would have found a ship using his father's connections. His last command, a fourteen-gun brig, was procured for him in this way, and had famously captured a privateer of nearly twice her size with remarkably few casualties. Now newly promoted and, for whatever reason, given *Pandora*, Banks looked forward to getting under way as soon as possible. He was established on the captains' list; if he stayed alive long enough he should assume flag rank by his early forties. And if he failed, if some stray, or intended shot took him, or if he fell to illness or disease, there would be few regrets. Life, like so many things, had been a gift to him, and Banks made a point of using every gift to the full.

The carriage ran through Petersfield, clearing the small town within minutes. He had been away from the ship for more than a week, organising his financial affairs for what was likely to be a long commission, and ordering the uniforms and stores that would be needed for foreign service. When he had last seen *Pandora* she had lacked topmasts, yards and most of her standing and running rigging. There had just been time enough to attend to all of this and the rest of the fitting out although, to be certain, he had made the right moves with the dockyard to see that they were not ignored. In addition *Pandora's* standing officers, the carpenter, boatswain, gunner, together with their crews, were sound, reliable men. He felt that he could depend on them to do their duties without the intervention of the first lieutenant; a man he did not know well and had yet to trust, respect, or like.

Banks was more confident about Fraiser, the sailing master. Although yet to prove himself as a navigator, he had already created a good impression with his attention to the ship's trim, having been making plans for the stowage of her stores even while she was still on the slips. Despite the fact that he readily admitted to preferring navigation to fighting, Fraiser appeared the ideal officer; conscientious, professional and sound; even without having met the majority of the others, Banks was glad to have at least one man he could rely upon.

The road was opening out now; they would be in Portsmouth before evening. He thought back over the last few days, his mind naturally centring on the final interview with Nepean at the Admiralty. Sir John Jervis was a true seaman; the kind men respected and would follow; it was ironic that, as soon as he had taken over from the somewhat cautious Hotham, the situation in the Mediterranean had deteriorated. After Leghorn had fallen and almost all Britain's allies had been systematically overrun by the French on land, many valuable supply bases had been lost. Then Spain, always a doubtful associate, turned against them. Nepean had been careful to say nothing definite, but Banks guessed that the days when British ships could sail the inland sea were numbered. The latest news was that Corsica had been abandoned and Elba was about to be evacuated. That would leave Gibraltar as the only British base supported, for the time being at least, by Portugal.

Portugal. For many years an ally, but now it seemed the French had other ideas. Nepean had told him candidly: a large invasion force, several thousand men, many heavy transports, and well protected by warships, was being prepared in Brest. British intelligence sources had been unable to discover the intended target, but in the Admiralty's opinion it would be Portugal, and her loss, together with the friendly bases at Lisbon, the Azores, and presumably South America, would be a devastating blow. Gibraltar could not withstand the pressure alone and the Mediterranean squadron would need to be withdrawn completely to reinforce the Channel fleet.

At home the recent harvest had been particularly bad; with that and Pitt's policy of repression, the average Englishman's spirit was at an all time low. There had never been, there probably never would be, a better time for the French to act: a successful invasion was almost inevitable.

It was into this confusion that they would be sailing, and there was no consolation in the knowledge that his would be a minor part; *Pandora* was a frigate, and faster than most. She and her like would be depended upon for communication, both within the squadron and beyond. Not for them the glory of a profitable cruise, nor could they stand in line and gain the mutual support of true battleships. It would be hard, exacting, and probably unrewarding work; responsibility would fall heavily on him, his ship and his men; he would have to be certain, equally certain, of all three.

CHAPTER TWO

The biscuits were being swayed up in large nets, each holding several one hundredweight bags. Wright was at the gangway over the open grating, watching the nets as they were lowered into the ship, where Fraiser, along with Lewis and Conroy, supervised their stowage in the bread room. Each bag held roughly seven hundred of the flat hard biscuits that were an important part of the seaman's diet; when fully laden *Pandora* would carry eight tons, enough to last over six months at sea.

"Next a comin'." Wright spoke in a clear voice that carried easily to Carter and Jameson, stationed on the lower deck. At the falls a team of waisters hauled up the net from the almost emptied lighter. There would be one more load, two at the most, and then a few moment's rest while the next lighter took her place.

Below, a team of stewards and holders were opening the nets and heaving the bags onto their shoulders. It was a short walk along the narrow wooden staging set above the casks of the main hold but, in her laden state, *Pandora's* deckhead was low, causing the men to seemingly bend double to clear it and making their work almost literally back breaking. Once past the hold they had the narrow passageway next to the magazine to negotiate before the bags could be stowed beneath the gunroom, well above the bilges and at the very stern of the ship.

Guppy, the master at arms, stood on the larboard gangway. His official duty was to care for the security of the ship and in that capacity he might as well be on the larboard gangway as anywhere. The men were far too busy with the stores to contemplate mutiny, desertion, or any of the more trivial crimes that were his province.

"That's it, last one!" Wright raised his hand as the heavy net swung up and over the side. He gave a wave to the crew of the empty lighter and looked across to where the next, sitting considerably lower in the water, was waiting. To either side of him hands cast off the first lighter and stood ready to receive the next. The December day was cold, although the weak sun still shone, and it was mercifully dry; Wright was quietly contemplating his grog and the dinner that would follow when he heard his name being shouted.

"Josh! Josh, over here!"

He looked around, uncertain as to who in the ship would call him so. The voice came again, and with a sudden realisation he looked for Jenny. Stupid though, she was many miles inland, and far further away in time: or so he thought. The shout was repeated; Flint standing next to him heard it as well, and then they both saw the waving figure in the second lighter.

"Jen', what you doin' here?"

Her face was alight with smiles, and her arm continued to wave as if possessed. The lighter crept closer until it was up against their side. It was madness: the woman he had just said goodbye to for what would probably be several years was standing less than twenty feet away from him.

"Father was comin' into town; he had a delivery for the victualling yard. Superintendent said he were loadin' your ship, and it were all right for me to come down."

The other men on the gangway grinned and began to make appropriate comments to Wright. Guppy, the master at arms, also started to show an interest.

"You shouldn't 'ave come, I got work to do." Wright's words, though stiffly spoken, carried a tenderness within and Jenny beamed back, pleased with herself and her ingenuity.

"What goes there? Eyes in the ship!" All stiffened at the voice of the first lieutenant, and even Jenny began to look slightly doubtful.

"Master at Arms, what's that a shoutin'?"

Guppy turned back to the quarterdeck. "One of the hands 'as recognised a friend, sir."

The spirit of the moment dissolved instantly as Pigot moved from the quarterdeck and on to the gangway, his tread echoing through the light decking.

"Take that man's name at once!" he bellowed, near enough for them to hear his boots squeak.

Guppy turned and pointed at Wright, a wicked gleam entering his eyes as he whispered, "You're for it now, matey!"

"Captain's to join us in three hours, ship not fully victualled, and the hands have time to prattle." Pigot was looking about for a boatswain's mate with a rope's end when he caught sight of Jenny standing in the lighter and read the situation.

"Madam," he shouted, "you are disrupting the King's work!" Jenny looked blank with amazement; in fact the blue jacketed figure pointing and ranting so almost made her laugh out loud before an inner sense saved her.

"Sir, I'm awful sorry if I caused a problem. I was only tryin' to see my man, Josh."

"Your man?"

"Yes, sir. We was married three days back."

Pigot took the information in, as he did the pleading look on Jenny's face. He looked to the master at arms for a second, then back at the girl.

"Bring her aboard."

The order caught them all unaware, and there was a moment's pause.

"Bring her aboard, I say!"

There was no man-rope rigged, but Flint laid hold of a length of fall and held it over the side to Jenny. A lighterman slipped the rope under her arms and took her to the narrow steps that led up at the break of the quarterdeck. Jenny reached for one of the wooden ledges, and clambered up in a confusion of dress and petticoat. The steep tumblehome of *Pandora's* side, a feature of her French design, made the journey relative easy, and in no time she was on the gangway, smiling uncertainly at the group of men around her.

"Madam, you should be aware that there is no wedding garland hoisted aboard this ship." Pigot's words were harsh, and his expression had not altered from one of acute distaste. "However, I understand that you are recently married, and am prepared to make an exception."

There was a slight, almost imperceptible muttering amongst the men who wondered, even at this late stage, if the first lieutenant had been unfairly judged.

"I'm sorry to have caused a problem, sir." Her voice was soft and low, but she sensed a victory and caught Wright's eye with a gleam of triumph.

"First, of course, you will have to be searched. I'll have no sailors' joy contaminating my people. See to it, Mr Guppy!"

Guppy stepped forward at the command, although he clearly felt awkward. He had searched countless doxies in the course of his duties, but very few legal wives, and never with their husbands looking on.

"I said search her, Master at Arms!"

Guppy reached forward and patted her waist apologetically.

"Search her, man!" Pigot pushed him out of the way and proceeded to run his hands down the girl's body. Flint took a sharp intake of breath, but Wright was totally silent; only the reddening of his cheeks and his clenched fists betrayed the anger that was welling up inside him.

"Brandy in a bladder, tobacco stitched into shifts; there's no tellin' with doxies," Pigot muttered, to no one in particular. "Reckon you've more than a touch of lace under here, my pretty one!" He had his hand on her skirts now, and with one quick movement, lifted up the material, together with the petticoat beneath. Jenny let out a gasp and most of the seamen looked away as a white thigh was exposed. "Known women carry any manner of things in my time." His voice had mellowed to the level of casual conversation, although his questioning hands continued to explore further. "She's clean," he said at last, a hand lingering for a moment about her. "Let her have ten minutes with her man..." He paused as if out of breath before continuing in a stronger snarl, "They takes more, I want to know about it!"

The men looked uncomfortably about them as Pigot walked away, and Jenny lowered her head. Wright approached her, his hands held out.

"You shouldn't have come, Jen'," he said weakly. "The man's a swine: 'es no gen'leman."

"I wanted to see you." All her previous joy had been ripped away and she appeared several years younger.

"Go for'ard," said Flint. "Take her to the foc'sle an' talk in private." The crowd of seamen separated allowing them to wander slowly along the gangway.

"Ten minutes, 'member!" Guppy called after them, his toothless grin marking him out as the only man still smiling. "Not a second longer, or the first luff'll hear of it." He paused to chuckle again, "Then there'll be no tellin' what he'll do!"

*****

"I've been reading up on the ship," Lewis told King as they finished their dinner. "Seems she wasn't meant for the Navy original."

King raised an eyebrow. "British built though, surely?"

"Aye, British, but not from an Admiralty yard." Small ships of war were often commissioned from private shipyards, but this was rare for any vessel larger than a sloop.

"Made for a foreign buyer then?" A reasonable assumption, although there were precious few countries that would need even a small frigate that were not actively at war with Great Britain.

"No, a privateer." That made more sense, although *Pandora* was large for a letter of marquee, and would have cost well over twenty thousand pounds, just for her hull.

"Expensive project. Must have been someone a trifle warm." King had pushed his chair back from the table and reached for a small mahogany box. It had been a rash purchase; one he had made just after *Vigilant* had paid off and before the money began to run out. King's family could never be called comfortable, and he had begun life in the Navy with a minimal uniform and equipment. His present dirk had been won over a game of whist, and even now his best coat was threadbare and well patched. The pistol had been an indulgence, it was too small for service use; totally impractical in fact, and yet it was beautifully made, a real gentleman's piece, and he liked it.

"Viscount Medwood, or rather his son," Lewis continued. "He's on the list: commander. Mind, he's hardly at sea more'n two weeks in the year, an' then it takes the other fifty to clear up the mess. Amazin' what interest does when it comes to making commissioned officers." Lewis dropped his voice at the end of his sentence as he remembered King's position, but the passed midshipman hardly noticed.

"So, can't his father get him a regular command? Something with a decent premier to keep him out of trouble?" He opened the box; inside, resting on a velvet fitted lining, was a small silvered pistol with an ebony butt.

"T'aint likely. After wrecking one brig and near causing two mutinies, Admiralty would think twice about giving him a powder barge in hell, an' that's in spite of his father."

"And poor little boy still wanted a ship, so Daddy bought him one?" He eased back the hammer on the small pistol and checked the flint, before allowing a small amount of oil onto the frizzen spring.

"'s right." Lewis nodded. "Mind, he never saw her off the slip. Spent the time she was buildin' on cards an' horses, burning all the money put aside for fittin' her out. Seems 'is father felt he'd put up enough, and refused to give out any more. Threw his weight about a bit, and the Admiralty ends up with one more frigate."

"And a Jackass at that."

"Right, and you know what they say: too small to fight and too slow to run."

King shrugged. "Still, she's a fair ship; reckon they did a good enough job."

"Aye, least she's oak." Lewis patted a hanging knee with respect. "Better than them pine affairs. Ask me they won't last long enough to change the copper."

Collins, the marine servant, appeared briefly in the doorway. "Beggin' your pardon, gents, but we've 'ad a signal from shore. Captain's comin' aboard in an hour."

Both warrant officers stood up, and Lewis brushed the biscuit crumbs from his shirt. "An hour, that doesn't give us long." King replaced the pistol in its box and gently closed the lid.

Lewis shrugged. "Oh, it's all pretty tight. Mr Fraiser's well up with the storage, just got to run through the last supplies with the purser."

"Wish we could say the same for number one."

"Mr Pigot a bit behind, is he?"

"Watch bill's still in draft; I dreads what the captain will think when he sees the dockyard returns."

"No nap for the first luff today, then?"

"Nor me, neither; do you thinks he'll bail himself out of this on his own?"

*****

The captain was received on board that afternoon with all due ceremony. Lines of sideboys stood to meet him, along with the petty and commissioned officers, the latter in full dress uniform. Banks came up the prestigious starboard steps, rather than the larboard, so recently used by Wright's wife. His hand was raised to his hat and as his foot touched the deck he turned towards the quarterdeck in the naval tradition, saluting a crucifix that had not been present on Royal Navy ships for several centuries. The shrill whistle of the boatswains' pipes ended raggedly, and Pigot stepped forward to shake his hand.

"Welcome aboard, sir."

"Thank you, Mr Pigot," he turned to the group of officers waiting. "Gentlemen, my respects. I look forward to meeting you all shortly, but first I'd be obliged if the hands could be called." Even phrased in the form of a request, the captain's order was acted upon instantly and, urged as much by their own curiosity as the boatswain's mate's starters, the men assembled.

"Off hats!"

The captain reached inside his breast pocket and shook out the folded paper within. The men were silent as he read out the orders that confirmed him as their commander, and should see the ship clear Spithead with the afternoon tide. King, standing slightly apart from the commissioned officers, looked at the faces of the men as they stood in the waist. It was the usual mixture: young and old, all variously dressed and, for the most part, regular man-of-war types. Something in their expression disturbed him though. It was not quite the usual blend ranging from keen anticipation, through mild curiosity, and ending with outward disdain. Each man's face was his own certainly, but they appeared to stem from a common root, or were being looked at through the same coloured glass. They held a similarity that was at once potent and disquieting. He perceived a power that drew its strength from being shared. Alone, each was worth very little, but together; together there was nothing they could not achieve.

He had never sensed this from British seamen before. Of course no one who shipped before the mast was without complaints; their country had been at war, and most of them at sea, for more than three years. Conditions were not good, and only a few were genuine volunteers. But there was something else; something more fundamental, more direct; something that was not part of the usual sailors' lot had clearly upset them. Banks was still speaking when, as if in answer to his question, Pigot coughed once, immediately drawing the eye of every man standing in the waist and realisation dawned on King. He was aware that Pigot's intimidating ways were unpopular, but this was the first time he had noticed the effect. At the order to stand down the men did so, but not with the usual relief and chatter; they moved slowly, in silence, and on their own terms. Their attitude worried King, and as Pigot called out to a boatswain's mate to start a man he considered to be taking too long, his concern grew.

*****

She weighed as dusk was turning into night. Banks had intended to take the earlier afternoon tide, but there were problems raising the second anchor. He had had to wait, fuming, under the amused eyes of the Channel fleet, while Caulfield investigated the difficulty, and it was a good two hours later that the Solent's second high took them out.

The matter had not been eased by the fact that, rather than being foul as reported, the anchor had only required a little extra effort to free it from the Spithead mud; by the time this had been discovered they had lost the flood. Caulfield rounded on Conroy, the new master's mate who had been detailed to supervise capstan work, and was disconcerted by the man's reaction. Conroy was clearly cautious, not so much of doing damage to the ship and her equipment, but of taking action on his own initiative. Ships sailed and the Navy existed at all because men took responsibility; there were numerous occasions when it was not possible to consult a superior. Caulfield could not conceive how Conroy had been promoted to his present rank if he was really as hesitant as he appeared.

"You should have ordered more effort, doubled up on the bars; rigged swifters if need be," the lieutenant told him under his breath. "What were you frightened of, parting the messenger? Twisting a fluke?"

Conroy had joined *Pandora* two days before, and had already encountered Pigot and his ways on several occasions, and the knowledge that such a man was on board did not make him inclined to take chances. Caulfield dismissed him, deciding that he should be given a greater opportunity to acquaint himself with the ship before further judgement was passed. In fact Conroy was gaining that very experience now, working double tides for the next forty-eight hours.

Caulfield had still to report to the captain, and while on his way to the quarterdeck he spotted Lewis, the other master's mate, and a man he was familiar with, they having been together in *Essex* until a few weeks ago. Caulfield took Lewis to the empty gunroom pantry, a place of relative privacy, and asked him what he knew of Conroy. Lewis had been noncommittal, a reaction Caulfield would have expected when any man was being questioned about a colleague. Still, he did say something of importance, something that bothered Caulfield even now. It was a chance remark, made almost under his breath, although Lewis made it quite clear that, had he been in charge of the cable, he might well have shown the same caution; an amazing admission from a man with enough enterprise to pluck himself up from the lower deck.

Caulfield's report to the captain was as bland and indefinite as he could make it; he had no intention of raising more questions, or implicating Conroy further. But the problem was still there, and would have to be faced in the future. Until then one thing was certain: when working under Pigot the men were not inclined to show initiative.

✳✳✳✳✳

Rose, who berthed with Dorsey and Cobb, was the youngest of the young gentlemen, and had yet to reach the dizzy height of midshipman. The son of a Lincolnshire farmer, he had spent almost the whole of his fourteen years in the village, amongst people he had always known, and even within this protected space, the lad had shown little inclination to move beyond the boundaries of his father's farm. Though no slouch—he was always ready to work long hours during lambing, or when the fences had to be repaired—he also liked his own company, and was content to read all day, if the chance were given.

The idea of going to sea had been completely his father's, and in no way was the intention meant to be unkind. He was genuinely concerned for his son. He knew that before long the boy would have to start himself out of books, and other childish things, and begin to take some responsibility. Rose had two sisters, but no brother. One day the farm would naturally pass to him; what good would stories be when it came to getting the best possible price for mutton, and paying the least for supplement? The sea seemed an obvious choice, even though the nearest shore was more than a day's ride away. Rose's uncle, who had died of an unconfirmed ailment in the West Indies, had been a purser, and his mother's cousin was a master in the East India Company. She had suggested that her son be sent to join him as a servant but her husband was against the idea. The East India Company may be honourable by name, but the old farmer had vague suspicions about the position and exact duties of an officer's servant.

The Royal Navy was another matter; a respectable service where the lad could do well, maybe make a small sum in prize money, before he left the sea and with it all traces of boyhood. And so he had used what influence he had, and a rather greater sum of money, and secured him a berth as first class volunteer in HMS *Pandora*.

The fact that all the major decisions should be made without reference to the lad was of no surprise to anyone; it was naturally assumed that parents should know and do the best for their child. Rose was allowed ten days of increasing dread, from the time he heard his future to the day he began experiencing it. The first officer he had met on boarding *Pandora* had been Pigot; it had been an omen of the worst kind, and from that day his nightmare had begun.

The intervening time seemed to merge into one black image; his world had changed in every way possible and yet, throughout the numerous novelties of adapting to life in a warship, it was Pigot, and his constantly impending presence that appeared to dominate each hour. Never before had he experienced such a rich vein of evil in one man. At a time when Rose was trying to master many new things, he found room to learn hatred for the first lieutenant, almost to exclusion.

That afternoon had been the worst. The delay in weighing had infuriated every member of the crew to differing degrees, but Pigot was the one to channel his annoyance. Rose had been in charge of the party on the forecastle that would cat the anchors as they were raised. Perhaps being in charge was unfair, as it was the first time he had ever witnessed the procedure, whereas the hands under his command consisted of almond-brown men whose iron muscles were the product of many such exercises.

The first anchor had come up, almost without effort, and Rose had needed to do nothing more than nod at the quartermaster as the cat tackle was threaded through the ring, and the entire weight manhandled up to the cathead. Once there, Rose found himself relegated to the position of spectator. The anchor party had the fish tackle rigged ready, and hauled the anchor horizontal, stowing it safely away from the hull of the ship, while two men released cable and plugged the hawse hole. The hands turned from their work, grinning to each other. Raising the anchors was the signal that they were really going back to sea, for most their natural element, and the physical effort involved, the final confirmation.

The strain began on the second cable, and all waited to repeat the procedure, none more so than Rose, who had missed some of the complexities of the cat tackle, and wanted to view the exercise again. For several minutes they waited, with the cable wringing water from its fibres as, further aft, men strained at the capstan. It was only natural for his party to look to Rose for orders, although there was precious little he could do about the situation. He wriggled awkwardly in his stiff new uniform, uncertain what exactly was called for from him. Eventually he turned back to the quarterdeck, looking for reassurance and advice. Instead he found Pigot.

The memory would stay with him. His stammered questions met by the cold, stone mask of antipathy. Rose knew nothing about Pigot's own internal anger at being shown up in front of the fleet, and he could not tell of the modicum of satisfaction he supplied as the first lieutenant allowed him to dig deeper and deeper into his supposed offence. When he had finished his halting account of how he had failed to fish an anchor that had not been weighed, even then it was not the end. A brisk order from Pigot had seen the gunner raised from whatever depths he frequented when leaving harbour, and under the amused eyes of all, Rose had been swept down to the main deck, to suffer the most degrading public beating imaginable, over the breach of a gun.

The pain had all but dulled now, but his brain was not so easily mended, and ever since he had suffered a constant repeat of the incident as his mind refused to leave him be. To make matters worse there was an invitation, an invitation that carried the same force as a command, to dine with the captain that day. There could be no doubt that the first lieutenant would be there; that very evening he would be looking into his eyes, that very evening suffering more humiliation as Pigot ground him further into the dust. The fact that he had been on his father's farm, safe, loved and many miles from the sea, not three weeks ago, escaped Rose for a moment, which was all that kept him from taking some desperate and final action.

*****

On the lower deck the hands were sitting down to eat. This time it was not the newness of the ship that caused the stifled silence, but something rather more sinister. A few knew of the incident with Wright's wife, and many others had episodes of their own to feel bitter about. The remainder were merely resentful; resentful that any one man should take the trouble to make their lives, already uncomfortable enough, just that little bit worse. Flint had tried to break the gloom early in the meal, but soon stopped, when all attempts at geniality were met with mournful expressions. It was only at the end, and Carter, the mess cook, had cleared their platters away, that the talk began.

"I'm goin' to kill the bastard," said Wright softly, as if deciding upon a particular cut of tobacco. No one was worried by his words; the sight of a commissioned officer on the lower deck during supper was, by tradition, unheard of and apart from Guppy, who messed elsewhere, there was no junior or petty officer who did not understand or even share Wright's sentiments.

"He's a pig by name, and a pig by nature, and there's no mistaking," Flint said mildly. "But that's no reason to take risks." As he spoke he fiddled with the handle of his tankard, teasing the leather away and folding it back. His expression would lead anyone to believe that this was his sole source of interest and although he spoke in a soft measured tone, all the men listened. "Year or two from now things will seem different; ship might even be paying off. Then you got your whole life ahead of you. Spend it ashore, if you will; sounds like you live far enough inland to miss the press."

"Aye," another voice joined in; Lawlor, a Welshman who played the fiddle. "Sit on yer hands, take up your money; bit of prize mebee, and buy a place. You need never see the likes o' him again."

Wright was unmoved, staring into his drink with a vacant look. The silence lasted for several minutes before the rest of the mess began to talk quietly of other things and did their best not to distract him in any way.

28

Guppy appeared towards the end of supper, when the starboard watch, which included Flint's mess, were about to go on duty.

"Now hear this!" he said, his voice carrying easily through the subdued messdeck. "We'n settin' for the Channel, an' after that down south. Time bein' it's gonna be cold, an' First Lieutenant's ordered we berth watch together, harbour fashion." Now the murmurs began to rise. Berthing watch together as opposed to watch on watch meant that rather than enjoying the best part of four feet of room per man, they would be crammed into eighteen inches; one man's shoulders resting against his neighbour's, an almost unheard of and unnecessary annoyance in any well-run ship at sea.

"You'll thank us, you'll thank us!" Guppy's voice rose above the din. "You'll thank us when it comes to blow. You'll be warmer'n dry; no draught to get the chill in."

"They could do as much with screens," Lawlor muttered.

"Aye, they rigged 'em in the old *Boston* when we were on that Newfoundland convoy, back'n ninety-four," Carter added. "Kept the warm in lovely, they did."

Guppy left the lower deck to cries of derision far too universal for punishment. The noise grew, almost drowning out the bell that sounded the setting of the new watch.

"That's us, lads," Flint informed them, although none of his mess made to move. The noise rose once more then levelled out before dying, as men of the starboard watch shuffled towards the hatches. The ship was barely clear of the island, and yet already this was turning into a bad voyage. Flint gave an inward sigh; the colliers had been hard, monotonous work, but nothing like this. He never dreamt that within a week he'd be missing them.

*****

Banks usually dined at three but, with the ship only just clear of Spithead and many departments still shaking down, dinner with his officers had been repeatedly delayed until it turned into supper. Even then it was late, by naval standards, and rather less than the splendid meal normally expected when a captain entertains his officers for the first time. He acknowledged this to them simply; neither apologising nor blaming the situation that had caused the delay. Younger than most of his guests, Banks carried himself well, and Caulfield, for one, felt his confidence grow.

The gathering ran the course usual in these affairs; the officers seated in order of rank in the great cabin, with Banks at the head of the table, playing a role somewhere between agreeable host and wary headmaster. The talk was stilted and reserved at first, while the captain's personal servants handed out large welcoming glasses of Madeira along with some sweet biscuits that were all but monopolised by the youngsters. With the first course, a rich turtle soup, the men began to relax, and by the time the fish was served they were starting to get on well together.

Even Pigot; that was the strange thing. Caulfield studied him as the captain began to carve into a large saddle of mutton. All traces of the irrational tyrant had vanished and it was as if a new and totally different man had appeared in his place. Of course he had taken more than a glass of wine, but there was no fault in that and he could never have been called drunk. Rose, the volunteer first class and by far the youngest present, was talking now; a chance remark had grown into an anecdote, and the boy was slightly flushed as he realised the whole room, from his captain to the marine servants, was listening to him, and him alone. He finished the tale gamely enough, and there was a roar of appropriate laughter, which gratified Rose, making him blush once more. Pigot laughed as loud as any, and as the conversation turned away he caught the lad's eye.

"Splendid story, Rose," he murmured, nodding appreciatively. "Wine with you, sir?"

Caulfield watched as the lad cautiously raised his glass to the man who, only that afternoon had seen him bent across the breach of a gun and beaten.

A knock at the door heralded the arrival of Cobb, the midshipman of the watch. Cobb, a well-built lad, entered the cabin with the assurance of a man, and took in the loaded table and the smug expressions of his two messmates in one glance.

"Mr Fraiser's duty, sir, an' the watch is 'bout to be set."

Caulfield wiped his mouth with his cloth and turned to Banks. "If you'll excuse me, sir, I have to relieve the master."

"Of course, of course, Mr Caulfield. Perhaps you'd be so kind as to ask Mr Fraiser to join us for pudding, if he can spare the time?"

The air on deck was clammy and dank, although there was no actual rain. Caulfield approached Fraiser, standing next to the binnacle, and smiled.

"A choice of drowned baby or spotted dog, I believe."

Fraiser's watch coat carried a sheen of damp and his face was rosy with cold. He rubbed his hands in anticipation.

"An' the company of gentlemen, of course." There was a gleam in his eye that might almost be called wicked.

"Of course," said Caulfield, promptly, and they grinned at each other. To have said otherwise would have been altogether wrong.

*****

Four hours later, when Caulfield came off duty, everything had changed. He stood outside the gunroom door and shook the rain from his watch coat. A steward appeared, looking pensive and troubled. Caulfield handed him his coat; there was silence from within the gunroom; not unexpected at the late hour, although he could also feel a tension in the air. He opened the door and stepped through.

Inside a group of officers were seated about the table. Pigot was at the head and, even partially obscured as he was by the mizzen mast, his face showed crimson and bloated. The other officers: Stuart, the surgeon, Martin the marine lieutenant, and Soames, the purser, looked half asleep. In front of each was a bumper glass of brandy and the scent of alcohol was strong. Then Caulfield spotted Rose, the volunteer, sitting uncomfortably at the foot of the table. His shoulders were hunched and he sat low in his chair, as if seeking to hide in the dim light. He also had a glass in front of him although his appeared untouched.

"Mr Caulfield," Pigot greeted him, sitting back in his chair with elaborate disdain. "How fine it is to see you. I suppose I cannot tempt you to a glass of brandy?" The other officers took little notice, although Soames let out a wet belch; only Rose, ashen faced as if in shock, turned to look imploringly at him. "Mr Rose here has been entertaining us," Pigot continued, his voice thick and low. "Tellin' us tales of his youth, weren't yer, Mr Rose?"

Stuart gave a drunken chuckle; the midshipman nodded but remained silent.

"It's very late," Caulfield said. "I think I should turn in." He paused. "I think we all should."

"Do!" Pigot gave him a half smile. "Go now. Mr Fraiser is already abed. As for the rest of us; why, we are enjoying ourselves, is that not the case?"

The other officers signaled their approval in various stages of inebriation and Stuart, the surgeon, drained his glass and looked pointedly at the empty decanter.

"Steward!" Pigot's voice rose, although not to a shout; Caulfield guessed he had no intention of waking Fraiser. "My guests are running low." The steward departed. "I'll have no one go short at my table; you're not dining with the captain now!"

"What has the captain to do with matters?" Caulfield could not resist the question.

"Why, you only have to see the way he serves wine!" Pigot sat back and considered his glass.

Soames, the purser, looked about, smiling in a way intended to be ingratiating. "Aye, reckon we's in for a dry old cruise with this one."

The steward returned with two opened bottles and reached for the decanter.

"Leave 'em, leave 'em," Pigot waved the man away as if he was an annoying fly. The surgeon reached out for a bottle and filled his glass with deliberate concentration and what could almost be called love. Caulfield had already judged him a man who enjoyed his drink, although of them all he seemed strangely sober.

"Another story, Rose!" Pigot commanded, tapping the table with his finger.

The boy jumped visibly. "I, I don't think I know any."

"A song, then?" The first lieutenant was smiling, while his eyes held a glare that was evil and intense. "Come on, man, you entertained us so well at the captain's table. Sure there is a wealth of talent in that young body."

The boy was silent.

"W-well what about one of the ones you've told already, eh?" Martin, the marine, had a cultured voice; distorted by liquor it sounded feeble and comic. "The time you fell into the sheep dip?"

"Pushed!" added Soames, with glee.

"Aye," Martin again, "that was a good one, eh gentlemen?"

There were general nods from the other officers, although none took their eyes from their glasses.

"I think Mr Rose has had enough for one night," Caulfield said pointedly. "I think everyone has."

"You do?" Pigot eyed him with apparent interest.

"I do." There was no point in any further discussion. "Mr Rose is on watch in under four hours." Turning to the lad, his voice took on the tone of command. "Take yourself back to your quarters, right now."

For a moment the boy stayed put, as if frightened of obeying Caulfield's order. Then he cautiously rose from the table and made for the door, his eyes meeting Caulfield's only briefly. Pigot watched him go, before switching his gaze back to the lieutenant.

"Mr Caulfield, you have broken up my party," he said. His tone was cold and there was no trace of inebriation as he spoke. "I do not like juniors who take such things upon themselves, in fact I do not like presumptive people in general. And I do not like you, Mr Caulfield, I do not like you one little bit."

CHAPTER THREE

The afternoon was dark and cold with a thin, but persistent, drizzle that had been constant since first light. Lewis stood next to the quartermaster, his woollen coat gaining weight as it steadily soaked up the rain while allowing just enough past the collar to make him thoroughly miserable. Beneath his feet *Pandora* moved with a steady, rhythmic motion, pressing through the leaden waves with little show of effort. The light, fitful wind came on her larboard quarter, and with topsails, forecourse and topgallants set, she was making reasonable progress; nothing more. Only occasionally would she hint at her true potential when a sudden blast of cold wet air pressed her hull down, chilling the men who had to stand her decks, and changing the regular hum of her lines to a scream that grated the nerves like a baby's cry. There were still several hours of supposed daylight left, yet the low blanket sky gave the illusion of dusk. Lewis suppressed an involuntary shiver and rubbed his hands together while he told himself there had been plenty worse watches when he had been a lower deck man.

King strode aft, hands clasped behind his back in an effort to break the lifelong habit of thrusting them into his pockets. The toothache that had been bothering him on and off for the past day or so had gone for the moment, and he felt reasonably at ease. Lewis caught his eye, and the two exchanged a smile; it might be cold and wet, but to be on deck was a pleasant contrast to the oppressive, quarrelsome atmosphere that had become common below.

"We must be well clear of Ushant b'now," King said.

Lewis pointed back over his shoulder with his thumb.

"A few leagues astern. Plenty of room if the wind shifts."

"You think it will?"

"That or die completely. Glass is playin' strange japes."

Pandora had been making steady progress for the last few days although all on board sensed she could have done better; certainly she had shown little of the dash expected of a frigate fresh from the dockyard. No single reason could be found for this; no fluke of wind had carried away a vital piece of equipment, no error of navigation set them dramatically off course. Any delay was subtle, and possibly more a question of not being fully up to scratch; the men, though experienced in the main, had yet to shake down together and learn to work as a team. The officers were equally uncertain how to get the best from her rig, and even the master was still deciding on the optimum layout of stores; one that allowed everything to be within reach, yet left a tidy ship with a serviceable trim. Pigot made his way on deck, barely acknowledging the pair. Of course there may have been other reasons for *Pandora's* lacklustre performance.

"Deck there. Sail ho. Sail on the starboard bow!"

All eyes turned aloft to where the masthead lookout was peering out across a dark heaving sea.

"What do you make there?" Pigot's voice, loud and demanding.

"Lost it now, sir. It were no more'n a glimpse," the first lieutenant snorted with annoyance.

"Foremast, what have you?" There was a pause before the apologetic tones of the second lookout reported a clear sea. Pigot glared about the deck, his eyes naturally falling on the most able midshipman.

"You, King - get aloft to the main with a glass. Tell me what you see."

There was only one response acceptable when Pigot gave an order. King moved quickly, collecting the deck glass from the binnacle and strapping it across his back as he made for the main shrouds. He swung himself out with barely a thought, rapidly climbing up the sodden ratlines, letting the tight weather shrouds run through his hands as he went. Up to the main top, hang back for the futtocks, then on to the main crosstrees. Here the ship's motion could be felt more readily, with every movement magnified by the height of the frigate's main mast. The lookout was from King's own division and he knew him to be trustworthy.

"What did you make, Wright?" he asked, as they clung to the mast.

"Nothing to be certain of, Mr King. Looked like a ship, a warship or a big Indiaman; mebbe a liner or frigate, couldn't be sure."

"Where away?"

He stretched out a hand. "Two points off the starboard bow. Headin' west nor-west, or so it seemed." He stopped, then added more guardedly, "Might have got a sight of sommat afore, sir; a few points off the larboard beam, but I couldn't be certain, like."

King nodded and peered out. The horizon to starboard was indistinct; small patches of fog were rolling with the wind, and there was a band of heavy weather slightly behind the point that Wright indicated.

"Reckon it's closing in," Wright said, as the midshipman swept the glass along the horizon. It was true, even in the brief time he had been aloft *Pandora's* motion had lessened; the main topgallant was just beginning to loosen, although the air still felt as cold.

"Nothing to see now." King tried hard to mask his feelings. It was the worst sighting possible, no more than a peep, and that just by one man. Wright's report might easily change the ship's course. An enemy warship - perhaps a squadron, maybe even a fleet - could be heading up towards the Channel. At that very moment *Pandora* might be the first line of defence against an invasion.

But then, of course, he could be mistaken; with the best of intentions Wright might have taken the combination of fast moving cloud and poor visibility and made it into a ship. Instances had been known of two or three men making the same certain sighting, only to find their supposed squadron was no more than scud and spindrift. *Pandora* might be off course for days investigating the mirage. Then the wind could shift; they could waste more time fighting to regain their original course, and all the while her mail would be delayed, and Jervis deprived of a valuable frigate.

Topgallant and topsails were flapping now as the wind died further, and King felt the pain in his tooth return. Wright pointed out to windward. "There's a fog comin' for us. An' a thick'n, by the looks o' it." The midshipman glanced back across their quarter: sure enough the individual patches had spread into a dark grey wash that was rolling forward, eating up the horizon by the second.

He looked again, while Wright reported the fog to the deck below. Now there was something; a shape, nothing more, several points behind that which Wright had reported and almost abeam of *Pandora*. King felt the blood drain from his body as he raised his glass. Yes, that was definite. He nudged Wright, pointing at the break in the cloud. As he watched the image detailed into a ship: a warship; hull up and a Frenchman, judging by her bow. There was also a trace, no more than that, of other sails. Not merely another vessel; two, maybe three, further forward. He held his breath, straining to make the misty shapes more distinct.

"Maintop, there - what d'ya see?"

It could have been his imagination, or did Wright stiffen slightly at the sound of Pigot's voice? The seaman's eyes were more accustomed to the work. He handed the glass across without a word; Wright took it, and focused on the spot.

"What do you make of that?" King asked, after several seconds had dragged by. The seaman passed the glass back and shook his head sadly.

"Nuthin' I can see, sir."

King took the glass and raised it again; no, the cloud had thickened and now sat like a rug over his sighting. There was no ship; certainly no squadron: that was assuming there ever had been to begin with.

"What do you see there?" Pigot's voice was edged with anger as it drifted up to them. King swallowed; here was a quandary. He could say nothing, he could stay safe; or he could report exactly what he had, or thought he had, seen. Report it and accept the consequences. If Banks believed him and altered course only to find him wrong he could kiss goodbye to any hopes he might have of his commission being confirmed.

"Masthead, make your report!"

"Ship sighted to windward, sir; mebbe two or more," he shouted back, with barely a shake in his voice. "Headin' west norwest."

King gave Wright a grim smile, while the seaman looked at him with renewed respect; now he had really started something.

*****

38

The air in the great cabin could never have been called warm, and yet King's coat steamed liberally, while his damp nankin trousers (breeches were only for ceremony) cloyed about his legs making him long for a hot, dry towel, and his sore tooth ached like it was five times the size. Banks wore a heavy dressing coat over a baggy shirt and his feet were wrapped in old flannel carpet slippers, although his manner and poise remained very much that of a captain.

"For how long did you see this ship?"

King swallowed and repeated his story once more. Banks nodded, "What do you think, Mr Pigot?"

The first lieutenant appeared composed and thoughtful; very different to the man King had met on returning to the deck. "I've been in the same position m'self, sir. I know what it's like, expectin' to see somethin', and only half certain. Still, what Mr King says hardly constitutes a sightin'. I don't think we should take any action at present." Pigot smiled benignly at the midshipman, every bit the well meaning and supportive executive officer; King wondered how much Banks really knew about his second in command.

"Thank you, Mr Pigot. I feel Mr King is reasonably experienced, and there is also the matter of the lookout's earlier report."

Pigot stiffened. "May I remind you sir, that convoys from Lisbon and Quebec are at sea? Both are due about now, and both could be hereabouts."

"They could be in the area, certainly, but not heading west norwest." Pigot said nothing although King could almost sense him begin to prickle as Banks continued. "I had not intended to alter course, but I think this puts a different perspective on matters." He looked across to the tell-tale compass. "Take her two points to starboard, if you please; that way we should run into whatever it is Mr King has spotted. I could wish for a little more wind, but so be it."

King was prepared to go, but Pigot, it seems, had other ideas.

"Forgive me, sir, but that will delay our arrival at Gibraltar, as well as meeting with Admiral Jervis."

Bank's expression did not change, although his voice became marginally cooler. "That is so, Mr Pigot."

The first lieutenant opened his mouth, and closed it again. Any late rendezvous would reflect as badly on him as the captain. "I was just concerned, sir," he said, eventually. "Concerned that we would be wasting our time."

King closed his eyes. Pigot was talking himself into a hole, and the midshipman already knew how any displeasure encountered from the captain would be paid back many times over on those whom Pigot would consider rightly to blame.

"Mr Pigot, I have made my decision, and I do not wish to discuss matters further." The atmosphere in the cabin had suddenly become distinctly unpleasant. "If there is nothing else, I will not keep you from your duties." There was nothing else, and the two turned to go. "Not you, Mr King, I'd like a word. Thank you, Mr Pigot."

King felt a pain in his breast that almost overtook that in his jaw; in one action he had caused the ship to alter course and fallen foul of Pigot. The latter would be seething from the interview with Banks and the fact that King had also been witness to the captain cutting him down to size and present when he was dismissed from the cabin, would not have made him any more popular. The door closed, and they both could hear Pigot's boots as he stamped out along the upper deck.

"Mr King, I recollect that you have passed your board but not been made, is that right?"

King said that it was.

"I have no need for another lieutenant in this ship, but I am aware of the risk you ran this afternoon. Many would have chosen the easier path and not reported the sighting. If you are proved in any way correct, I will be happy to speak for you."

"Thank you, sir." Banks was clearly influential; a word from him, or his supporters, would secure King's commission.

"Very good, you had better return to the deck now. I am sure the first lieutenant will appreciate every sharp eye." Was there just the flicker of humour in that face? It could be that Banks was not totally ignorant about Pigot, although King could not be sure. "And I do hope you are right," the captain added, as King left the cabin.

*****

The fog had reached the ship by the second dogwatch. A dense, evil mist that coated her every fibre. At times it was so thick as to hide the forecastle from the quarterdeck, with only the occasional break, when an area of fifty, maybe a hundred feet would show clear, and the black night was allowed in to fill the temporary void.

As the watch wore on Caulfield stared vainly at the traverse board. There had been no change of course since that ordered by the captain, but the wind had also shifted several points, and their speed had altered, dropping to barely three knots despite the addition of jib and staysails. They could increase sail further, although creeping through the fog as they were, without any audible warning, was the very edge of folly. Caulfield looked up to where the main lookout, only recently relieved, would be settling in. The previous man had reported dense cover, and Caulfield guessed it was likely to remain so for the rest of the night. King appeared, summoned by the inescapable urge to be where the news would come first. To stand on deck, smell the fog, pace up and down, to hope; only to return below, as he had done for every half hour or so since Caulfield had taken the watch.

"You'll be on in no time," the lieutenant informed him, approaching out of the gloom. "Better get some rest while you can."

King shook his head. "I'd be happier out here, if that's agreeable, sir. The waitin's far worse below."

"Very well." Caulfield turned away; it was not the night for conversation, even if there had been anything to say. King might have been right in his sighting. Even now, an enemy force could be crossing their path, heading for the Channel and invasion. Colpoys' offshore squadron would miss them in this fog, as would the main force of Bridport's Channel fleet, currently sheltering in Spithead. They might be there, they could be within a mile of them at that very moment, but there was nothing he, nothing anyone on board *Pandora*, could do while this darned fog persisted.

Flint was on watch, along with Lawlor and Jameson. The three were sheltering in the lee of the larboard gangway. No action had been called for from them for several hours and they were cold, their kerseymere jackets wrapped tight about them and woollen caps pulled down over their ears.

In the cockpit Lewis was looking at his glass, peering at the gauge in the dubious light. The reading was low, very low, with barely a flicker of movement since that afternoon. The tension had eased slightly since King went on deck, but there was still an aura of hushed expectancy that filled the entire ship. Lewis shivered suddenly, rubbing his hands against his forearms to warm himself as he moved back and sat down at the table. In front of him was the cold and fast congealing portion of lobscouse that Collins had served over an hour ago. He looked at it with surprise, and picked up his fork to annoy it for a moment or two, before sitting back in his chair. There was a Guernsey top of his chest, fine knitted from heavy wool, and just waiting to be put on. He leaned forward, still shivering, and pulled it over his head, stretching the tight garment around his body. The rich smell of lanolin came out to greet him, and he gratefully pressed his arms into the sleeves. He knew that in a few moments he would start to grow warm, although now it seemed the Guernsey was merely trapping his damp shirt against him. He shivered again, considered turning back to his food, dismissed the notion, and pulled off the Guernsey, before getting up to study his glass.

In the great cabin Banks had supped sparsely and alone and now lay, fully clothed but without his jacket, on the upholstered stern lockers. His eyes were closed, his breathing deep and regular although he remained wide-awake and ready to move at a moment's notice. On a clear night it would have been relatively easy to miss another ship, even a whole squadron, if they were properly darkened. With this fog it would be strange, no a miracle, if anything was spotted, and yet still he remained alert, still ready for the call.

Stuart, the surgeon, had heard of the supposed sighting, but gave it little consideration. The ship, so recently fresh from port, was healthy, and until anything came along to cause him a nuisance he was content to allow illness and injuries to appear in the normal way. Certainly there was little enough for him to do; the amount of preventative medicine available to him was too small to consider. He had the standing orders from the physician of the fleet, and his medicine chest and tools were in order; Manning, his mate, had seen to that. Some might spend this time of relative leisure in reading, although Stuart had no intention of improving, or even changing his mind. New techniques might have been developed, but in the end the human body remained the same. In his youth he had attempted several surgical operations, some with reasonable success, but now he had no desire to open a body that had not already been penetrated by injury. He could remove a man's leg in four minutes, far less if it was a lad and the saw sharp. He could tell a case of scurvy, and identify most of the more common types of shipboard ailment. He was especially good with venereal disease; few were novel to him and most could be, if not cured then at least delayed long enough to allow the sufferer to pay the regulation fifteen shillings for his trouble.

He walked into the cubical partitioned off from the gunroom that was his berth. On the spirketing next to his head the carpenter had erected a small shelf for him to keep a few personal possessions. It was to this shelf that he reached now, and removed a large blue bottle. Laudanum, the alcoholic tincture of opium, was one of his more powerful tools; one of the few drugs that actually made a positive impression on his patients, although Stuart was in no way deceived by its healing powers. Still, for a bored and indolent man it was exactly the right prescription and he added a generous measure to the half filled wine glass that he had taken from the gunroom. This would give him just the right amount of comfort to see him through a cold night. He drained the glass, feeling the warmth of the drug run pleasantly throughout his body, before filling it once more. From somewhere far, far away he heard the tolling of *Pandora's* bell as it marked the half hour, but Stuart was no longer concerned with the ship's routine, or even time itself. He drank the neat dose, and fell heavily against his cot, gripping the sides and swinging himself in with practiced ease. Within seconds he was snoring heavily, lost to the ship, the world, and anyone who might need him.

Back on the quarterdeck the tension persisted. "No ships yet, Mr King?" It was Pigot, presumably the waiting had affected him as well, and he was reacting in the only way he knew. "No fleet of invading Frenchmen, ready to burn our homes and cut up our wives and sweethearts?"

"No, sir." It was the safest reply.

"I suppose you'll ask the captain for a change of course shortly?" Say, we must 'ave missed 'em on our first pass, time to go back for another?"

"No, sir." King swallowed. He was on duty shortly, and Pigot would be the officer of the watch. Just his luck to run into him now, a good hour before he was officially due on deck.

"I'd send you aloft, young man," Pigot continued in a conversational tone. "Send you aloft; masthead you for the rest of the night, but I fear for what we might run in to. M'bee a school of fightin' whales, hell bent on takin' the ship an' sailin' her to China? Who can tell?"

He was going to evoke the first lieutenant's wrath whatever happened, so when the next glass was turned, and Pigot became distracted by the casting of the log, King did go aloft. He took a slow passage; the ratlines were thoroughly soaked and slipped beneath his feet, and he was in no rush to reach the masthead. Once there, however, he found the situation was starting to change.

"Mist's fadin', Mr King," Lawlor, the Welshman informed him. "Not clear nuff to report, but I gets a proper view everso often. Give it a couple of moments and we'll be fair." King nodded, and together they stood looking out into the blank mist.

Then, as Lawlor had predicted, it lifted. Lifted, but only for them, only for those many feet above the soft waves. The light from the half moon began to break through, and then they were in clear air. Clear air, over a bed of cloud, a bed that sat barely eight feet below their position. They could look out for several miles in each direction. It was a strange experience to be many feet above the deck, and yet apparently safe over a dense floor of solid mist. King looked about as Lawlor reported the situation to the expectant deck below. No sign of topmasts, no break in the solid rind of cloud. There was an empty ocean, and *Pandora* was in the middle of it.

"Bad luck, sir," Lawlor muttered.

King smiled grimly as his toothache returned to pester him once more. Now he really would be for it.

The boy Rose tapped at the door and Banks' eyes opened instantly.

"Mr Caulfield's duty, sir, an' the masthead's clear of the fog."

"Anything in sight?" It was an obvious question but one he had to ask.

"No, sir."

"Very good." He closed his eyes again as Rose left. So that was it, a wild goose-chase. King had either been wrong, mistaken, or just plain unlucky; whatever, they had ventured off course and far deeper into the fog than was necessary. They should turn back right away. Now that the threat had gone he realised just how tense he had been. For a moment he considered staying as he was, maybe dozing for a moment. It was a feeling that had become rather common of late; possibly the onset of old age. That was the exactly the right thought to stir him into action, and he sprang to his feet and made for the quarterdeck, the very essence of youth and vitality.

*****

44

"A fleet, he says. An invasion fleet!" Pigot's voice was low, but dangerous. "Saw a bunch of liners, did yer?" The face was barely inches from King's and his breath clashed horribly with the clean cold night air. "Took us on a right little rainbow hunt, didn't you my lad? Well, I'll tell you what! I'll tell you what you can look forward to once the watch is called." He turned away and caught the eye of Rose who was acting as the midshipman of the watch, and sheltering unhappily by the binnacle.

"Pass the word for Mr Smith," he said. Smith, the gunner, was the officer traditionally responsible for discipline amongst the midshipmen, although King, with his age and experience, had not had to face such a situation in years. Pigot turned to King, an evil expression on his face. "I'll show you the correct punishment for barefaced cheek."

Smith made his appearance fully dressed; only his eyes, still bleary with sleep, showed that and he had been roused from his hammock.

"Mr Smith, Mr King here wishes to become intimate with your daughter." To kiss the gunner's daughter was the euphemism given to that particularly humiliating punishment that Rose had experienced so recently.

"Mr King, sir?" Smith was not so wide-awake as to accept Pigot's suggestion without question. "But 'e's a lieutenant, sir, near as can be!"

"Mr Smith, you will do your duty!" Pigot's voice rose unnaturally in the still night. Smith stood uncertainly for a second, before his eyes became fixed on someone approaching from behind.

"One moment, Mr Pigot, if you please." King drew a sigh at the captain's voice. "I think we will discuss this matter in my cabin." It would be wrong to countermand Pigot's order in public, although Banks had no intention of allowing King to suffer any form of punishment, simply for doing his duty.

For several seconds the lieutenant remained staring at King before the spell broke.

"Yes, sir." Pigot's voice was sulky, and he turned to follow Banks toward the companionway with a look of thunder on his face.

"Very good, Mr Smith, you may go below." Caulfield, this time. He gave King a sympathetic smile. "It might have been better for you if the captain hadn't turned up," he said, softly. "When that bastard gets back he'll want more than just blood."

King's eyes fell. Caulfield was right; he could not rely on the captain's protection forever. In his elevated position Banks would always be unaware of the subtle unpleasantries that Pigot could inflict at will. And Pigot was no fool; he had eyes, and knew exactly when it was safe to use a rope's end on the men, unheard of for a commissioned officer. He knew just how many beatings and mast-headings he could inflict on the midshipmen, without arousing comment; how often he could have the same man flogged and it be ignored. There had been many supposed instances when one un-popular officer wrecked the lives of many. King had even known an oldster midshipman who swore he had been passed over for treading on the port admiral's dog. But this was real, and happen-ing to him. The captain's words about having his commission con-firmed came back to mock; there would be little likelihood of that once Pigot got his teeth into him. Any lieutenant had the power to make a mere midshipman appear incompetent: a first lieutenant could do it without leaving his cot.

"You'll be on duty in less than half a glass; get something hot inside you." Caulfield again, speaking sense and giving more than advice, although there was little he could actually do to ease the situation. King turned to go below, when a voice cut into his thoughts.

"Sail ho! Two points off the larboard bow!"

Caulfield waited while the report was repeated.

"What do you see there?"

Topmasts; two ships, no three. Tops'ls set, one looks to be a liner, headin' west nor-west."

Topsails, in this weather, hardly likely to be Indiamen. Caul-field smiled at the midshipman. "Mr King," he said, as the ship erupted to the call of all hands, "I think we might have found your squadron."

CHAPTER FOUR

"Take in tops'ls, stays'ls and jib, if you please," the captain's voice was steady, with only the barest trace of excitement as he bounded up the companionway from his cabin. He caught the eye of Caulfield, still the officer of the watch.

"How far off?"

"Lookout reports a fair way, sir. Fog's levelling but the horizon's obscured."

Banks nodded. "Mr Caulfield, have the maintop lookout replaced; I'd like to speak to him. You can dismiss the old watch at eight bells." The call for all hands might have been slightly premature, although there was little point in releasing them now, so close to the end of watch. He looked about the deck, taking in the situation. A few seconds ago he was handing out a reprimand to his first lieutenant; now, for all he knew, there was an enemy fleet bearing down on them. Pigot made a more sedate entrance behind him but Banks chose to ignore the man for the present. "Mr Conroy, perhaps you would take a glass to the maintop? Mr Rose, I'd be obliged if you would do the same at the fore."

In fog it was easy to creep almost within hailing distance before danger became apparent; Banks drew a breath of relief as he realised that this was not the case. In fact, judging from the density of the mist, and the distance from the enemy, he was reasonably sure *Pandora* had escaped detection; it was one thing to spot a number of ships in fog, especially when they were expected, quite another to notice just one. Besides, if they had been seen, it would be little trouble to drop back into the mist. Even without the windward advantage, *Pandora*, with her new copper and fresh spars, would be lithe in stays. Her people might not be working quite as a team yet, but they included a good proportion of experienced sailors: more than a match for Frenchmen cooped up in port for goodness knew how long. The lookout slipped down a backstay, and swung himself in from the main chains. He approached the officers knuckling his forehead.

"Make your report, Lawlor," Banks told him gently.

"It were five ships for certain, sir," the man said. "Others I couldn't be sure of, then I started to lose them as we fell back."

"How far off?"

Lawlor shook his head. "Can't rightly say, not with no horizon, like. Several miles, though, a fair distance."

"What about their size?" Caulfield prompted.

"Liners, were they?" Pigot this time. The tone was brash but Banks noticed his face held a set expression, as if he was trying to hide his emotions.

"One was, t'others I couldn't say, but reasonable, sir. Mebbe frigates, mebbe heavy transports."

"Silence there!" Fraiser's voice cut through the general hum of comment that followed Lawlor's report. For several seconds everyone on the quarterdeck held their breath as they listened. A faint whistle could be heard as the wind cut through the shrouds; there was the constant muttering from the stem and the periodic slop of the sea hitting her hull, but nothing else.

"What is it, Mr Fraiser?"

"I thought I heard something, sir," Fraiser said, stubbornly. "Sounded like gunfire."

They were quiet once more, before a fluke of wind brought the noise to them all. A deep rumble, not unlike gunfire, but more regular and constant.

"They're beating for fog," said Caulfield. For a group of ships to avoid collision in poor visibility some sort of loud regular sound was invaluable. "I suppose you wouldn't expect them to fire a gun."

"Pardon me, sir, but that noise is off our larboard quarter." It was Lawlor, the lookout. Of them all his senses would be the most primed.

The officers exchanged glances. The different bearing, together with the fact that sound was reaching them, meant there was at least a second group of ships, and closer to them. "Very good, Lawlor." The silence returned to the quarterdeck as Lawlor made his way forward. No one could accurately determine the direction of a fresh sound in fog, although once the suggestion had been made it was hard to believe that the noise was coming from anywhere else.

"Larboard quarter means more'n a squadron," Lewis whispered to King. "Reckon we got ourselves a proper fleet."

King shook his head; it was equally feasible for two groups of ships to have separated in the fog, although his heart seemed to be beating extremely fast.

"Sail ho!" Conroy, the master's mate, bellowed out from the main top. "Sails on larboard beam - an' quarter!"

"Bring her around, Mr Fraiser," the captain's voice cut through Conroy's report. "Take her three points to starboard."

"Seven in line an' more, off the larboard bow." Rose's voice this time, the excitement causing it to crack up the octave.

"A fleet all right," Lewis muttered.

"What course in the main, there?" Pigot hailed the masthead.

There was a pause while Conroy considered this. "No change, sir. West nor-west, near as makes no difference."

Banks waited until the ship settled on her new heading. The fog was starting to disperse, and would be gone before long. When it did *Pandora* would have to show her heels, but he wanted to stay close enough to make as accurate a sighting as possible. He took a turn along the deck while his mind raced. This could only be the fleet he had heard about; presumably they had either avoided or annihilated the blockading squadron off Brest and escaped into the North Atlantic. Nepean's theories about an invasion of Portugal could be forgotten now; they must have another target in their sights.

The heading ruled out a Channel invasion, although they could still be making for Devon or Cornwall with a wide margin for error. But Plymouth and Torbay were right on hand and in winter, with many ships in harbour, there would be little difficulty in mounting a reasonable force to stop them. Or they could be heading for Wales, a popular choice in the past. Not so heavily defended, and with a minimal militia compared with the South Coast. Then there was Ireland.

He stopped at the end of the quarterdeck level with the fife rails, and peered forward through the mist. It might have been his imagination, but the fog seemed to be clearing as he looked. Ireland it would be: he was sure of it. Admiral Kingsmill had the station and at the best of times there would be no more than one ship of the line and a handful of frigates, nothing like enough to dissuade a determined enemy. As for military, Banks could not be sure but at a time when England was scouring all her forces to serve more vulnerable areas, he would be surprised to see more than a few thousand regular troops, and a minimal militia.

"Deck there, fog's clearing further." Conroy's voice cut through the gloom and all on the quarterdeck turned to windward, although there was still nothing to be seen.

"More ships in sight, sir. Hull up, an' headin' west nor-west." Rose at the foremast lookout this time. The fog must be falling away quite quickly and the wind, now on their beam, was also strengthening.

Banks turned to Caulfield. "I want the jib, and forecourse on her as soon as I give the word."

"Aye, sir. Jib and forecourse." Caulfield nodded, "Prepare to make sail." Banks had been wrong; all hands would certainly be needed before the end of the watch, and possibly for the rest of the night.

"Here it comes!" Pigot this time. Banks noted that his first lieutenant had been almost silent since the sighting. This might have something to do with the dressing down he had just received; then again there could be other reasons. Sure enough the mist was moving in the strengthening breeze. Deep swirls of dark and light moved about the ship in complex marbled patterns, while all eyes stared towards the enemy that still lay hidden.

Then they were hidden no more. The half moon broke through clear air, giving enough light to pick out the details of their rigging. Real ships, and large ones, just as they had been promised. Banks stared across the short expanse of dark water while Pigot, Caulfield and Lewis made notes. There must be thirty or forty out there, less than six miles away. The majority were apparently warships; frigates and line of battleships, were it to be an invasion fleet some would be armed *en flute*, their guns removed to make space for soldiers. Otherwise, they were looking at the most powerful fleet currently at sea. Eight bells rang out: the end of the watch, although few noticed. They had stayed long enough; it was time to be moving.

"Make sail, Mr Caulfield. Jib and forecourse at first. See if she'll take more after that."

There was nothing that *Pandora* could do faced with such a force, and the information she now carried was worth a good deal more than her tender hull. The enemy had the windward advantage and could press a close action; he might wear away now, but adding sail first would make the manoeuvre faster. The deck bucked beneath him as *Pandora* picked up speed.

"Very good, take her round, heading east."

"All hands wear ship!"

She turned neatly, almost within her own length, and soon was tearing through the water, heading away from the enemy fleet and vaguely in the direction of the French coast. There were still some patches of fog ahead, and Banks was confident they could disappear into the night within a few minutes. He looked up to the maintop. "Any movement there?"

"No, sir." Conroy's voice was reassuringly positive. "One's showing three blue lights, but they're still keeping to their..."

"Sail ho! Sail fine on the starboard bow!" Rose cut through Conroy's report. "She's a heavy frigate, sir, hull up an' headin' straight for us!"

Banks dodged round to the windward side of the quarterdeck but the night was dark and with the forecourse set he could see nothing.

"No colours showin'," Rose continued. "But it's a strange pendant; not British."

"Must have lost the main body in the fog," an anonymous voice came from the darkness. Yes, that made sense. Banks toyed with the idea of raising French colours, but rejected it almost at once. This was not through any sense of decency; it was a common enough ruse to show foreign colours to deceive an enemy and providing he didn't open fire while doing so, no offence would have been committed. *Pandora*, like all British ships, carried a selection of ensigns, although his course and sail pattern would mark him out as anything but French.

That being the case, now would be the time to change course, to turn to larboard and try and shake the other ship off before it had a chance to respond. He opened his mouth to give the order, then closed it again. The fog was clearing all the time and altering course might only prolong matters, stacking the odds in favour of the larger ship, and giving them time to call for support. Then they would be trapped, with superior forces on each side, and all their hard-won intelligence would follow them into captivity. Better perhaps to try and slip by, and take cover in what was left of the mist.

"Bloody lucky," the mystery voice continued. "Leaves them fair set to take us out."

Not if he had anything to do with it. Banks turned back. "Clear for action and send the hands to quarters, if you please, Mr Pigot."

Pigot touched his hat and bellowed across the waist of the frigate. Immediately the men began to clear away the guns and break down bulkheads, making a clear gun deck from forecastle to stern. Banks watched them as they went. Some, the newer members, seemed uncertain as to their duties. Most were taken in hand by older men, but there was still too much noise and confusion in the operation. The marines were forming up on the quarterdeck. One collided with a member of the afterguard and dropped his musket. Banks closed his eyes; but the men could not be blamed, it was desperately early in a cruise to go into action; the conditions could hardly be worse, and it was difficult for the captain to ignore the deep, heavy feeling of foreboding that lay inside him.

*****

On the upper deck Flint was already with his guns. According to the watch sheet he had overall charge of both number four long nines of the main battery, although he usually gave the care of the larboard piece to Dobson, the second captain and reliable, despite his less than sanguine attitude. Jameson joined him; the last time they had tended a gun together the lad had been the powder carrier. That was more than a year ago though, and he had done quite a bit of growing since then. Without a word the two began to release the tackle. It was a procedure that neither had followed more than once before, there being little time for practice. Flint swallowed as they loosened the ropes and eased them through the blocks. He had been in action many times before, but the last occasion had almost cost him his nerve. The knots unravelled under his experienced fingers, and he told himself that this time it would be all right.

Bennet and Johnston appeared, and began to clear away their equipment: the flexible rammer, worm, feeder and crows of iron, while Dobson broke out a cheese of wads and drew fresh water for the butt.

"Where's Lawlor and Carter?" Flint asked. Billy, the lad, was with them and had drawn a charge, the three pounds of cylinder powder needed for a standard round, and Johnston was sprinkling sand and water on the deck around the gun. A shout came from above as a man slipped, stumbling against the launch stowed on the skids above their heads. For a second or so he groped for a purchase, before falling away from the boat and tumbling down onto the deck beside them.

Laughter, followed by shouts of "Butcher" came from the gun crews, as Jameson and Wright went to help him.

"'S'all right, matey," Wright informed him, lifting him up by the forearm, and helping him back to his feet. "Jus' a tumble, no damage."

The man looked up to where his mates, still rigging the *sauve-tete* netting twenty or more feet above their head, were grinning and pointing down at him. "Never done that afore," he told Wright as he limped away. "Never in more than ten years at sea."

"Here's Carter!" Sure enough the Londoner came running towards them, with Lawlor a little way behind.

"Bleedin' crusher caught us," he complained, taking the flexible rammer from Bennet. "'ad us carr'in' cabin furniture to t'old. I says we was gun crew, but he weren't 'avin' none of it, not on y'r Nelly." Lawlor took off his shirt and rolled it up into a bundle, before stowing to one side of the shot locker.

"Ne'r mind, you're here now." Flint looked across to Dobson. "Better nip across and help with the larboard. Wright, you go an' all, 'though I wants you both back as soon as you're done."

"Out starboard tompions!" Caulfield's voice carried along the deck, repeated by Cobb, the divisional midshipman. The gun ran in easily on the tackle, Flint pressed the quoin under the breach and Jameson whipped the wooden plug from the muzzle, before the gun was run out once more. Flint removed the lead apron that covered the touchhole, pressed his thumb over the vent and worked the gunlock twice to check the spark. Satisfied, he then went across and collected a two-foot length of slow match from a gunner's mate. The match was lit and smouldered eerily in the dark. Flint spun the length around in the air until the red glow grew yellow and bright, then placed the match in a central tin tub, where it could serve either gun if the need arose.

When at war the guns were kept loaded at all times, but left unprimed to prevent accidental discharge. Flint attended to this, spilling a small amount of lightly mealed powder mixed with spirit from his priming horn into the touchhole, closing the frizzen gently over the powder and easing the hammer shut. Bending down behind the sight he raised his right hand and the servers moved the gun until it was pointing as far forward as the port would allow. He stood back and uncoiled the lanyard leading to the closed gunlock and looked over to Cobb. They were ready.

*****

Below them, Stuart the surgeon was missing. Before the call to clear for action, Manning, the surgeon's mate, had organised the loblolly boys. The warrant officer's sea chests were liberated from the forward storeroom and arranged to form two operating tables. Worn sailcloth was then thrown over, while four lanthorns were slung from the deckhead to give as much light as was possible. Manning had considered laying out the surgeon's tools as well, but his master was known for his short temper, and he decided against it. Now though, with the ship almost ready, action imminent, and still no sign of Stuart, he began to grow uneasy.

"You there, Stamford, go up and see what's keepin' the surgeon." The elderly loblolly boy digested the order for several seconds before slumping off, only to stop in utter confusion as he saw Stuart coming towards him.

He was bleary-eyed with sleep, and wore a face that was flushed and bloated. Without a word to Manning he lowered himself down to the main chest and lifted open the lid. After removing two retractors, a probe and a fleam-toothed saw, he set them on one side, then sat back and sighed, rubbing his eyes at first, then holding his face with both hands.

"All right, sir?" Manning asked after a reasonable period had elapsed. Stuart turned an angry, dilated eye upon him.

"Get on with your work!" he said, before raising his hands past his forehead, running them through his greasy hair, and releasing a generous belch.

*****

On the quarterdeck men were clearing away the carronades while two files of marines had taken up position next to the hammock-packed netting that lined both sides. Banks now paid no attention to the chaos that was erupting all about him; his mind was totally fixed on the frigate that lay just ahead. The best he could wish for was to pass as quickly as possible, then hope to lose the enemy in the night.

"Ship cleared for action, sir," Pigot's voice cut through his thoughts.

"Thank you, Mr Pigot." He turned as a group of men by the forward chaser gave a small cheer; it seemed that the enemy frigate was in sight, although the forecourse still hid it from the captain's view.

From the forecastle, Lewis gave a sigh as he peered under the roach of the sail. "She's a big one, a right thumper, an' no mistake!"

Caulfield clambered up to the main chains and looked out. Twenty great guns a side at least, he reckoned, and eighteen-pounders, that's if they weren't twenty-fours. At least twice the weight of *Pandora's* main armament, and far more of them; they would be lucky to get past without severe damage.

Pigot also considered the ship and swallowed dryly. He had been in action before, twice in fact, and both times survived without harm. Still, this was not the way he preferred to spend his nights, and he would be mightily glad when it was over.

Two yellow flashes spat almost simultaneously towards them as the enemy fired off her bow chasers. One shot splashed off their starboard beam, the other fell without trace.

"How are you loaded, Mr Caulfield?" Banks' voice came from the quarterdeck.

"Single round shot, sir. Do you want the guns drawn?"

Banks shook his head; there was no time. If he was to carry out what he had in mind a large proportion of the gun crews would be needed to help manoeuvre the ship. He walked across to the quarterdeck rail, leaned over and spoke more quietly to the lieutenant.

"Are you able to provide me with both batteries in action?"

"Both batteries? Yes, sir."

"And I require those of your men who are designated trimmers to assist in manoeuvring the ship."

"Sail trimmers, very good, sir." Caulfield's reply came without hesitation. Banks nodded briefly, before turning back to Fraiser and Pigot.

"Gentlemen, I intend to steer to larboard. Fire the starboard guns, and continue round, is that clear?"

"Pass him to starboard, sir?"

"No, Mr Pigot, I expect him to turn to meet us. But we will continue round, tack, and pass to larboard. There's still a deal of cover off our starboard bow; with luck we should lose him."

"But that'll present our stern, and we'll be dead in the water!" Pigot's voice held just a hint of panic.

"No, beggin' your pardon, I think we can do it, sir." Fraiser's voice was quiet but positive and Banks looked his gratitude. Of course Pigot was right; to even think of attempting such a manoeuvre with a fresh crew was asking for trouble. In less than a quarter of an hour *Pandora* might easily be in irons and ripe for a pounding, although if he could pull it off they should slip by with just the one, or maybe two, broadsides to weather.

"Mr Fraiser, you will conn the ship, to allow Mr Pigot to take over from me should I fall." Banks had no intention of allowing Pigot control when *Pandora* tacked. Beside the fact that Fraiser was the better seaman, the captain had a low opinion of the first lieutenant both as an officer and a man. "Are you both clear about what I have in mind?" They nodded in the darkness; there was little time for argument.

Two more stabs of light from the French frigate followed this time by the crash of wood being struck, and a slight jolt from the deck beneath them. Banks ducked down and stared across the forecastle to where the Frenchman's hull could just be made out. They were still three or four cables off, but he wanted to have enough room for the turn. "Very good, take her round, Mr Fraiser!"

The ship healed and wallowed slightly as the rudder kicked over, forcing her into a savage turn. Yards creaked as they were pulled round, desperately trying to keep pace with the wind.

"Fire as you will, Mr Caulfield!"

Caulfield had his sword raised as he looked along the line of gunners; some he knew, though the majority were still relative strangers: the next few minutes would tell a lot more about *Pandora's* men than he had learnt so far in the commission. "Starboard battery, ripple fire broadside from number one, on my word!" He caught the eye of a gun captain, who nodded confidently in return.

The enemy was still heading straight for them, although Banks thought he noticed a slight heal. Yes, she was turning also, but not fast enough to avoid being raked by *Pandora's* broadside.

"Fire!" Caulfield's voice rang out, but there was no answering shot from the first gun. A misfire, by God; if they left it too late the moment would be lost.

After no more than a second, number two fired, and the broadside continued, ragged and with little attention to accuracy, until the last quarterdeck carronade had done its work. The captain turned away from the final shot that fell a good eighty feet from the enemy's bow. There was nothing to be said; the men were untrained and he was asking a lot of them. It had been impossible to detect any damage to the Frenchman but, with luck, they would have caused enough of a stir to allow the ship to survive the next five minutes. Fraiser was looking up at the sails with cautious apprehension. "Very good, Master, carry on."

Fraiser touched his hat before leaning back to bellow. "Bring her round, lads. All hands to tack!"

*****

At Flint's gun Carter and Lawlor, who were nominated as trimmers, clambered up to the forebraces. Flint and the rest attended to the gun, swabbing out and reloading the warm barrel. To their left the crew of number one were also working with singular deliberation, keeping their eyes on their work, and preparing to meet the inevitable reprimands, official from the officers and, far more wounding, the jibes of their fellow men. The linstock flint had failed: split in half when it hit the frizzen, and the gun captain was slow in following up with the match. Their gun had only fired towards the end of the broadside, and by that time the shot had probably gone very wide, although in the confusion, no one could be absolutely sure.

"Well that was a right bloody shower!" Cobb's voice cracked near to them, but his remarks were directed at the entire battery. "That your idea of frightening the frogs - make 'em think they're fighting lunatics?" He caught the eye of Caulfield, looking from his station by the mainmast, and continued in a more official manner. "Secure your pieces, and prepare larboard battery."

Flint nodded to his men as the gun was pulled up tight. They moved across to where Dobson was ready with the larboard gun. Now the action had started the only doubts in Flint's mind were not for himself. The crew was untrained, the biggest bunch of lubbers he had ever sailed with. He could only agree with Cobb; the last broadside had been a proper mess, even though everyone was prepared for it. Heaven alone knew what would happen if the action continued for any length of time.

"We're going about, all right," muttered Dobson, handing the powder horn across. He had heard the orders, and watched as the men ran to the braces, but still the idea of tacking in front of the enemy seemed unbelievable.

"Captain don't mind stretchin' the men," Flint commented, shortly.

Dobson nodded. "God help us all," he said, and the ship continued to turn.

Thankfully the majority of the topmen and petty officers were experienced enough, if not to read the captain's mind, then at least to understand and follow orders. As the quartermaster took her round, keeping every breath of wind for the final ounce of impetus, Banks felt his shattered confidence recover slightly. But now they were stern onto the enemy, stern on and facing a broadside of twenty or more heavy guns.

The flash, seen from their angle, was almost blinding in the black night. Banks found himself ducking down beneath the taffrail, as if a couple of inches of oak would hold back what was heading for them. *Pandora* seemed to slump lower as the shots slammed into her timbers. Her stern windows disappeared, along with the flag locker and two lanterns. The aft starboard carronade was also hit and rolled off its slide onto the healing deck. Men were screaming on all sides, and Banks caught sight of Pigot, peering from behind the relative safely of the mizzen mast.

"Do you have steerage?" Banks shouted back to the quartermaster.

"Aye, sir," the man's tone was completely untroubled; it could almost have been the captain's grandfather speaking. "Rudder's safe, never you mind."

They had lost a good deal of momentum, although the ship was still turning.

"Meet her, meet her." The voice of Fraiser was also reassuringly calm.

Now they were passing the eye of the wind. Banks swallowed. Two, maybe three minutes should see them under sail; otherwise they would stay as they were until the enemy destroyed them. He looked back to the heavy frigate, a line of dim lights showed where her stern ports had opened to allow the guns to be swabbed out and reloaded. It would have to be soon, very soon.

"That's it, bring her round!" Now Fraiser's voice rose, although he was still in complete control. Banks breathed out; *Pandora* was moving again, moving and moving faster than he had expected.

"Forebraces, there!" The yards of the foremast were hauled round to catch the wind once more, and the ship's momentum increased.

"Larboard battery, broadside on my word!" Caulfield's voice came up from the waist; clearly he had no intention of trying a ripple fire again.

A small fire had started at the break of the forecastle. Caulfield would be more than able to cope with it, but Banks was strangely eager to get rid of his second in command.

"Mr Pigot, supervise the fire party forward, if you please." Pigot paused for no more than a second, before leaving the quarterdeck.

Now the enemy was off the larboard quarter, and would be in range within seconds. Banks noted that she was attempting to pull back round to meet them, but it would be too late to use her full broadside.

A shot rang out from *Pandora's* side.

"Wait for it!" Banks all but screamed.

"Check, check, check!" Caulfield's voice this time, but not fast enough to stop another gun firing, and another after that; by the time he had the remaining guns under control the ideal moment had passed.

"All right, Mr Caulfield, fire as you will!" There was no point in trying for a controlled broadside now; the only important thing was to hit the enemy before her vulnerable stern moved out of their sights.

The ragged salvo sailed towards the frigate. Those that had not been let off early were poorly aimed, and any that hit did so to little effect.

Banks watched without emotion; the most he had dared to hope for was to get free without important damage. They had hit back to some extent but now the main thing, the only thing, to do was run. *Pandora* moved away into the night, her speed increasing as she went, and soon the fog began to thicken about her.

For a moment Banks considered setting topsails, but decided against it; with the wind as it was they would do little good and the extra pressure would force the hull down, while straining the yards and making *Pandora* more obvious in the mist.

The wind was growing steadily, taking what cover there was, but giving them extra speed; with luck they should be free of danger before long. Then the night was split with the flash of another broadside from the French, but either it was badly aimed or simply let off for good measure as no shot came close to them.

Fraiser was looking at his captain expectantly. Banks shook his head. "Keep as she is, Master." There was little point in changing course; he didn't feel the Frenchman was likely to chase after them. The crack of a shot rang out forward, followed by the slump of something heavy hitting the deck. Some fool of a marine had let his musket off, no doubt. Banks hardly cared at that moment. He looked back over the shattered taffrail. Somewhere out there was a powerful fleet, and somehow they had to be stopped. Later he could decide what to do; probably head for the Brest offshore squadron, either that or make for Plymouth or Torbay. First he must attend to his ship, but before that a moment or two for himself. He closed his eyes and felt the tension ebbing from him as he breathed in the cold night air.

After several minutes Caulfield approached, his face blackened with burnt powder. He looked apprehensive. Banks opened his eyes, gave him a brief smile and nodded. "Had a few problems, I collect, Mr Caulfield?"

"Yes sir. I'm sorry; the hands are not as practised as I would like."

"It is to be expected, and I'm sure you did your best." He moved away from the shattered taffrail and looked about the quarterdeck. Fraiser was standing next to the mizzen mast looking up to the sails. The fire at the forecastle had been stifled, although Pigot had yet to return. Banks remembered him with a stab of conscience; it had been a selfish action, to send his first lieutenant off like that. The man had every right to walk the quarterdeck; he was hardly to blame if his captain couldn't stand the sight of him. He turned to Dorsey, the beefy Irish midshipman standing near by.

"Mr Dorsey, present my compliments to the First Lieutenant. If he has finished his duties, perhaps he might join me for a glass of port."

The master looked around and caught his captain's eye. Was he mistaken, or had the frank, honest look suddenly disappeared from Fraiser's face?

"Mr Pigot, sir? I'm afraid he was wounded."

"Wounded?"

"Yes, sir. Shot."

"That last broadside, I suppose?" Banks was guiltily aware of no great feeling of concern about his second in command.

Caulfield broke the silence. "I think it was small arms fire, actually, sir."

"He's been taken below." Fraiser again, and again with a touch of uncertainty. Banks tried to clear his mind. The sighting of an enemy fleet, followed by a sudden action, had all but deprived him of the ability to reason.

"That's right, sir." Caulfield this time. "I saw him being carried down.

But this was madness; Banks was certain *Pandora* had been well clear of anything other than the frigate's heavy guns throughout the action, and there had been no scream of case or grape; round shot had been used throughout.

"Of course I only saw him for a moment." Caulfield paused and drew breath. "But it didn't look good, sir. He'd been shot in the head."

CHAPTER FIVE

The next morning broke with no sign of ill weather. Banks stood at the open deadlights that covered what remained of the stern windows. A fragile but welcome sun played upon his face, and the sea, calmer now with barely a trace of white, refracted the light into a thousand cracks of phosphorescent brilliance. He took a deep draught of cold, clean air, exhaling slowly as his mind wandered over the events of the previous night.

Caulfield had done well. From the moment Pigot had fallen the second lieutenant stepped into his place with confidence and ability. They had been fortunate in taking little damage (Banks gave scant credit for his own actions), but no ship survives raking fire without some important repairs being necessary. Caulfield had attended to it all, from the shattered sternposts and larboard mizzen chains to the deadlights that were in front of him now, and had allowed Banks a few hours of precious sleep. Above him he could hear the sound of the carpenter's crew setting up a new taffrail. The sail maker and his men would also be busy stitching a new suit of signal flags, while the boatswain, his mates, and whatever topmen could be spared had been running fresh shrouds, stays and braces since the end of the action. Caulfield had organised much of this, although he had done so with the full cooperation of every man in the crew. It might have been the action, the action that had come upon them unexpectedly, and caught many out: frightened the new hands and made fools of the old. It might have been the nearness of the enemy, an enemy that some had only read about, yet now appeared actual, alive and deadly. It might have been the relief that death had passed so very close, and yet left them to live a while longer. It might have been any one, or a combination of many other smaller factors, although Banks knew that there was a far simpler reason for the oppressive atmosphere that had been part of *Pandora* since she had first set sail, to suddenly lift.

His mind registered the scent of fresh roasted coffee and, turning he saw Dupont slip quietly into the cabin with a loaded tray.

"Breakfast, sir?"

Stupidly Banks always felt a slight shock on hearing the French accent after being in action with Dupont's countrymen, even though the man had served him for many years, and was an ardent Chouan. The captain turned and seated himself at the dining table while Dupont brought in the rest of the meal. The sound of the ship's bell was followed by the usual shouts from each sentinel. With Pigot gone the watch system was in disarray, and Banks felt mildly guilty that he had been sleeping peacefully while *Pandora* was one watch-keeper down. Fraiser should have the deck now, allowing Caulfield to go below and finally rest. Banks sipped at his coffee; it would be far better to talk to the lieutenant here, in the cabin, besides he would sleep all the better with a good breakfast inside him.

"Pass the word for the second - for Mr Caulfield, if you please, and lay an extra place." Dupont nodded and wafted from the cabin.

The lieutenant arrived simultaneously with a covered plate of devilled kidneys, and accepted Bank's invitation to join him. They ate guardedly and in silence, each conscious of the novel situation, and the many events of the previous night that would have to be dealt with. In fact it was while Caulfield was spreading salted butter over toasted soft tack that Banks began to speak.

"I'll take inspection later this morning, although I have every confidence in what you have done. Before that I want at least two hours on the great guns. There's nothing like an action to show the people what they should be about."

The lieutenant nodded; formality could not be upheld over buttered tommy.

"Bosun reports we'll be in full rig afore noon, sir."

"What speed are we making now?"

"Six knots at the last call." It was a fair pace for a ship under limited sail.

"Very good, but we should make all haste." Colpoys' squadron could be barely over the horizon, or many miles away. It might even have ceased to exist, but whatever, *Pandora* was carrying vital information; every effort must be made to pass on the news of the French invasion fleet. Both had finished eating now and Banks paused, a little self-consciously, before continuing.

"There is still one matter we must address; something that, I will confess, is beyond my experience."

"Indeed, sir?"

Their eyes met and Banks very nearly smiled, although heaven alone knew the situation did not merit humour.

"Indeed; the loss of the first lieutenant." He paused for several seconds; Caulfield's face remained totally impassive. "Tell me," Banks continued, "just how did Mr Pigot die?"

*****

Banks was right - the exercise with the great guns took on a far greater importance. Freed from the tyranny of an overbearing number one, and yet deeply conscious of the disgrace they had brought upon themselves, the gun crews fell to work with a will never known in *Pandora* before. Watched by the boatswain's party aloft, and the carpenter, his mates, and any idlers not involved in repairing damage below, the heavy guns were run back and forth, with the straining servers and tacklemen giving everything they had and still more. The early morning sun lingered, and the men's backs were wet with sweat when King blew the silver whistle that marked the end of the exercise.

"Secure your pieces and stand down." Once more the trucks rumbled along the deck, this time to be trussed up soundly. King descended to the cockpit. The berth was already half full; Lewis sat at the table with a needle and thread darning his better woollen waistcoat that had been torn in the action, while Manning was reading up on common ailments. He hoped to have his position as surgeon's mate confirmed at the end of the commission, and was already researching the many subjects he might be tested upon when he finally stood in front of his betters at Surgeon's Hall. His current subject was syphilis, the mysteries of which were fast turning him into a confirmed bachelor.

Lewis looked up as he entered. "Good exercise, Thomas?"

"Aye, the men did well."

"Trying to make up for last night?" Manning asked.

King eyed him uncertainly. "How do you mean?"

"The balls-up they made of those broadsides." There was no malice in the words and the surgeon's mate stayed with his book.

"I seen an Indiaman filled with monkeys do better," added Lewis.

King pursed his lips. "Well we won't be needing your apes, not if this morning is anything to go by."

"Improvement?"

He nodded. "You wouldn't credit they were the same men." He looked about; Collins had returned his possessions to his locker, although he noted that his pistol case was not properly closed. On impulse he opened the other clasp and looked inside. The ebony butt glowed in the half-light, and the maker's name *"Whitehern of Abingdon"* stood out on the side of the lock. A mark on the barrel caught his eye and he picked the pistol up, examining it carefully. The pan was heavy with soot and there was an unmistakable scent that could only mean that the thing had been fired. He dropped the gun back into its box, almost frightened to hold it. The other two were taking no notice of him, and for a moment he wondered if he should tell them what he had found. He thought back over the events of last night. Both cockpits had been cleared during the action. Despite the fact that the deck housed no guns, space was needed to tend the wounded, and everything would have been bundled into the storeroom forward.

King looked at his locker; his other possessions appeared in order, in fact were it not for the mark on the gun and the faint aroma he would have said nothing had been touched. He wondered over the likelihood of someone taking a pistol before going in to action. It could not be mere personal protection; pistols, muskets, cutlasses, pikes - even tomahawks were on hand for those who felt the need of them. And however accurate his piece may be, the charge and calibre were too small for the rigours of shipboard fighting. His mind wandered, and a chill began to grow inside him. All of the ready use weapons were heavy, clumsy affairs. They were also stored in open view, although under the scrutiny of a warrant officer. He suddenly became aware of Manning's eyes on him, and snapped the box shut.

"Hiding your guilty secrets?" Manning enquired.

King forced a grin. "Any secrets I had wouldn't be kept in here," he said.

There was a tap on the deal bulkhead and Collins appeared at the door.

"Captain's sendin' for you, Mr King."

"The captain?" King looked blankly at Manning.

"Yes, nice man with a big hat, you must remember."

"All right, but what does he want with me?"

"One way to find out." Lewis grinned at Manning and went back to his darning as King hurried from the cockpit.

*****

The mood of the ship had lifted after the successful gun exercise, and improved still further with dinner. To date this had been a solemn meal with only the rum issue and hot food to lighten stilted conversations that were carried out *sotto-voce* across the mess tables. Now there was a far more healthy murmuring and several times actual laughter could be heard above the clatter of pewter plates and wooden platters. Flint took a pull at his beer and grinned at Jameson.

"Aye, were a perfect mash, but at least some good come of it."

"You mean Pigot?" Lawlor asked unnecessarily. "Ask me, the Frogs did our work for us."

"Our work?" It was not unusual for Jameson to find the conversation race ahead of him.

"That's right, Matt," Flint said, pointing at Lawlor. "We got a right firebrand here; Lawlor was all set to finish Mr Pigot off by the next watch, ain't that the truth, Sam?"

"Stranger 'as 'appened," Dobson cut in, his eyes hardly moving from the table. "Seen it afore, seen it many times; fallin' top hamper, rollin' ball, trippin' over a combing. T'aint too 'ard to lose a man, if the people is willin'."

There was a brief silence as each considered this. Flint himself had known of one instance when a young and well-connected midshipman had made a living hell for every man in his division. It had taken nothing more than fifteen seconds' work to send him over the side during a moonless graveyard watch. Two men did it while five kept watch; every man in the division knew the details, and the entire ship was in complete agreement, but for all the fuss the lad's family raised, the court of enquiry could do nothing. No one said a word, no one was any the wiser, and the death was finally put down to shipboard accident.

"So, Lawlor would have taken care of Mr Pigot?" Bennet asked, the pieces finally falling into place. Bennet had joined the ship as a landsman and only now was starting to find his voice.

"More'n likes," Lawlor nodded complacently. "That, or he'd a been exchanged first opportunity."

"Exchanged…" Dobson said, wistfully. "What in Hades d'you reckon we'd have got in exchange for Pigot?"

"You can see the proclamation," Carter bashed his tankard down. "'Bastard wanted, in swap for same'."

Those within hearing laughed easily and it was a good sound. It was the laughter of comfortable men, laughter that would have pleased any officer unaware of its cause. But Wright said nothing, his eyes remaining fixed on the tabletop.

"Anyways, we ain't got a worry." Flint looked about for the currant duff that had been promised. "Pigot is gone, and we can get to being a proper ship."

"Thanks to the French," Jameson reminded him.

"Aye, thanks to the French," Flint agreed.

"God bless 'em…" Wright added. His voice was strangely hard, although his eyes remained fixed and distant.

*****

All vital work was completed before sunset, and with the information about the invasion fleet still burning inside him, Banks spared no thought for men or fabric. It could well be that Colpoys' squadron had been destroyed by the French; at that very moment they might be heading for a collection of mastless hulks or worse. But as she made sail and set her stem to intercept, *Pandora* moved with true purpose for the first time in her short life. Cutting through the grey seas with the dash expected of a light frigate, the icy winter air cleansed the memories of Pigot and the dismal action from her timbers, and she truly began to live in the minds of the men.

From that day onward a new air of enthusiasm appeared, and grew with each passing hour. There was no more shirking of responsibilities; men became eager for challenges, and competed with each other in simple tasks. The exercise with the great guns was followed by another with small arms, this under the joint direction of Martin, the lieutenant of marines, who was well versed in the gentlemanly art of swordsmanship, and Williams, the gunner, who had been on more than one boarding party and knew the value of a well placed boot. Skylarking was seen for the first time, and more than one mess evening ended with the men drawing together to bellow out the "coalbox" of *Spanish Ladies* or whatever popular song had taken their fancy.

The change in atmosphere had a more tangible side as well; hammocks were packed neatly in the nettings, mess tables swept clean, and the men themselves took on a smarter appearance, their pigtails being properly dressed by tie-mates, and the ship's barber called upon other than on a Sunday. Throughout his time, all Pigot's bullying and intimidating ways had failed to raise the decks to anything like the expected splendour, and yet now, with little encouragement and certainly no coercion, the strakes shone bright and white as newly laid paper.

And it was on that very deck that Pigot's body was laid later that morning. Packed in his closed cot, with two round shot at his feet, it was alone; although several were likely to follow, no one, bar him, had actually died in the action. As the captain read the burial service over his late second in command, he was conscious that the solitary body only brought attention to his death, and invited speculation as to how he had died. It would have been far better for Pigot to have been amongst several of his shipmates, he thought, then instantly recoiled at the image, and the wish that had been part of it.

"We therefore commit his body to the deep." The cot slid from the grating lifted suitably enough by Guppy, probably the only friend or ally Pigot had known. As the body hit the water the captain came to the end of the service.

"On hats!" Caulfield's voice sounded relieved; indeed every man turned away from the scene eagerly, some pleased to see the end of a particularly nasty individual, others simply comforted by the fact that another funeral had been completed and, once again, it had not been their turn.

*****

Later the great cabin had an air of formality as the officers entered. Banks rose to meet them, but there was no smile on his face, and he indicated the waiting chairs with a silent wave. Caulfield seated himself carefully. He had known that this would be a difficult meeting, and was now uncomfortably aware of a prickling of sweat beneath his shirt, despite the damp winter air that whistled through the shattered stern windows. To his right, the surgeon, Stuart, balanced awkwardly on his chair. He too had been expecting an uncomfortable time, and had taken measures to see that he was properly relaxed. Rather too many measures, if Caulfield was any judge. Fraiser entered last, and sat down without a word, fingering his collar and stock nervously in the silence.

"Thank you for coming, gentlemen. I trust this will not take us very long." As Banks spoke he managed to hold each with his eye long enough to give the impression he spoke to them, and them alone. "We are all aware of the regrettable death of Mr Pigot, and I think no one can be ignorant of the manner in which he died. Mr Stuart, perhaps you would like to elaborate?"

Stuart moved awkwardly on his chair. "Shot in the 'ead, sir," he remarked thickly. He reached into his pocket and withdrew a small, flattened piece of metal. "My assistant removed this from 'is skull during the forenoon." He passed the lead ball to Caulfield who took it reluctantly. It was small and light, unusually so. Much less than half the weight of a musket ball, and far smaller than grape or canister shot. He passed it on to Fraiser, who seemed equally unwilling to take it.

"Small arms bullet, probably from a private piece," Fraiser said, turning the shot over in his hand. "A pot house pistol, minimal power, limited range, and probably inaccurate. Certainly not from the enemy; we weren't anywhere close enough for a ball like that to reach us."

"Pardon me, Mr Fraiser, but do you detect any marks?"

Fraiser looked again. Sure enough there were a series of thin but regular lines on the rounded side of the ball. "Yes, sir. Yes, you're correct. There are rifling marks."

"Exactly. Which means a slightly different matter. No cheap pistol has rifling, this is a more sophisticated piece." He paused, with just a hint of theatrics. "But the main point is, whoever shot Mr Pigot was not a Frenchman."

The implications were vast.

"I was not unaware of Mr Pigot's unpopularity." Banks accepted the bullet back from Fraiser and placed it on the table where they could all see it. "And I am also sensible to the ways in which a disliked officer may be dealt with. However, we are in the very early days of our commission. There can be no excuse, no reason good enough for a man to die barely days after leaving port."

In the silence each officer nodded. They were well aware of their tenuous hold on authority. Mutiny and insurrection were not uncommon in British warships, and Pigot's death would serve as a positive indication of the power that the men of the lower deck held.

"Naturally I will have to present a full report as soon as we reach Admiral Jervis; until then I wish for you all to be particularly alert for any murmuring amongst the people. Any chance word must be reported to you, and subsequently to me. If it comes to it I would rather see a dozen innocent men in irons than run any risk of mutiny."

Once more the three officers nodded, and Caulfield felt the tension ease slightly. The matter had been dealt with, and they were going to move on, although there remained a nagging doubt inside him. There was something that did not fit, something that he knew, or had known, something that he should be recalling now, although for the life of him he could not think of it.

"If we may just turn to the watch-keeping arrangements. Mr Caulfield, you will assume the position of first lieutenant."

There were few other statements that would have distracted him so successfully. His reply was brisk and automatic, although it was difficult to keep a smile from coming to his mouth as Caulfield absorbed the news. Fraiser looked his congratulations while his mind raced; a move to second in command was not likely to be overridden by a subsequent appointment, and he was now next in line for promotion to commander, should *Pandora* fare well in action.

"I have already spoken with King; he has passed his board, and will be supporting you as acting lieutenant."

Doubly good for the lad, Caulfield thought, and a move he richly deserved. The feeling of well-being grew; maybe this would not be the disastrous commission he had anticipated. It should only be a formality for Jervis to confirm King's promotion, and with such a popular and competent subordinate, Caulfield was reasonably certain of knocking the crew into shape. Then a chilling thought struck; one that took all the pleasure out of the recent news. It suddenly occurred to him that he was assuming, they were all assuming, that a lower deck hand had dealt with Pigot. The pistol bullet seemed to draw him like a magnet as he realized where he had seen just such a piece. No one had considered it might have been an officer. No one until now.

*****

Whatever doubts the captain may have had about the crew were totally unfounded. Mutiny could not have been further from any mind, and the improvements continued, until it was hard to remember the suspicious and frightened men who had so very recently made up the lower deck. The weather also changed; the wind rose and remained strong and constant, and *Pandora* began to make excellent progress, her dark tarred shrouds screaming as she ripped through the black Atlantic with a white crust of spray rising from her stem.

They spotted one of Colpoys' frigates on the morning of the third day; by noon they had closed with the squadron, and shortly after *Pandora* lay hove to as Banks clambered up the flagship's steep tumblehome. Caulfield and King watched him go, conscious that the frigate's battered appearance was attracting a fair amount of comment from the men of HMS *London* and the offshore squadron.

"Admiral dines at three, reckon we won't see him back before the first dog."

King nodded, it was a fair enough prediction, but the tooth that had been nagging him for the last few days was playing up again, and he could not get excited about an admiral's dining habits.

Martin, the lieutenant of marines, came over. "Sir John has his nephew, Griffith, as captain; the pair of them keep a fair table I hears."

Caulfield nodded. "Their premier's Peter Bover; we served together as midshipmen. Rest of us always said he had worms, judging by the rate he ate; seems he's found the ideal berth."

"Belike we could have ourselves a bit of a feast as well. What say you to one of the suckling pigs? We could have it killed, drawn and roasting in no time."

The thought of biting his way through heavy pigskin made King wince. Noticing this, Martin slapped him on the back and laughed.

"Come on, none of that sissy 'hide me in the cable tier stuff' - you're a lieutenant now. Get used to the company of gentlemen, and eating like one!" Martin chortled loudly, and went off in search of the cook.

Caulfield grimaced. "There's some that ain't as gentlemanly as others," he said, nodding towards the departing marine. "An' some who wouldn't deserve the name if it were tattooed upon their forehead."

Together they watched the men in the three-decker in silence for a moment, then Caulfield turned to him.

"You have a pistol, I believe?" he asked. King sucked at his sore tooth, too distracted to note the change in tone. "Do you carry it with you?"

"No." King became aware of Caulfield's words and their implications. "Why do you ask?"

The older man was still looking at the flagship. "No reason, I just wondered if you could account for it during the action."

His collar had suddenly become tight, and King felt a warm flush sweep over his body. He knew his cheeks had grown red, and hoped that the chill air would be blamed.

"It's too small," he said softly. "I only keep it for going ashore."

"But has it been fired on board this ship?" Caulfield asked, turning to him.

King nodded. "Yes." His voice was barely a whisper.

"Aye, I thought as much." Caulfield gave him a grim smile. "But better mind who you tells that to," he said.

*****

Banks surprised them all; within an hour he had boarded his barge, and before he was half way back to *Pandora*, a line of signal flags had broken out from *London*.

"Private, to the squadron," Dorsey, the signal midshipman, reported. "They're making sail, they'll be a headin' soon, no doubts," he added, with an assured voice.

"They'll have to move some to catch the French," Lewis commented.

"If that's what they're about." Fraiser looked meaningfully at the captain's barge, now just approaching the larboard entry port, where Banks could board without ceremony. "Reckon it'll be little of our concern whatever they do, *Pandora*'s not gonna make one *iota* of difference to this lot, or the Channel dodgers, an' Jervis is crying his eyes out for frigates.

"So it's south to Gib, and sunshine?" Lewis asked him.

"I would say so," Fraiser nodded.

"And blackstrap, and singing, and dark Spanish ladies," he grinned at the master. "There're worse ways of spendin' a war."

*****

It was the first time that Caulfield had taken his 'cello from its case since they had sailed. He did so now, a little guiltily, tightening the strings and bringing them gently up to pitch with a delicacy few would have credited him with. The bridge had slipped slightly, and the lieutenant gently eased it back into position, remembering the caution that the maker had given him over the tender oil varnish. Caulfield looked at the finish in dismay; what had once shone with a deep and full lustre was now saddened by a bloom of condensation. He took up his silk and rubbed at it to salve his conscience, before reaching for his bow and tightening the tortoiseshell frog. The 'cello had been an indulgence; similar in part to King's pistol; it was the sort of thing a sailor bought when on shore and with money in his pocket. The lower deck equivalent would probably be a parrot, or a gaudy gold watch, although Caulfield had wanted a good 'cello ever since he had first started to play.

This particular one had been bought from Hills, and had their distinctive fittings. The bow was also made by them and in addition to the tortoiseshell frog, was gold mounted with a fine logwood stick. He plucked a stray hair from the bow, and adjusted the A, which had fallen flat. Then, bringing the bow down onto the gut strings, he drew it across. The low, reverberating noise filled the officers' store, a place he had chosen as being about as far as anyone can get from the rest of humanity in a Jackass frigate. He closed his eyes and played again, gradually carrying up the C major scale, on and on until he was pressing the very edge of the fingerboard. His vibrato was appalling, but that was hardly to be surprised at. He descended, passing through each of the strings, finally ending on a low and mournful open C. Then he began to play a piece he had learnt as a child. Simple, but fulfilling, his fingers readily fell into the well-remembered patterns, while his mind was free to wander over the events of the last few weeks.

Caulfield usually regarded himself as a good judge of character. Certainly he had summed up Pigot in a trice, yet King had surprised him. He had every time for the lad, and honestly thought he would make an excellent officer, although that would all be for nothing now. There was bound to be a court of enquiry and, despite his own warnings to the boy, these matters had a way of coming out, especially in a ship as small as *Pandora*. The piece was ended now, and Caulfield began to play another, again from his youth, again from memory. One thing was quite certain - if King was revealed as the murderer, he could expect little quarter. In a service that had seen an admiral executed on his own quarterdeck, there was small chance of a mere acting lieutenant avoiding the same fate. He stopped, mid phrase, and brought the bow down, before gently releasing the tension and replacing it, and his 'cello, in the case. His mood had changed, as moods do, and suddenly he had lost all desire for music.

*****

The tooth would wait no longer. King made his way to the sick bay assuring himself that whatever immediate pain there might be in pulling the thing, must be worth ending the prolonged agony of the last few days. There were four hammocks rigged for men recovering from wounds received in the recent action, and a cot secured to the deck held Powell, a topman with a head wound. A distracted groan came from one of the hammocks, and King recognised the voice of Carter, who had been badly wounded and wasn't expected to make it. Stuart looked up from his counter as King entered. His face appeared flushed in the shaded lantern light, and King suspected he was already three parts inebriated.

"A tooth you say? I've men dying about me, and you come botherin' with a tooth?"

King swallowed; he had little taste for arguing with a drunk, but the pain had now reached the stage when he would gladly resort to violence if it meant even temporary relief.

"If you've no mind to pull it now, so be it. I'll take a dose of laudanum, and be back to you in the morning.

"Ah, so it's my laudanum you're after, is it?" Fresh colour now filled the man's face, and he eyed King suspiciously. "Ach, talk to my assistant, he'll do for you. Reckon there's little he can muff in pulling a tooth."

King turned gratefully, and headed back towards the cockpit where Manning would be found. He would prefer to trust the tooth to the mate. Although young and relatively inexperienced, Manning inspired confidence, and was almost certain to be sober.

He opened his mouth as wide as possible while Manning peered and poked about inside, his free hand holding a lantern above King's head.

"To the right you say?"

King nodded, and tried to talk further, but Manning was blessed with large fingers that almost filled his mouth.

"There's two there that need 'tending to," he said, finally removing his hand. "One looks like the tiger; care to have them both out and be done with it?"

King shook his head. "Stick to the one that troubles."

Manning nodded wisely, "Aye, you could die tomorrow, and then there'd be a waste."

He reached for his brown leather bag and produced a small metal key with a wooden handle. It was about the size of a corkscrew, but in place of a spiral it had a straight metal bar with a recess, and a small fin to the end, not unlike the foresight of a gun barrel.

"Just have another look about," Manning said, deftly feeding the tool unnoticed into King's mouth. The tooth was locked into the recess in the key, and twisted free of the gum in under a second, less time than it took King to feel a sudden stab of pain and grunt in surprise.

"There's the blighter!" It was big and appeared almost entirely black in the dim light of the cockpit. Manning looked up to where King was exploring his mouth with his tongue. "Better wash out with hot sea water for next few days. Gum'll heal in no time."

King thanked him and left the cockpit. Since his promotion he had been allocated a cabin in the gunroom. He would be on duty in under an hour; there would just be time to get a steward to boil up some salt water. Stuart weaved into his path in the dim light. He had a stupid smile on his face and King guessed that now he was well into his cups.

"Something I thought you might like to see, if you've a moment," he said, raising a beckoning finger. Unwillingly King found himself following the man as he swayed along towards his small cabin. Once inside he fumbled with the lamp for several seconds, before turning back to King with a look of smug triumph on his face.

"I have to take the watch shortly," King said, his face still smarting from the extraction.

"All in good time, all in good time." Again that stupid smile and King felt anger replace his annoyance. Then Stuart reached under his locker and brought out a small package wrapped in canvas.

"I thought you'd like to see this, knowing how fond you were of our late, lamented first lieutenant." The surgeon's voice was thick, and King watched as he began to unwrap the bundle.

"Some folks gets upset, but we medical men, well, its jus' the stuff we works with."

All memories of the tooth left him now, as the contents of the package became obvious. King tore his fascinated gaze away, and looked at Stuart's face.

"I'll bottle it proper soon as I gets the chance, but it'll never look the same preserved." There was an evil pleasure in the surgeon's expression that neither his drunken state, nor the poor light could disguise.

"There, what you says to that?"

King felt his body chill; reluctantly he switched his gaze from the surgeon to that of his package, and found he was looking straight into the bloodshot eyes of Pigot's shattered head.

CHAPTER SIX

Pandora was heading south, but still the icy winter held her firmly in its grip. The weather deteriorated shortly after they left the inshore squadron and it had been slow progress, logging ninety, a-hundred-and-three, and eighty-nine miles on each subsequent day. But now the air cleared as the wind picked up, tightening her canvas as the ship gathered speed.

Caulfield paced the quarterdeck as the dark night showed signs of giving way to gloomy dawn, and looked about. Apart from the fresh timber that had yet to be painted there was little visible sign that *Pandora* had seen action. Certainly the boatswain had set all to rights aloft, and even without reference to the traverse board, he could feel the ship bite into the black seas under the press of canvas. He turned to Dorsey, the midshipman of the watch.

"Take a glass to the masthead and report."

Dawn; one of the few times a well run ship can be taken by surprise, and Caulfield was determined not to be caught napping during his first week as first lieutenant. When light broke at sea all manner of dangers might be uncovered; after twelve hours of relative security, they must be prepared for anything.

The cry came from Lawlor at the masthead, well before the lad had reached the maintop, making him quicken his pace in an effort to join in bearing the news.

"Deck there: sail in sight, fine on the starboard bow!"

Caulfield's pulse quickened. "What ship?"

"Hard to tell, sir. She's hull up an' headin' for us; 'bout four mile off. Look's like a heavy frigate, maybe somat smaller."

The first lieutenant turned to send a boy for the captain just as Banks appeared on the quarterdeck.

"Good morning, Mr Caulfield. We have company, I hear."

Caulfield touched his hat and tried to assume the captain's air of nonchalance.

"Much lighter than a liner, but well built," Dorsey's voice squeaked with excitement as it cut in. "Not flyin' no colours, though she's sailing trim enough, and showin' a deep roach to the forecourse."

"A warship, sir!" Caulfield could not resist the comment; Banks barely grunted in acknowledgment. The light was still bad, although the strange vessel would be visible from the deck as soon as day properly arrived. Banks still seemed unconcerned; with a hand to his brow he was looking up at the yards, as if inspecting the boatswain's work of the day before.

"I can see just the one line of ports." Dorsey again. Every man on board was listening to his words, and clearly the lad was relishing the rare power. "But she's a big 'un, more'n forty for sure."

Almost any size of frigate would be larger than *Pandora*; it was plain bad luck to pick one of the heaviest of her class. Caulfield swallowed as he turned to the captain, expecting some form of action. He was not disappointed; Banks took three paces to the weather mizzen shrouds and reached up to the deadeyes. Swinging himself out, he raced up the ratlines in true seaman fashion, the shrouds slipping through his hands as he climbed. Up, and out along the futtock shrouds under the mizzen top, before continuing up the topmast shrouds to the masthead. Fraiser made his appearance just as the captain reached the crosstrees, and was holding a glass to the sighting.

"What's afoot, Michael?" the master asked. Caulfield shook his head.

"We got a heavy frigate before us."

"Colours?"

"Not as yet."

Not as yet, although both were fully aware that there should be no lone British frigates in the area. The nearest would be one of

Kingsmill's squadron, probably *Kangaroo*, and she was stationed more than two hundred miles to the north.

"Could be a scout from a convoy."

Caulfield nodded. "Aye, but whose?"

Fraiser digested this for a moment. The likelihood that this was yet another of the invasion fleet was surely slight; they had travelled a good way since they had met the main body, a straggler would never have been so far adrift. He thought further; nothing was impossible, and the North Atlantic in winter was known for its contrary weather. Assuming the French had come from Brest, one or two ships may well have separated earlier on and then hit adverse winds. That being the case they would expect to find just such a ship heading north, almost exactly the heading of the sighting. In fact the more Fraiser considered, the more likely it was that they were facing yet another Ireland bound vessel.

From the mizzen crosstrees the captain looked down and hailed.

"Take in the forecourse, sharply now. Then slacken the foretopmast shrouds."

Caulfield stared up for several seconds while he considered what the captain had said before springing into life, repeating the order in a manner that was automatic.

Working only under topsails and driver *Pandora* began to wallow as she lost way. All about the men began casting worried glances at the quarterdeck as the topmast was allowed to creak forward and slightly to one side.

"That'll do, secure it." Banks gave the order in a clear, measured tone as he swung from his perch, and began the descent.

"Very good, Mr Peters," Banks shouted as he reached the deadeyes and dropped nimbly onto the deck. "Now slacken the main top and mizzen stays, weather side, and ease all braces to spill." The boatswain was looking at the slackening shrouds with an air of disbelief and for a moment a look of rebellion flashed across the old man's face. He turned to Caulfield in protest. "She can't take a sail like that, sir. First extra stitch and all will be ahoo!"

"Make it so, Mr Peters."

Lewis appeared, slightly dishevelled and obviously still half asleep. He looked about in amazement as the ship began a choppy roll.

"What's about?" he whispered to Conroy, who gave a subtle shrug of his shoulders.

The fore topmast creaked alarmingly, while the main topmast was allowed to fall slightly to leeward; even in the dim light, their rig looked ungainly in the extreme.

Banks turned to one of the master's mates. "Mr Conroy, I'd be obliged if you would have the deadlights removed from my cabin, and ask the carpenter to start the pumps to the weather side."

Caulfield looked as if nothing would surprise him again as Conroy cautiously repeated the order. Exposing their damaged stern was pure lunacy, although quite in keeping with the captain's previous orders. In the space of a few minutes they had gone from a well-found ship to one that would look as if it had been severely mauled in battle. The light was coming quickly now, in no time they would be in clear sight of the strange vessel; then realisation dawned. Caulfield caught the captain's eye, and smiled.

Banks smiled back. "She's an armed transport," he said, simply. "Caught a sight of uniforms packed 'tween the gangways, and she's stowing on the quarterdeck."

"Soldiers, sir?"

"So I believe."

"And the guns?"

Banks pursed his lips. "Hard to say. Chances are some will be quakers, but they'll have a good few working, you can be sure of that."

Caulfield mused to himself. If the captain was right the mystery ship wasn't quite the threat she once appeared. Removing some guns would create extra space, but at the obvious cost of firepower. However her timbers would be every bit as strong and carrying maybe three, four hundred extra fighting men would settle matters very quickly if they allowed her close enough to board. The wind was off the starboard beam, putting both ships on opposing tacks; they would have to keep their distance; that meant turning, and as soon as possible. Then it would become a stern chase. The reduction in sail, together with the slackening of the shrouds that Banks had ordered would make *Pandora* considerably slower, even ignoring the time and space that would be wasted in bringing her about.

"She's visible from the deck now." King's voice cut in to their thoughts, and sure enough Caulfield could just make out the ghostly outline of topsails becoming more solid as the ship emerged through the gloom of dawn. A murmur went about the men, instantly stifled by Guppy, the master at arms. But Caulfield sympathised entirely, the ship looked huge, far bigger than the normal British thirty-two or thirty-six. Her lines were sleek, with a broad beam counteracted by an unusually long hull, making her appear nearer in the growing light.

"Reckon she'll carve us by three knots," Conroy muttered. Lewis nodded; it would be at least that considering *Pandora's* current state of rig, although Lewis guessed the Frenchman would be clumsy in stays, and possibly slower in an outright chase.

One of the carpenter's crew came up from below and approached Caulfield, knuckling his forehead.

"Carpenter reports the well's nigh on dry, sir."

"Very good," Banks interrupted. "Ask Mr Everit to start a couple of water barrels, and be sure the dales are working to windward. To windward, do you hear me?"

Despite the novelty of being addressed by his captain, the man hesitated before knuckling his forehead once more, and disappearing below. Starting the fresh water was common practice to add speed to a ship, but why did the captain insist the drained water be pumped to windward, when surely the enemy would be able to see?

"Colours, sir!" All turned as one on King's report and, sure enough, the French national flag had broken out.

"Hoist ours, if you please, and prepare to wear ship." The British ensign began to flap as the ship was taken about. Fraiser called out the orders without the aid of a speaking trumpet, the frustration evident in his voice as the ship came ponderously round, and gradually began to take up speed on the opposing course. Every man on board knew that the slack shrouds would make *Pandora* a very untidy sight as she presented her beam to the enemy.

"Set forecourse and jib, but take your time, lads. This isn't a race, you know." A small murmur of laughter could be heard from the topmen as they clambered aloft. By now every man in the crew was becoming accustomed to a powerful Frenchman bearing down on them; the captain's strange sense of humour only served to add spice to the situation.

Banks caught the boatswain's eye. "Mr Peters, we've shown how bad we can be. Tighten the shrouds up, but as quietly as possible."

"Aye sir, an' the braces?"

"Continue to spill, if you please."

Partially mollified, the boatswain went to attend to his limp shrouds while, muttering under his breath, the quartermaster and three helmsmen struggled to hold course as the wind played havoc with the poorly set sails.

"She's drawing on us fast." Caulfield was talking to Fraiser, but loud enough for the captain to hear; as strong a hint as was possible.

"Very good, Mr Caulfield." Banks smiled. "You may clear for action and stand to quarters, but please leave the guns inboard for the present."

The men moved with a purpose, in many cases thankful of having a positive duty, rather than simply watching as the enemy drew closer. Already the gilded beakhead could be made out, and they could expect fire from the bow chasers at any moment.

"Ship's cleared for action, sir," Caulfield reported, as the activity around them died down. Banks nodded, smiling, and stepped forward to the break of the quarterdeck. He cleared his throat, conscious that he had the ear of most of the men, and that those who could not hear would be informed of his words within minutes. He paused; this was important, probably the most important speech he had ever made. It was vital that he put his idea over to the men - men who had worked together for just a short time and had failed to impress on the only occasion it had been asked of them. If they could grasp his intention they might come through this, and may even take the enemy ship; otherwise it would be disaster and defeat.

*****

"Rum deal, an' that's a fact!" Wright scratched his head as he and Dobson prepared to put the captain's plans into action. The men at the great guns to either side of them had already moved across to the larboard side, leaving their pieces run in and unmanned. Four men, including Dobson and Wright, would be needed to run their nine-pounder out, the others of the gun crew were already preparing the larboard battery, seemingly the side that would not see action immediately.

"Trimmers to the braces!" The boatswain's voice cut through the general murmur, and there was silence as the afterguard took up their positions. "Take up there, let's see some tight canvas!" The relief in the boatswain's voice was obvious, and the ship began to pick up speed and even healed slightly as the braces tightened.

"Prepare to wear ship!" The increase in speed, together with the tightened shrouds would make this a far more professional manoeuvre than before. The splash of a round shotl took them by surprise as it skipped by on their starboard beam. A dull thud followed shortly afterwards. The French were trying the range and presumably they were well within it.

"Wear ship!"

Once more *Pandora* turned, although this time it was towards the enemy.

"Starboard battery, run out!" The captain's voice was cool and measured as seven of her main armament were heaved into the firing position, leaving as many lying idle, their muzzles still secured above the open ports.

"There's a fine sight, an' no mistake!" Dobson muttered sarcastically as the ragged line of nine-pounders faced the enemy. "Bet the Frenchies are fair shakin' in their boots, seein' that lot!"

Certainly *Pandora* did not look the part of an efficient fighting ship, but she was still turning, and by the time the enemy was close enough for an effective broadside, she would be heading almost straight for her.

"Do you think she'll wear?" Dobson asked. Wright shook his head. "Hard to say. If she don't we'll meet her beakhead to beakhead, an' that'll be a right to do. If she does, she'll spend her first broadside."

Dobson nodded. "Maybe that's what the cap' has in mind. Seeing this lot," he indicated the ragged battery, "the way we been handlin' and the damage, they'll think we got no fight left in us."

*****

It was what Banks had planned, and the fact that the lower deck men were broadly in favour of his tactics may well have gladdened him, were it not for the doubts that still haunted his racing mind. Standing on the quarterdeck he held his glass to the enemy ship, now less than a mile from them as *Pandora* continued to turn. There was possibly just the slightest movement from her foremast braces, although even now might be too late for what he was intending.

"She's comin' about!" Caulfield's voice confirmed his suspicions, and sure enough the ship began to turn, presenting a full row of broadside guns to *Pandora's* irregular battery.

"Penny to a pound more'n half of them are quakers!" Conroy muttered to Lewis. When guns were removed to save space and weight it was customary to substitute actual weapons for painted wooden half barrels that looked the same from a distance. Just how many would have been replaced in this way was still impossible to say, despite Conroy's odds.

Now *Pandora* was ninety degrees from her original course, and running before the wind. With the enemy ship turning, this would be the point that they should let off their feeble broadside.

"Keep her going there!" Caulfield had noted that the quartermaster was instinctively correcting the wheel. The ship continued to turn, just as the enemy became committed to her new course.

"Larboard battery prepare to run out." The guns were double shotted, and would need to be relatively close if they were to cause any real damage.

"She's opened fire!" King again, and all turned to look as the smoke billowed from the French ship's side.

"I make it eight," Banks said calmly. Eight out of a possible broadside of twenty heavy guns, plus carronades. They could not tell what the French would be mounting, but it was bound to be bigger than *Pandora's* little nine-pounders. Probably eighteens, possibly even twenty-fours.

It took barely a moment, and yet the time hung, ending finally in a collective sigh that seemed to come from the ship herself. The broadside was poorly aimed and fell short, only one shot struck the hull and that, after skipping off the water, did not penetrate. Caulfield looked across at Banks, their eyes met, but neither spoke.

"Larboard battery, run out!" They were still turning and now the bow was pointing straight at the enemy. If the French captain had guessed their manoeuvre this would have been a far better time to loose off his broadside. King was looking up from his position in the waist. They were closing fast, and at any time the expected order would come. "Very good, Mr King. Ripple fire on my word."

King nodded, and drew his dirk from its scabbard. They had almost finished their turn now, and the trimmers were hauling in on the braces, pulling the wind back into their sails forcing the hull over. The gun captains were compensating for the heel by adjusting the wooden quoins under the breach of each barrel, although the range was closing fast, and in no time they would be within pistol shot of the enemy.

"Open fire." King's raised dirk came down almost simultaneously with the discharge of the first gun, and for the next fifteen seconds the air was rent with the concussion of the slow, rolling, broadside. It was a sharper note than the deep boom of the enemy's guns, but as King raised himself up against the main chains and peered through the smoke he saw that their shots were far more effective, hitting the hull in several places, and bringing forth screams from the tightly packed Frenchman that could be heard long after the guns had ceased.

Banks had little time to admire his handiwork; *Pandora* was passing the enemy at quite a rate, and would soon be in range of her starboard broadside. He looked down at the men on the larboard battery, now reloading their pieces; it would be several minutes before they would be able to fire again. The men on the starboard battery had been joined by the trimmers. They had cleared all the guns and were now standing ready.

"Larboard trimmers man the braces; prepare to tack!"

Given time and the chance to consider his move, he may have chosen differently, but the French captain had already shown himself to be a slow thinker, and Banks had learned that in a single ship action, it paid to take the initiative.

"Bring her about!" Fraiser was at the conn, the speaking trumpet now to his lips as he commanded the ship with calm assurance. Her head came into the wind, the sails flapped, and for a moment it looked as if the enemy would yaw to fire, but instead a flurry of movement aloft showed that she was making more sail in an effort to be rid of *Pandora*.

"Got her on the run!" Dobson said with obvious pleasure as the enemy's maincourse was set and their intention became obvious. "Reckon they've tasted a touch too much of our iron for their likin's."

Flint nodded, although in his mind he could see the heavy frigate's decks, packed tight with men, men trapped by stores and equipment, men who were in the main unable to fight back. *Pandora's* broadside had hit them hard, and he guessed that panic would not be very far away, and impossible to control if ever it took hold.

Her head had passed through the wind now, and the ship was creeping round onto the opposite tack. Powered by her extra canvas, the French ship was pulling away, and already stood several cables off. *Pandora* picked up speed once more as the wind found and filled her sails. Her bow came round further until the gun captains of the starboard battery were signalling their pieces ready and sighted. Banks nodded at King, and the broadside rolled out.

This was longer range, but the French ship was neatly straddled, with several shots clearly hitting her stern. An indignant blast from her two chasers roared back, but no shot fell near *Pandora*, as she continued to turn in pursuit.

Now she was pointing directly at the enemy. For a moment they held the same course, and Banks had a chance to gauge their relative speeds.

"Keep her as she is," Banks told Fraiser, who was preparing to turn her deep enough for the larboard battery to open fire. Banks had a suspicion that the enemy would turn to larboard.

Sure enough the braces on the French ship began to swing the yards round, as the rudder kicked over. Banks opened his mouth, but Fraiser had also noticed and was ordering the change of course.

"Forecourse, and stays'ls if you please, Mr Caulfield." This was the time for *Pandora* to show what she could do, and the devil to caution. The frigate heeled under the fresh spread of canvas and the wind shrieked in the lines as she began to tear through the water.

Caulfield felt the deck lift under him as her speed increased. He glanced across at the captain, and was surprised to see him grinning like a child. "Sails pretty under a bowline, think you not?" His face was clear of worry as if this was nothing more sinister than a pleasure cruise.

"We're closing on her," Fraiser muttered, peering under the roach of the forecourse.

Banks glanced across the deck. "Mr Lewis, the come up glass, if you please."

Lewis touched his hat, and made for the binnacle. The come up glass had a split element that gave a clear indication of the state of a chase. Lewis sighted the enemy and adjusted the element to form one whole image. There was a pause of no more than ten seconds before he looked back at the expectant group of officers.

"Aye, we're closing. Sure as a gun!"

Pandora was doing well, although the heavy frigate was carrying a disadvantage in the extra men that even her additional main course could not counteract.

"She won't stay on this heading for long, not once she learns we're closing," Banks said, and sure enough the yards soon began to move once more, and the enemy turned to starboard. Again Banks opened his mouth to speak, and again Fraiser unconsciously anticipated the order, bringing the ship round with a smooth, polished ease that lost very little of the lead they were steadily winning back. The ship's bell rang for the end of the watch and brought no change; every hand was at their action station, and it was doubtful that any would have stood down, even if they had been allowed.

"Nine-and-a-half, sir." Rose, who had taken over from Dorsey, reported to Caulfield before noting the speed down on the freshly wiped traverse board. Nine-and-a-half knots, the French could hardly be doing more than eight, which meant they would be in effective range in less than fifteen minutes. Martin, the marine lieutenant, had his men formed up, although Banks had no intention of straying too close to an enemy so well served with soldiers.

Banks nodded to his second in command. "Ask the gunner to begin with the bow chasers." Caulfield touched his hat and relayed the order. It was still long range but better to be doing something than nothing, besides they could expect the French to open fire with their stern mounted guns at any moment.

Exactly on cue a shout from the forward lookout, followed by a sharp crack, told where an eighteen-pound ball had hit them, smashing into the warrant officers' round house, and blowing the fragile shelter apart. There came a couple of ribald comments from the men, followed by a general roar of laughter.

"Silence, silence there!" Dorsey shouted, his adolescent voice cracking in anger. The men might find it amusing, but they hadn't just watched their only place of privacy blown into a thousand splinters. The officers on the quarterdeck were grinning also, although neither spoke, for fear of undermining the young man's authority.

Then came a second cry from forward. Almost unnoticed the enemy had spilled her wind, turned to larboard and backed sail. Now she sat almost dead in the water, broadside on, her battery run out to meet them; ready, poised to fire upon her fragile bow.

Banks cursed inside; the Frenchman's relative inaction had lulled him into a false feeling of security, now he had to act fast, or risk losing his ship. He open his mouth and let loose a stream of orders that would lay *Pandora* on the opposite tack, and take her away from the danger, but even as he spoke he knew inside that it was too late. From forward Dorsey's voice could be heard once more, this time to urge the men at the braces to haul her round. The boy's face was still red from his recent anger, although memory of the incident had already been forgotten by all. Suddenly being under fire did not seem funny any more.

CHAPTER SEVEN

There was no time to secure the men; eight enemy guns spoke almost as one, and were well laid. *Pandora*, in the act of turning, was struck fair on her bow, creating a cloud of splinters, and a shock wave that carried throughout her fragile frame.

King, moving forward from his position in the waist, roared out for axe men to cut away the shattered wreckage and torn shrouds that were still falling. The foremast had been hit, but still mercifully held, but the jib boom seemed strangely out of shape, hanging several degrees below its normal rake. Presumably the forestay had parted, taking the jib, which was now dragging to leeward. The boatswain led a team aloft; each had a length of coiled line across their shoulders, while more made their way forward; the foretopmast had been robbed of forward support, and would be vulnerable until they could replace the missing shroud.

A sudden crack came from the foretop, and the forecourse yard began to creak alarmingly. King shouted for the sheets to be released, but it was too late, the yard parted and fell, dragging the sail with it in a mushroom of canvas that enveloped many of those working below. The sail missed Flint by inches and he, Dobson and Wright began to bundle the damp canvas into some sort of manageable lump, while the trapped men beneath struggled free.

On the quarterdeck Banks surveyed the scene. *Pandora* was all but stationary, with those sails that were left flapping impotently out of control. He could tighten up what canvas he had and attempt to manoeuvre, but the boatswain's party was still working to replace the shrouds: any movement might unsettle the foretopmast, besides slowing the men in their work. And all the time they were facing the enemy; exposing their vulnerable bow to a second broadside that could be expected within the next few minutes.

He glanced up at the mizzen driver, still set for the turn. There should be just about enough leverage to move *Pandora*, despite the fact that without forward momentum the spar, and even the mast, may be weakened in the process. The boatswain was busy forward; it fell to Caulfield and Lewis to organise the sail, hauling the boom forward to catch the wind, and controlling the spar as it slowly wrenched the hull over.

By the time the second broadside came they were almost round, the two hulls very nearly parallel, with *Pandora's* shattered bow in line with the French frigate's stern. The shots came high, killing three of the boatswain's crew, and parting two further shrouds, but causing no other significant damage.

Banks caught sight of King as he was helping to bundle the remains of the forecourse over the starboard side, and pointed significantly at the larboard battery. King nodded and left what he was doing to bellow for the gun crews to return to their pieces. Within thirty seconds the guns were run out once more, and King was looking for instructions.

"Aim high, lads," Banks bellowed at the line of waiting gun captains. "And reload with bar!"

A broadside falling amongst the French in the act of loading would probably delay the next barrage, but it was more important to disable the ship. The gun captains crouched over their pieces, squinting along the crude sights, standing back and raising a hand when all was ready.

Pandora's guns spoke in a ripple of fire, the shots raining down on the enemy with remarkable accuracy, although there was no apparent damage, apart from a split sail and several parted stays.

"Ready forward!" The voice of Peters, the boatswain, came from the foretop. Banks glanced up. The mast was reasonably secure now; they could reset the topsails, and possibly even risk another jib on their weakened bowsprit.

Banks gave the orders and the ship gathered way once more, urged on as much by the sigh of relief that came from every member of the crew. The enemy were showing signs of coming back to the wind, their movements slow and ponderous; doubtless the extra men and stores they carried made any manoeuvre more awkward.

Pandora gathered speed, and was about to pass out of the field of fire when the enemy's broadside rang out. This time part of a stanchion was knocked down and several marines fell. Splinters flew about the quarterdeck, the oak and pine shards more deadly than the hot iron that had caused them. Conroy fell, his leg ripped open, and the boy Rose was struck senseless by a tightly rolled hammock knocked free from the larboard rail. Caulfield felt the wind of something passing close by, and was surprised to see the sleeve of his right arm partially separate from the jacket.

"Keep it at the spars, Mr King." King raised his hand to the captain and passed the instruction to the gun captains.

The British broadside rolled out again, and a hearty cheer followed this time that no one bothered to suppress. The French ship was in the act of turning, and was caught on her starboard quarter. The barshot flew about her rigging, peppering her mizzen and main, and after the briefest of pauses the mizzen topmast began to fall, taking most of the main topgallant with it.

"Check, check, check!" Banks shouted unconsciously, then in more measured tones. "Back mizzen tops'l, lay her to."

Pandora hove to, with the enemy's stern directly in front of her larboard broadside "Mr King, reload with round and alter your aim to the hull, if you please."

With the enemy temporarily disabled and seemingly at their mercy it was now time to strike the killing blow. Banks looked across to where the French seamen were rushing to clear the wreckage, as they themselves had done only minutes before. The first British gun captain was already signalling his piece ready. Closing his mind to the effect his actions would have, he nodded to the lieutenant, and another broadside rolled out.

*****

Below, Stuart and Manning were dealing with the first of the casualties. Though grisly, Manning found the work infinitely preferable to the waiting that had gone before. The waiting that Stuart had filled with long rambling reminiscences and frequent swigs from his bottle of Hollands. They had felt the concussion as the bows were struck, the shock had sent one of the loblolly boys tumbling onto the deck, and caused Stuart to break his indecipherable monologue to take an extra hefty swill. For a while nothing happened, the men on deck being too busy securing the ship to have time for their wounded colleagues. Then one of the gun crew from the larboard bow chaser had been brought down, his right arm hanging limp and an ugly bruise spreading across his shoulder, and from then on a veritable floodgate opened.

Manning was currently working on a topman with a splinter to his chest. The slither of oak had hit him just below the armpit, and been deflected along the ribs until it sat, dark and swollen, just under the skin, and directly over the man's heart.

"All right, Adams, this will hurt for a couple of seconds, then you'll feel a lot better." Manning gently explored the wound, noticing how the man's breathing was fast and shallow. Adams, besides being a lithe and able topman, was also a first class wrestler. Several times Manning had watched while he had unsettled bigger men, sending them spinning to the deck, only to be jumped on and locked in a grip that owned as much to experience as strength. In all his bouts Adams had never shown a flicker of fear and yet now, with the prospect of an operation in front of him, his eyes sought reassurance with a mixture of hope and terror.

The splinter was wide but thin, and by its feel had been bent round by the rib cage. Manning reached for a scalpel and held it well out of the man's sight while Nairn, a loblolly boy, secured Adams' hands behind his head. Adams' chest was dirty with burnt powder and sweat; Manning looked for a wet swab to wipe it, and noticed Stuart's bottle of Hollands, lying just where the surgeon could lay a hand to it whenever he had the mind. Manning reached for the bottle, and trickled some of the liquid onto the place where he would have to cut. Adams started, then breathed a sigh and seemed to relax.

"Feel good?" asked Manning.

"Cold," Adams replied, nodding slightly.

It was a point worth remembering, and as Manning made the first incision he noticed that there was very little response from the patient.

He tied up the wound with horsehair, neatly spacing the stitches so as to make the best of a ragged cut. He reached for a piece of dry tow, and soaked it in more spirit, before wiping the wound. There was very little blood now, only the need for one layer of bandage. This Manning deftly wrapped about the chest, one arm supporting the topman's body, before laying him back down on the midshipmen's sea chests that formed his operating table.

"You're done, now," he smiled, grimly. "And there'll be no duties for you for yet a while."

Adams nodded softly, and whispered a word of thanks that was completely buried under a deluge of oaths from Stuart, who had discovered his bottle of spirits to be missing.

*****

The French ship had taken three broadsides on her exposed stern. The first two had swept the quarterdeck clear of men and the third neatly removed most of her larboard quarter-gallery. The mizzen and main masts were now almost unsupported and the foremast leaned forward and to one side at a drunken angle. There was no question of her moving or fighting further, and Banks was keen to stop the slaughter that their shots must be causing deep within the hull. A small fire could be seen through the shattered stern windows, and Banks delayed the next broadside in the hope that she might strike. But the flames were soon extinguished, and the two stern chasers continued to return the British shots as deliberately as before. The temptation to close and finish it was strong but, battered though her hull may be, the enemy still outnumbered them in men, and a boarding action would see the French victorious.

"At the yards!" Martin had noticed how several brave souls had made their way to the larboard topsail yard, and were feverishly trying to rig a stunsail in the hope of turning the ship. His marines took note, and soon volley after volley of musket balls rained about them. The range was long, but one man fell by the second salvo, and another after the fourth.

Meanwhile the great guns continued as before and it was fifteen minutes later, when four more broadsides had raked her through the stern and a fifth was about to be fired, that she struck, the surrender being signalled by a young aspirant waving something white above the shattered taffrail. Caulfield ordered the ceasefire with some relief, although he made sure that every gun remained trained on the frigate, ready to open up once more should the situation demand it.

"Mr King, you may have the honour," Banks said, a slight smile cracking his smoke-stained face. "The starboard cutter is undamaged, I believe. Take a midshipman, Dorsey's the most experienced, and a party of topmen with you. Mr Martin, you can spare your marines, I am sure? Mr Caulfield, would you select some men for Mr King?"

Caulfield paused for a second. If what he suspected was true, the man Banks had just placed in charge of the prize might someday stand trial for murder. He glanced at King as he prepared to leave the ship; it was hard to think ill of him. Besides being a friend, he was an excellent officer, one that by nature would do what was right for the service. But he had to detail a prize crew without delay, and here was Everit, the carpenter, coming forward to report. All thoughts and implications were brushed aside as Caulfield allowed himself to become immersed in the running of the ship.

King touched his hat to the captain, and went to supervise the launching of the cutter. He would be taking no more than twenty men with him, twenty men to quell an enemy of perhaps five, six hundred. But an enemy that had withstood raking fire was likely to have had the stuffing knocked out if him, and strangely it was not the thought of opposition that worried King as he took his seat in the sternsheets of the cutter and ordered it away.

They drew close to the French frigate, approaching by the stern where the damage could be more clearly seen. *Pandora's* shots had penetrated in several places, and King thought he could hear the sound of running water as it found its way into the shattered hull. The name *Aiguille* could still be made out across the counter. Dorsey, sitting next to him, was making some comment, but King had no mind for conversation.

"Starboard side, Cox'n," he grunted, his voice purposefully curt in an effort to hide his doubts. The elderly seaman turned the boat neatly, calling in the oars and brought her to rest against the French ship with hardly a bump.

King stood up and straightened his dirk. There was no man-rope rigged; he would have to make the difficult assent unaided. He reached up to the first of the wooden steps that ran down from the entry port. It was wet and sticky. He pulled his hand away and was momentarily sickened by the sight of fresh blood on his fingers. For an instant he hesitated, before reaching for the step once more and clambering up.

On deck the first sight that met his eyes was a young man in a blue and white uniform not unlike his own. The officer took a pace towards him and bowed briefly.

"My name is King," he announced, awkwardly.

The Frenchman bowed again, and muttered a name that King did not catch. He then reached for his sword, and drew it. King controlled the instinct to take a step back as the man quickly reversed the weapon and offered it to him, hilt first, the blade resting across his left forearm. King accepted the sword and gave a shallow bow, before returning it to the officer. The Frenchman looked hard into his eyes, as if trying to read his mind. He nodded briefly, and a faint smile spread across his face as the sword shot back into its scabbard.

King was conscious of Dorsey and the rest of his party clambering up the ship's side, and it was with some relief that he turned to see the marines forming up, and fixing bayonets. He looked about the quarterdeck that was almost empty, then turned forward and glanced down to the waist.

This was crowded with the blue, red and white of soldiers' uniforms with the occasional less regulated dress of the seamen dotted about amongst them. Some were wounded, and more than a few dead. The bodies lay, unattended, amid groups of squatting men who appeared sullen, and did not look up to meet his stare. A scuffle from his left caused King to turn, and he looked straight into the eyes of a soldier rushing at him with a pike. King ducked down and to one side, avoiding the thrust but putting himself off balance at the same time. His hand reached down for the deck to steady himself while the soldier, who had all but passed him in his rush, now swung round for a second try. The Morris brothers, two burly British seamen, moved in without a word. Working as a team the younger plucked the pike from the Frenchman's grasp while the other swung a heavy left fist up and onto the man's chin. The blow lifted him slightly and, suddenly unsupported, his body seemed to flop down to the deck in an untidy heap.

"There'll be no more from that one, sir." Pug Morris, the man who had thrown the punch, looked about the rest of the crew as if eager for another opportunity, as one the Frenchmen shrank back from his stare and it was clear they had little fight left in them.

King recovered himself and looked back to the marines.

"Corporal, arrange your men along the gangways; at the first sign of trouble, I want you to blow a whistle. There will be no firing unless I, or Mr Dorsey order it, do you understand?"

A loaded weapon retained its threat, whereas the marines could be overwhelmed in seconds as soon as they had fired their muskets.

"You there, Smith, and Dobson." The two sailors had been looking about the stricken ship with an air of disbelief on their faces; they jerked back to reality as he spoke. "I want a swivel loaded with canister and trained on the waist, can you see to that?"

They both nodded. Dobson spoke. "We could rig two, beggin' you pardon, sir. That ways we'd cover both ends."

"Make it so." He turned back to the French officer. "You captain?" he asked in a loud voice. The Frenchman shook his head.

"Capatian es mort," he said briefly. *"Toutes officers dessous; dessour, s'il vous plait."*

King hesitated, guessing at the young man's meaning. To go below would be a risk. The ship was still packed with men, most of whom had every reason to want him dead. He glanced across at *Pandora*, still riding hove to, with her guns run out. The cutter was just returning, and a further party of marines would soon be joining them. "Very well," he said, and ignoring the questioning eyes of the midshipman, King allowed the French officer to lead him to the companionway.

He descended to the next deck just forward of what was presumably the captain's quarters, although as he looked back and through the shattered stern windows there was little sign of opulence. To one side a heavy gun had been overturned, and a man still lay beneath, moaning gently while his comrades tried to lever the metal beast off him. King turned away to see more injured and dying men, the majority left unattended. He caught sight of the French officer, his face was working slightly, although it became suddenly wooden when he noticed King was looking at him.

"I will get help," King said briefly. "I will order medical assistance."

The Frenchman nodded and his expression softened once more.

Down to the next deck, the berth deck in a British ship, the scene changed. They were level with the waterline, and in the half-light there was very little actual damage. Although the deck was crowded, being surrounded by shattered limbs, bodies and, in two cases, minds made it no less horrific. King was led to where a middle-aged man lay under a single sheet. His head was almost bald, and he seemed peacefully asleep. The Frenchman reached for a lantern and held it above, and the eyes opened revealing a man of intelligence and possible culture. The two exchanged words that King could not comprehend, then the wounded man spoke in clear English.

"You have come to accept our surrender?" he asked, his voice faint, but with an air of confidence. King assumed he was used to being obeyed.

"Yes, sir," King said, automatically. "And to render what assistance we can."

The man nodded. "That will be very welcome. I am afraid *Le Captain de frégate* Pahlen was killed early in the action. I am *Lieutenant* Segond; I was in command until one of your round shot did for me. I would offer you my sword, but I fear I cannot account for it."

King nodded, almost apologetically. "It is of no matter, sir, I accept your word."

"We will give you no trouble," the officer continued, his voice now perceivably softer, "although I might not say the same for the soldiers."

A man approached and for the first time King was pleased to see the bulk of Lieutenant Martin looming up behind him.

"You have all the marines aboard. Cap'n said I was useless on my own, so I'd better come across and help you."

King was grateful, both for the brisk return to normality and the knowledge that he had a good number of disciplined fighting men with him.

"Would you see to the soldiers? There seem to be a fair number on board."

Martin nodded, "I'll take care of them. Meantime we're promised a few more to help out as soon as they can be spared from *Pandora*.

The marine turned and left, striding past groups of wounded men as if they did not exist. King turned back to the lieutenant, who was closing his eyes once more, and seemed on the verge of sleep.

"I will request medical assistance immediately," he said, somewhat awkwardly. The man opened his eyes again, and smiled faintly.

King drew himself away from the scene and made for the companionway. The novelty of being on a beaten enemy ship was fast disappearing and as he came up on deck again, he looked about for a familiar face amongst the many who watched him.

"You there, Dorsey. Has the surgeon arrived?"

"No, sir. Reckon he'd be needed back in *Pandy*."

"Then send a message, ask for Mr Manning, or even a couple of loblolly boys."

Dorsey touched his hat and reached for his block of paper.

A shout from aloft was followed by the clatter of falling top hamper that rained about them for several seconds.

"What the devil goes there?" King bellowed, staring up to the remains of the mizzen top.

"Sorry 'bout that, sir." It was the voice of Thompson, one of the boatswain's mates. "Bit of a mess up 'ere, an' we was try'n to make some sense of it."

King made towards the break of the quarterdeck; his movements were slow and laboured, as if he was wading through a deep river. There was so much to take in, so much to think about that he had to regulate his stunned mind to face each decision as it came. He looked down into the waist, ignoring the appealing cries from a wounded boy. Below the marines had formed up and were organising the French soldiers, watched by Dobson and Smith who had rigged one of the smaller carronades to bear down on them. Dobson was silently spinning a length of burning slow match, and there could be little doubt that he would use it, albeit at the risk of injuring the marines.

Dorsey was saying something and he had to concentrate hard to understand the words. "Beggin' you pardon, sir. But shouldn't we see to the hull?" Of course, they were bound to be taking in water; in fact there was even a chance the ship might sink beneath them.

"Take a party and sound the well," he said, his voice disguising any sign that he had been remiss in his duties. "Are there any English speaking officers on board?"

Dorsey looked blank. "Not that I've noticed, sir."

"I speak English."

King looked round to see a young man of his own age dressed in the international uniform of a sailor, standing next to the fife rail. He was clean-shaven, and wore his dark hair cropped about his ears in the modern fashion.

"What's your name?"

"Crowley."

"You're British?"

He shook his head. "Irish, if you please."

King considered him for a moment; there would be time later to sort out the rights and wrongs of Crowley's situation, at that moment he needed someone who spoke the language."

"Very good, Crowley. If you give me your word to do right, I'll see you well cared for."

"I'll do right by the men in this ship, you can be sure of that."

King's heightened senses detected an ambiguity in the remark; he took a quick breath. "This is not the time for Nationalist principles, Crowley. It is this ship, and the people in her that I am looking to save. If you will help, then so be it. If not, you may get back to the scuppers where you belong." His voice betrayed the exasperation he felt, and he was somewhat surprised to see Crowley's soft brown eyes twinkling into a smile.

"Then I'm your man," he said, pausing for a second, and adding, "sir."

*****

On board *Pandora* Banks was having problems of his own. The damage to the forecastle had not been confined to the masts. A shot had hit them just above the waterline and slightly to larboard of the stem, shattering several planks and opening up a sizeable hole. There were few worse places to take damage; the structure of the hull meant that access was difficult, and any repair would have to withstand the entire weight of the ship pressing against it and the water as she made forward progress. Banks stood on the lower deck with Caulfield and the carpenter, as they surveyed the damage.

"I've nailed two lead plates over the spot, and shored 'em up, best I can," Everit explained in his usual slow drawl. He shook his head as he regarded the damage, and it was difficult to believe that he did not derive some mild pleasure from the situation.

Caulfield had been bruised by the shot that damaged his jacket; at the time he had felt no pain but now his arm ached terribly. "What about from outside?" he asked.

Everit shook his head again. "Tried all we can, young Griffin and Glass went over the side on a bosun's line, but they couldn't get a patch over the spot. Too near the stem, you see."

"What about packing it with canvas?"

"They stuffed some oakum in the hole and sealed what they could, but it'll not take a heavy sea."

Banks had already received a message from King; the enemy frigate sailed without any spare spars; this was not surprising, considering the lack of supplies the French were enduring due to blockade, but it did mean that she would make slow progress under what was effectively foremast alone. The main had been weakened in two places, and could not be considered sound enough to carry canvas.

"So, little chance of us making a tow?" he asked, his tone completely neutral.

Everit shook his head. "Ask me I'd rather see us takin' a tow than making one, sir. An' that'd be stern first an' in choice weather."

"I see." There was a moment's pause as Banks exchanged glances with Caulfield, who was surprised to see a smile flicker across the captain's face. "And what about transferring some of our spars to the Frenchman?"

"And let her tow us?" The obvious disgust in Everit's voice broke his usual monotone.

"By my word, sir, I hadn't thought of that!" Caulfield fought hard to control his voice, although Everit was too upset to be aware of any manipulation.

"Beggin' your pardon, sir, I don't think it need come to that." Everit's depressed expression had become agitated now. "Reckon she'll do as she is, if she's treated gentle."

Banks shook his head in a credible imitation of the carpenter's previous attitude. "Can't guarantee that, I'm afraid. Nearest port's a good few leagues, and you know the Atlantic in winter as well as I do."

"I'll go an' take a look me'self, sir," Everit said with sudden determination. "Fair bet we can 'fect a repair, even if it means shippin' some weight back temporarily, to raise the bow an' give us room." There was more than just lower deck stubbornness speaking now, Everit was a standing officer; he had been present almost from the moment *Pandora's* keel had been laid. Despite the fact that she had been at sea for so very short a time, the ship was clearly dear to him and the idea of her being pulled backwards through the water by what he would probably always consider an enemy ship disturbed him greatly.

Banks laid a reassuring hand on his arm. "Ask the master for any help you need with altering our trim. The important thing, the only thing for you to worry about is making this bow watertight again." Once more the smile returned, although this time it was open and more general. "We'll leave the towing option 'till last, I assure you."

*****

Manning appeared on board *Aiguille* two hours later, in which time King, assisted by Crowley, had set two teams of French prisoners to work the pumps, and routed out the carpenter and his mates to attend to the damaged stern.

"Pretty picture," Manning commented dryly, looking about the shattered frigate. "Thought more'd be sorted, bearing in mind the time you've had."

"Didn't seem much point in starting early and cheating you of your share," King replied in turn, but as he led the surgeon's mate down to the horror that was the lower deck, all attempts at banter vanished.

"I'll need some help," Manning said, looking about at the misery that surrounded him. "Not skilled, but someone to sort things. Maybe a midshipman?"

"We've none of us with the language, but there's one who has who'd give you a hand."

"A Frenchman?"

"Irish, but sound. He's been more than a help to me." This was true; almost all that King had achieved was due in part to Crowley, and the support he had given.

Manning nodded, trying not to meet the eyes of the desperate men who all but covered the deck. "I'd take help from the devil himself on this one. Have they had no medic on board at all?"

"No physician, no surgeon, not even an apothecary. It seems they were to sail in convoy, and thought none necessary."

Crowley joined them and the job of sorting out the patients into those who might survive, and those who could not, started. Several of the soldiers were impervious even to Crowley's particular brand of French, but eventually some order was made, and Manning began work. He had no loblolly boy to assist, and it seemed completely natural for Crowley to help him. A succession of shouts from above told that the topmen were rigging fresh backstays. King told himself there were other things for him to do elsewhere, and with more than a twinge of guilt, left the deck in the hands of capable men.

CHAPTER EIGHT

The captain came on board at the beginning of the afternoon watch, and was met by King. With few words he allowed the younger man to lead him on a tour of the capture, noting the salient points and reckoning the likelihood of both ships reaching harbour once more.

The French frigate was still leaking badly, although the measures King had taken: setting both pumps into operation, stopping the accessible holes and fothering two sails beneath her hull to reduce those that could not be reached, meant that she could be kept afloat. Using French soldiers to man the pumps by rota also served to keep many of the disproportionate number of prisoners he had to attend to occupied.

Manning seemed to be coping well with the wounded, although there remained a large number of swollen canvas parcels awaiting burial on the gratings. Banks made a mental note to deal with these reasonably quickly; nothing could depress or upset a defeated enemy more than to have their dead left unattended. A swift sea burial would also put an end to any question of interring the bodies in their ballast, a vile French practice that Banks was determined not to have any truck with.

Aloft, the mess of rigging and top hamper had been sorted to a good degree. The foremast was now secure, and would take moderate sail, staysails could be rigged from the truncated but stable main, and it may even be possible to set some sort of canvas on the stump that was all that remained of the mizzen. Martin had organised his men into two watches, the second of which had just come off duty as the captain arrived and were now dozing on the small area of lower deck that had been allotted to them. Too tired to eat, or rig their hammocks, the marines huddled together in a way that reminded Banks of his father's hounds at the end of a day's sport. Watching them, Banks realised quite how tired he was himself. It was barely nine hours since he had been roused from his own cot, and yet the strain he had gone through since then was beginning to tell. He would have gladly found a comfortable spot to catnap, were such an unthinkable idea possible.

"You have done well, Mr King," he said, when the inspection was over. "There is still much else to do, of course, and *Pandora* needs several hours yet before we can move, but I think we may be able to make sail afore nightfall."

"Thank you, sir." They paused while a group of waisters came past, their shoulders bent under the weight of a fresh foretopsail. "Beggin' your pardon, sir, but where would we be heading?"

"Gibraltar," Banks said simply.

"Of course, sir."

"Admiral Jervis may well be there, either that or Tagus. We can look in there on the way." Banks raised one ironic eyebrow. "And are you happy to stay in command here?"

That was a question. King looked about the stricken deck, noting the weakened rigging, the clank of the pumps and the groups of morose prisoners that greatly outnumbered their guard; happy was very much a relative word. A smile had replaced Banks' look of enquiry, and King found himself grinning in return.

"I'd be greatly honoured, sir," he said.

*****

In fact it was barely five hours later, although quite dark, when *Pandora* showed the white light at the main that was the signal to make sail. King ordered the acknowledgment; Smith at the fore showed one red light before being all but swamped by thirty of his fellows as they rushed past, eager for the novelty of setting foreign canvas. The ship gathered way, and King heard the rhythmic mutter from the jury rudder as she swung round to point vaguely in the direction of the Spanish coast some four hundred miles away. She was moving under an odd mixture of foretopsail, forecourse, and staysails; the wind was strong and steady, coming conveniently over her starboard quarter, and as Dorsey and another ran the log, King was reasonably pleased with the four-and-a-touch knots they reported.

Looking back, *Pandora* appeared far more normal, although the foreshortened bowsprit was out of proportion. King took a couple of paces up and down the quarterdeck. His men had been fed this last hour and were now distributing hard tack and water to the prisoners. Tomorrow they might experiment with the coppers to cook up something hot but before then there were several hours of darkness to endure. Three lanterns hung above the waist, giving the deck an eerie, flickering glow, while forward, at the forecastle, two marines stood next to the rockets that would be lit at the smallest sign of trouble. This agreed signal should bring *Pandora* bearing down on them, although King suspected that despite these measures the British ship would keep them under close supervision throughout the night.

The bell rang twice, the deep unfamiliar note jerking King from his daydream. He had eaten nothing all day other than some cheese and biscuit several hours ago, and was suddenly hungry. Dorsey was at the conn, with Broome acting as quartermaster. King took a quick look about the deck, decided that there was nothing that warranted his immediate attention, and hurried below to find supper.

He looked in at the captain's quarters, but little had been done, other than to secure the four guns mounted there. He moved on down to the gunroom. Here there was order at least, the officer's cabins had not been cleared for action, and the assortment of watch coats and discarded boots gave the place an air that was almost homely. A large table ran down the middle of the room; King made towards it, and was aware of a deep growling sound from beneath. He stopped, and glanced under the table to see Dobson fast asleep, a dark bottle clutched affectionately against his breast.

"Marine!" King bellowed, and shortly afterwards a shirt-sleeved corporal entered. King pointed at the sleeping man. "Get rid of that, if you please."

The corporal clambered under the table and together with the two privates who soon joined him, dragged Dobson out and wrestled the bottle from him.

"Let him sleep it off, but see he reports to me at first light." The corporal, still holding half of the sleeping Dobson, saluted awkwardly before reversing out of the gunroom.

Once he was properly alone King sat at the table with a faint feeling of anticlimax. His stomach craved food and drink, although he felt no inclination to move, and Dobson's half-filled bottle held little attraction for him.

"Would you be wanting some victuals?"

Turning, he saw Crowley, the Irishman, standing at the doorway.

"I heard you shout," he said, by way of explanation. "I wondered if you'd care for something to eat?"

King nodded. "I'd welcome it."

Crowley disappeared without a word, returning less than a minute later with a heavily laden tray that he placed down on the table in front of him. It held a generous chunk of dark yellow cheese, together with some cold sausage and what looked like pickled cabbage. There was a long, dry loaf of bread, and a fresh bottle of red wine with the cork pulled.

"You prepared this for me?" King asked, his voice mildly tainted with suspicion.

Crowley smiled, "That I did, and it ain't spiked."

King considered him for a moment. Despite his apparent Nationalist stance the man had worked conscientiously at many tasks throughout the day. Apart from assisting Manning, and the numerous translations that had been called for, Crowley had been invaluable in dealing with the frosty French officers, as well as identifying key members of the crew like the carpenter and boatswain. His attitude had been constructive whenever it came to the good of the ship and the men in her, so much so that King had found it all too easy to trust the man far beyond the normal bounds expected between prisoner and captor.

"You'll be wondering why I takes the trouble over a King's man?"

King nodded, and silently reached for a piece of cheese.

"I respect no one who puts himself before others," he said simply. "You may be a British, and doubtless all manner of bastard by that count, but you've looked after the men here as best you can. An' it's only now you're eating, now the others have been well fed."

"And have you eaten?"

Crowley grinned. "That I haven't."

Their eyes met in understanding, and King also broke into a smile. "Then bring yourself a cup and pull up a chair."

*****

On board *Pandora* the captain was dining alone. He too had all but missed dinner, usually the main meal of the day, and was making up for it as best he could. In his case this amounted to a generous cut of pork liver paté, which he now spread onto a chunk of warmed soft tack. The bread had been dipped in goat's milk, before being toasted over Dupont's pantry stove, a process that had banished almost all the staleness from it. The fact that Dupont had done this, presumably at a time when everyone else was hard at work repairing two badly damaged ships, gave Banks a slight twinge of guilt, but then the bread tasted so good he was inclined to ignore it. The bell rang for the end of the second dogwatch, and he decided to salve his conscience by sharing the coffee, which was hot and plentiful, with the retiring officer and midshipman of the watch. A shout to the sentry (an unarmed landsman detailed to the duty; all the marines were with King in *Aiguille*) accomplished this, and two minutes later a tap at the door announced the arrival of Lewis and Rose.

Banks shouted for another cup; he had quite forgotten that in their reduced state, Lewis, a master's mate, and the volunteer Rose, were sharing a watch. Fraiser would have the current watch, and Caulfield would take over at midnight. He wondered briefly who his tired mind had expected to see: King, returning from *Aiguille* to fulfill his commitments? Or maybe Pigot? The exhausted look on both youngsters' faces drove the lunatic thoughts from his mind and he called for a further serving of soft tack; there was more than enough paté for all.

The memory of Pigot stayed in his mind as he watched them eat. It seemed such a short time ago that he, Rose and the late first lieutenant had been together at this very table. Since then *Pandora* had seen action twice, Pigot had died, and Rose here, now laying in to the food with a lad's appetite, had a glorious blue-black bruise on his forehead. In such a situation it was impossible to maintain the strict discipline usual at a captain's table.

"Better?" Banks enquired, when they had both finished. He was less than fifteen years older than Rose, and yet it was all too easy to look on him as a father might his son.

"Aye, sir, thank you." Lewis was older, but no less grateful. "Better than that we're given in the cockpit."

"They don't serve you paté?" he asked, his eyebrow raised slightly.

Lewis laughed, but Rose shook his head in all seriousness. "Nearest we get is toasted miller, sir," he confided. "Other than that it's salt horse, Banyan, and pork, with duff on Thursdays and Sundays.

"Miller?" Now both he and Lewis were smiling broadly, but Rose remained as solemn as before.

"Yes, sir. Gunner gives it to us as a treat when he's a mind."

There was an awkward pause of no more than a second before Banks asked the inevitable question.

"Are you aware exactly what miller is?"

Rose blinked. It was not a question his young appetite had asked.

Banks sat back in his chair and sipped his coffee. "We have strange habits, calling food by another name, just for the sake of it. Pork for pig, mutton for sheep."

"Salt horse, sir," said Lewis.

"Exactly," he looked at Rose. "Know what that is?"

Rose blinked. "Horse, sir?"

Banks shook his head. "Beef, which in turn is cow."

The boy was becoming confused. "So what is miller, sir?"

"What does it taste like?" Lewis asked.

He thought. "Chicken."

"Do you mean hen?" Both Banks and Lewis were smiling broadly now, and he was glad to see that Rose was not in the least intimidated.

"Goat?" Both men shook their heads. "Duck? Goose? Rabbit?"

Now the laughter was general, even Rose was giggling, while part of his mind struggled with the problem.

"Think what else we carry aboard ship," Lewis prompted. Rose's eyes grew round.

"Cat?" He hoped not.

Lewis banged the table while Banks rocked contentedly on his chair. Then Rose snapped his fingers and pointed at his captain in a way that some might regard as mutinous.

"I got it!" he shrieked with glee. The other two waited expectantly, their mouths open, ready to laugh once more.

"Rat!"

All three roared as one, while Lewis banged the excited boy on the back in triumph. Summoned by the noise Dupont watched the scene from the pantry, before shaking his head and turning away. He had been in the British Navy long enough to know that rats, often covered in a fine powder of flour from their scavenging, were known as millers, but the idea of eating such rodents was not to the taste of his more refined palate.

*****

The surgeon, Stuart, was already in his cot and sleeping heavily, as was his habit. *Pandora's* wounded numbered nineteen, three of whom were in almost as deep a coma as he was, although Stuart had little time for them even when he was awake and sober. A faint knock came at the door that screened off his cabin from the rest of the ship. He did not move. The knock was repeated, and the door pulled open, letting in light from a lantern, and the worried look of Nairn, one of his loblolly boys. Nairn had worked in the sick bay for twelve years and was hoping for a warrant as surgeon's mate eventually, although at that moment he had little thought for advancement.

"Mr Stuart, wake up, sir." He touched the sleeping body of his superior cautiously at first, then shook it with increasing strength.

"Carter's bad, sir. He's askin' for somthin' to kill the pain."

Carter, the Londoner from Flint's mess, had been hit in the upper thigh. It was a deep, dirty wound, and one unlikely to heal. Stuart would normally have removed the leg, except that Carter was skinny and there was very little sound flesh to make an agreeable stump. Rather than risk an operation that had a high chance of failure, Stuart had elected to leave the man to his own devices. Should he subsequently die, as he almost certainly would, no blame could then be attached to him.

"Shall I give him another dose of laudanum? He's 'ad it before, an' it would serve him to sleep." Nairn had seen Stuart's ready prescription for the drug, but was barred from doing the same. He shook the surgeon again to no effect, other than persuading a trickle of thick saliva from his open lips. Nairn considered the sleeping form for a moment, swore silently to himself, and left.

*****

The one, probably the only, good side to Pigot's tyranny was the fellowship that quickly sprang up between the other youngsters in the berth. Both Cobb and Dorsey were streets ahead of Rose when it came to just about everything, and neither could be accused of the smallest degree of sensitivity. Both had also suffered Pigot's cruelties, and yet there had been no sign of either of them passing the first lieutenant's bullying ways onto the younger boy. Now that Pigot was gone there seemed little evidence that things would change, and for the first time since he had left Lincolnshire, Rose was starting to enjoy himself.

This change was revealed in a number of subtle ways. He found that his appetite, even for the startling preserved food, so alien to a farmer's son, was returning. The hammock that had seemed almost hostile, where he had felt vulnerable and exposed, now became a comfort longed for at the end of a busy watch. And in what free time he was allowed, he found he could think of his family and even begin to write a letter, with no danger of falling into the chasm of misery that had previously threatened to swallow him whole.

He was writing that very letter when Cobb came into the berth, sat himself down at the table and shouted for one of the servants who looked after the youngsters.

Balaam appeared, a lad of roughly Cobb's height, but lacking his full frame, who bowed in front of the midshipman in mock deference.

"Did you squeak, sir?"

"Get me some cheese and biscuit, you idle bastard." The lads were too close in age to allow any difference in status to affect them. "And some coffee, if you haven't drunk it all, already."

Balaam rolled his eyes. "Only scotch coffee left, less you wants I borrow some from starboard berth?"

Cobb looked earnestly at the servant. "Think Collins'd notice?"

"Na, not if we don't make an habit of it."

"Make it so, do what you can, but don't drop us in it if you get caught." Cobb winked. "Beavered coffee always tastes better."

*****

The next morning saw both ships making reasonable progress. The sea was heavy, forcing *Pandora* to join her capture in manning both pumps. The wind blew strong but steady, and their jury rigs appeared adequate enough. Flint, who stood the forenoon watch with the rest of the starbolins, was resting himself on the prow of the forecastle; Jameson and Bennet, a landsman of about Jameson's age they were training up, with him. Since they had come on duty two hours ago surprisingly little had been called from them, and now the wintry watery sun was breaking through the iron clouds with just enough energy to bring them warmth.

"Mr Lewis reckoned we might raise Gib this sennight," Jameson commented. He, like Flint, had known the master's mate since he had been a lower deck man, although both accepted his promotion as just.

"Aye, an' what sight's we'll see then." Flint chewed his tobacco with satisfaction as he rested his back against the foremast. The fresh puddening on their damaged bowsprit was giving out a regular, hypnotic creak and he gladly allowed his mind to fantasise on the impossible prospects of shore leave, ample drink and clean, willing, women.

"Will we be there long?" Jameson asked.

"Long enough," he answered, although the mood was still with him and his eyes remained fixed somewhere in the middle distance.

"Reckon they'll have a job to do on us first." Jameson switched his attention to Bennet who, though not yet a proper sailor, was at least giving him some attention.

Bennet nodded. "Probably put us in dry dock," he said, using a term he had heard on more than one occasion.

"No dry at Gib," Flint commented.

The two younger men exchanged glances and raised eyes, but Flint remained in his private world. Then Bennet grew serious and leant forward.

"Tell you a funny thing," he said, holding Jameson with his expression. "But I sees a sight last night."

"What was that?" Jameson asked, intrigued despite himself.

"Mr Pigot." Bennet sat back again, satisfied.

What warmth they were enjoying from the sun suddenly vanished, and Jameson had to resist a shudder that made him draw his elbows in to his sides. Pigot had been dead for quite a time, considering what they had been through since, yet the name still carried power enough to disturb him.

"Pigot, you say?" Even Flint had been pulled from his fantasies, to listen.

"Aye, I know how it sounds, but it were him, sure as a gun."

"Whereabouts?"

Bennet pointed behind him with his thumb. "Upper deck, outside the galley." It had been in just that area that Pigot's lifeless body had been found.

"But the galley were cold," Jameson mused. Indeed the range, usually quite a convivial place to meet and the only part of the ship where men were allowed to smoke, had remained unlit and empty since the action.

"Aye, cold it were an' not a man abroad, bar the lieutenant."

"What was you doin' on the upper deck?" Flint asked.

"On my way to the heads."

"What time was this?" Matthew had now grown quite chilled.

"Jus' afore two bells, mornin' watch. Thought I'd take my ease 'for the idlers gets about." Bennet might not have been at sea for long, but he had slotted into shipboard routine very quickly.

"An' what did you see?"

"Pigot, least it looked like him. Wearin' his coat, an' standin' jus' outside the galley, as if he were warmin' his bum to the fire. Then he turned an started walkin' back past the manger."

"You sure it were?" There was no trace of teasing in Flint's voice; Bennet's story, however incredible, had the ring of truth about it.

"Sure as I could be in that light. I ducked down, like, thinkin' he'd see me."

"Well you would," Flint commented, dryly.

"Anyone else see him?"

"Oh yes. I gave it a while an' he didn't come back, so I crept after him." He broke his spell for a second. "I still needed the heads, after all." Both men nodded. "Then I comes up to the manger and no sign of him. So I looks about and sees Sammy." Flint and Jameson rolled their eyes; there could be little corroboration from that quarter. Sammy, the middle aged man who looked after the animals, was well known for being as daft as a brush.

"'You see anyone go past?' I asks him, and he says, 'Yes, Mr Pigot went by five minutes ago', an' he points to the officers' roundhouse."

"Lieutenants don't use the roundhouse," Jameson interrupted. "They got their own jakes in the quarter-galleries. Besides, the warrant officers' roundhouse got knocked to splinters."

"I seen a captain use the roundhouse when there was a need," Flint confirmed with satisfaction.

Bennet closed his eyes briefly. "An' so they're using the larboard now, an' that's where Sammy was pointin'," he said.

Flint shook his head almost sadly. "Can't hold for it m'self."

"Neither would I... I mean, neither would I if I hadn't been there, and if I hadn't seen it with me own two eyes."

"Yeah, an' you also saw him buried," Jameson pointed out. "Shot over the side like a good 'un, he did." It was one of his happier memories of the lieutenant.

"Aye, I saw that, an' I saw him again last night." There was no shaking the man, and despite themselves Flint and Jameson felt disinclined to argue further.

Cobb, the midshipman, spoke suddenly, appearing from behind, making Jameson and Bennet start.

"If you've no better there's a mile of splicin' the bosun wants doin'," he told them.

"Very good, Mr Cobb." Despite his size the lad was almost ten years younger than Flint although the novelty of calling any boy mister had worn thin long ago. All three rose up and brushed the dust from their trousers.

"Either that or cook's overhauling galley stove; you can help him if you've a mind," he added casually. "Makes no odds."

Flint caught the eye of his two messmates and grinned slightly. "We'll take the splicin' thank you, Mr Cobb." Tattletale or not, neither of them had a mind to spend any time near the galley, if they could help it.

*****

Carter was buried later that morning. Nairn stood next to the groggy Stuart as Banks read the well-worn words of the service. There was little emotion on the captain's face and even less on Stuart's, which was still bloated with the effects of his nightly draught. But Nairn found it unusually hard to contain his feelings and was in very real danger of breaking down in front of the assembly.

He had watched Carter die, and it had been a relatively peaceful death, thanks to the laudanum that he himself had eventually been forced to administer. The final, generous, dose that hardly made up for the hours of agony the man had undergone before. And all because the surgeon cared more for his own comfort than that of his charges. Nairn contained a wave of revulsion as the canvas bundle was launched from the upturned grating, hitting the water with barely a splash.

His eyes moved about, catching those of Wright, who had a fixed, wooden expression that spoke volumes. Nairn considered him for a moment. Wright had been Carter's messmate. They had tied each other's queues on many occasions, and as such it had fallen to him to set him in his hammock, place the two round shot, and sewn him in (all bar the last "snitch" stitch, which, by right, was the job of the sail maker). Wright had also been there towards the end, when it was clear that Carter was not going to make it, and Stuart could not give a damn either way. He didn't know about the laudanum, no one did, not even the surgeon had noticed the reduction in the jar. And he didn't know about Stuart being absent when he was most needed. Nairn fixed Wright with his eyes, deciding that he should, and would, be fully informed as soon as possible. Wright was straight, a popular seaman and very capable. He'd listen to Nairn, and know exactly what to do. After all, he'd been right on the ball when it had come to accounting for Pigot. Everyone knew that.

CHAPTER NINE

They sighted land on the morning of the fifth day, their progress having been steady and uneventful. King, standing on the quarterdeck of *Aiguille*, set his glass on the misty haze that marked nearby Cape Finisterre, a near perfect landfall, although he could take little credit for that. Despite the fact that she was the leading ship, *Aiguille* sailed under the eye of *Pandora* and it had been Fraiser's sightings and navigation that had brought them to this point. A further signal from the British frigate dictated a change of course and King shut his glass and returned it to the binnacle, while he ordered the ship round. The men strained at the braces as she took up her fresh heading. Behind him *Pandora* was just starting to press her helm, and before long both ships were set for Portugal. The wind, which remained strong and reasonably constant, now came across the beam, slowing their progress slightly and making the ships list to larboard. The bell summoned the men to breakfast. They would have burgoo and small beer, with a draught of hot tea for the boys and anyone else who wanted it. King felt mildly guilty over the last point. Several cases of tea had been discovered amongst the French military stores; presumably these were intended to help their officers through the bite of an Irish winter. Officially he had no right to touch it, being provisions stored below deck, but his men were working under extreme pressure and appreciated the novelty of the drink, almost as much as the warmth it gave them.

King gazed back at *Pandora*, quiet now after her change of course. Her bow was visibly battered by the recent action, but a closer look told him that there was no serious damage, other than a patch close to the waterline that might take four or five days to repair on its own. The ship was bathed in the light sunshine and a slight mist rose up about her. Presumably her decks were drying following holy-stoning and swabbing, a ritual he had been unable to observe in *Aiguille*. Despite receiving further reinforcements from *Pandora*, his prize crew were still greatly outnumbered by the French. On the British quarterdeck he could see the vague form of the officer of the watch, impossible to identify from this distance, and a party of topmen were working on the mizzen cross-strees. Something caught his eye, and he glanced forward; a lieutenant was standing at the beakhead beyond and slightly below the forecastle. The customary white facing to the lapels were quite distinct; it could only be Caulfield, although the figure appeared taller. King raised his arm in greeting to no response; either the man could not make him out, or was lost in thought.

King turned back and retrieved the glass. There was something about the figure that bothered him. He opened the telescope and trained it on the ship. Now the figure had gone, there was no one on the beakhead. He swung the glass round; Caulfield was on the quarterdeck, dressed in his old watch coat. Fraiser stood next to him, presumably in conversation. He returned to the head in time to see two seamen appear to take their ease. He lowered the glass and stood for a moment, unsure exactly what he had seen. A line of dark parcels was running up to the main yardarm. Dorsey appeared next to him and King handed over the deck glass as the coloured bunting broke out.

The midshipman shouted the numbers aloud, and continued to repeat them to himself while flipping through the signal book. "Make all sail commensurate with the weather," he said eventually. King nodded and looked forward. Banks was right; they could try a couple of staysails at least. He gave the order and watched as the freshly fed topmen raced aloft. The ship healed further as the wind filled the canvas, and there was a definite increase in speed. King looked back at *Pandora* who was in the process of setting her foretopgallant and main staysails. With this wind they would be off the coast of Portugal by night and presumably with Jervis, if he was at Tagus, within three days. It could not be fast enough for King, who was finding the strain of command a trifle wearisome. Already he had made a few stupid mistakes - giving a wrong order or forgetting something so obvious that he had had to be reminded by a hand. He glanced again at *Pandora's* beakhead and drew a sigh. It was empty and appeared completely normal, as he would be once he returned to her, and his regular duties.

*****

His estimates were remarkably accurate; within three days they were rounding Cape de Roco and creeping into the harbour. *Pandora* had taken the lead as soon as the Cape was sighted and now King stood on the quarterdeck with little to do, other than follow in her wake. The sun was warm enough to make his jacket unnecessary, but he had no intention of seeing his command into port in shirtsleeves. He took a turn about the deck, and noticed Crowley standing at the rail, watching the coastline intently.

"Your first time in Portugal?" King asked him.

The Irishman shook his head and smiled gently. "No, I spent many years here, back in the late eighties." He pointed at the large castellated building they were passing to larboard. "That's the Castle of Belim, you'll note the turret missing?"

King nodded.

"The work of Captain Payne, in the *Artois* nearly twenty years ago. The Portuguese don't rush to set things right."

"But we weren't at war then, surely?"

"Near as made no difference. Your man came in the harbour, friendly like, and the Government threatened to sink his ship where she lay. Sent out a bunch of papist priests to anathematise him into the bargain."

"And he didn't take kindly to it?"

"Set off one of his great guns, so he did. Near took their precious castle to pieces. 'Course he said later he had supposed the gun drawn, but that was more for appearance."

"What were you doing in Portugal?" King asked. Crowley had remained an enigma almost from the moment they had first met. Shipping with a French invasion force, King had naturally taken him for a Nationalist, yet there was little of the revolutionary energy he had noted in others of the cause.

"There for the good of my health, sir," he answered with a smile.

"You've no loyalty to any country?"

"Only myself, and the people about me. I've no knowledge of politics, nor desire for it."

King nodded, and met the Irishman's smile.

A fleet of bean cods, light fast vessels with angular rigs, shot out from the nearby land and in between the two ships. Their crews waved and shouted at the men of *Pandora* as their craft altered course and closed until they were almost alongside her hull. Some took to holding up small trinkets and in one case a live pig. They seemed to be ignoring *Aiguille*, other than to grace her with disdainful looks and scowls.

Crowley laughed. "Your ensign might be proud, but it's worrying the hell out of the Portuguese."

King looked up to the mizzen lateen yard where the British flag was flying victoriously over the tricolour of France. "You mean they think we're the enemy?" he said.

"Maybe, and maybe they're just not taking any chances. But there's no love for the French here, and I wouldn't give tuppence for any of your prisoners if they get set ashore."

Then they were round and looking deep into the harbour. King drew in a slow breath; it was vast, far bigger than any he had seen before. There were hundreds of ships, some of considerable size, at anchor. Many were British merchants, although a large convoy of Portuguese vessels was also grouped to one side. The entire harbour seemed to be alive with small shipping passing in between the anchored vessels, their bright sails making brief flashes of colour in the gentle sunshine, while the heavy, ancient stone buildings watched on from a distance like dutiful parents; any British port would appear small, mean and dingy by comparison.

A group of battleships could be seen anchored just off the bar. Dobson was at the main, and sang out as the anchored British fleet came into view.

I make it fourteen, sir, no, fifteen. Six are three-deckers; five have their t'gallants up, belike they've just arrived."

"What of the flag?"

"Aye, sir. There's a first-rate anchored to the east. Looks like *Victory*."

King nodded. Though a trifle old, *Victory* was a superb sailer, and the ideal command for an active admiral like Jervis. From where he was he could see a rear admiral's flag flying from the *Royal George*, a three-decker of 100 guns and less than ten years old. That must be Parker, late of the Channel Fleet. For him to be present meant Jervis had received reinforcements, and yet his command still only numbered fifteen line ships. It was possible that they had seen action already and sustained losses.

"There's what looks like a merchant convoy at anchor further in," Dobson droned on. "Topmasts up and ready to go."

"Two-decker in the van," Dorsey cut in. "She's making the private signal, sir."

"Very good... reply."

It was up to Banks in *Pandora* to make his number and report *Aiguille* as a prize, but the private signal would at least persuade the anchored fleet that he was no danger to them. They crept further into the bay and all its shipping opened up to them as they went.

The dull report of gun fire rang out as *Pandora* began to salute the flag. King had worried over this point for some while; *Aiguille* was legally a prize, and as such not expected to observe the normal naval courtesies, although he was equally conscious that not doing so might cause offence. Eventually he had decided to remain silent, assuring himself that any firing of guns, when they were so overcrowded with prisoners, was to be avoided.

"Flag's signalling, sir!" Dorsey was alert enough, his eye to the coloured flags that could just be made out on *Victory's* main.

"*Pandora's* number, sir. Anchor three cables to west, send boat."

The wind, which had been dying since they rounded the point, now became fitful and fluky. The foretopsail flapped and soon *Aiguille* began to drift with the tide as *Pandora* swept to starboard, under a more balanced rig of topsails and forecourse.

"Anchor in our lee, Mr King," Caulfield's voice boomed as the forecourse was gathered in. King waved back, and turned his attention to the forecastle where three hands were waiting to knock *Aiguille's* starboard bower away.

"She's takin' in 'er tops'ls," Dorsey reported and sure enough the frigate was coming to a gradual halt, almost exactly where the flag had ordered. King gauged the distance nervously, keen to give both ships room to swing, yet remain close to *Pandora*.

"Very good, Mr Dorsey," he said. *Aiguille* spilled what remained of her wind and the anchor dropped. Momentum carried her the last remaining yards as the bower bit, and the cable ran out. Topmen swarmed up to take in her canvas, and she came to halt with a slight snub. On board *Pandora* men were rushing to launch the cutter, while Banks stood on the quarterdeck, resplendent in full dress uniform. He would be calling on the admiral, and have quite a story to tell. Watching him without envy, King exhaled a breath he felt had been held inside him for almost a week.

*****

"I'd like a word, if you please," Nairn said, as Wright sat renewing the messenger cable. The seaman looked up from his splicing; even in a ship as small as *Pandora* there were some that you rarely came in contact with. Wright had to think twice before he placed the man, and then was reasonably sure he had never exchanged more than a greeting with the loblolly boy before.

"It was about your mate, Carter. I was with him when he died."

"Aye, I remember." Wright looked at him without expression. "You cared for him, I'm obliged."

Nairn nodded. "Happy to, but there's those who weren't quite so concerned."

Wright waited for the man to continue. Nairn sat down next to him, and carried on in a softer voice.

"Mr Stuart, the surgeon. He's a bad lot, he is."

The seaman nodded philosophically. "I've heard it said, but then I also heard it 'bout most sawbones."

"Aye, but he's a wrong 'un, and no mistakin'." Nairn shuffled uneasily, conscious that what he said was tantamount to mutiny, and might even see him face the noose. "I'm not speakin' for myself, but I wouldn't want to be in no action with him to sew me up afterwards."

Wright listened while Nairn detailed the care Stuart had been giving to his patients. Carter was one, but some of the others had fared no better. "So, what you think?" he said, when he had finished. "Reckoned you were the one to tell if any."

"Me?" Wright snorted. "I'm no crusher."

Nairn eyed him cautiously. "You know how to handle yourself, more important, you know how to put others in place."

Again Wright held his peace.

"I saw you taking that pistol from the reefer's berth. I saw you stick it in your belt, under your shirt, and I was there when they took the bullet from that bastard, Pigot. Weren't no regulation gun that fired a pellet like that, were the kind officers carry."

Still Wright remained silent, although his mind raced. As far as he had been aware no one knew that he had accounted for Pigot. There had been no planning as such; finding the gun had given him the spur: the weapon was ideal, small enough to conceal, and yet accurate. It had just been a question of waiting for the right moment. He had fired from the shelter of the empty galley, the flash had been minimal and all but hidden, and any sound went almost unnoticed in the heat of action. Returning the piece had been equally easy. Now though it looked like complications were appearing. Little though he knew him, Nairn did not appear to be the kind who indulged in blackmail; but then he could not be sure.

"I hear'd what you saying, and I'm not interested." Wright spoke softly, although his voice carried a definite edge. "You tells who you likes, and what you likes, but Pigot was about as popular as the flux, and you'll earn no friends by peaching on me."

Nairn considered this for a moment. "Aye, I thought as much," he said, finally. "Reckoned you wouldn't mind me asking, though."

"Don't mind at all." The tension had eased with the level of the men's voices. Wright sat back and drew a sigh. "You can do something yourself of course; in your line of business there must be plenty of ways to sort Stuart out."

"Aye, and that's the truth." Nairn got up to go but Wright stopped him.

"Best remember, though; as a surgeon he may not be up to much, but we won't get another, and a bad one's better than none at all."

Nairn nodded and walked away. The ship's bell rang; Wright would be off in half a glass. He returned to his splicing, content that a potential crisis had been avoided. Nairn was almost a stranger, but there was an understanding amongst seamen, and he knew there would be no further trouble from that quarter. He dug the fid of his knife into the fresh end of rope, and began teasing the separate strands free. Within minutes he was lost in his own world, dreaming of his other life, and the wife who would be waiting for him at the close of the cruise.

He had no mind for anything else as he worked, and Guppy, the master at arms, who had been standing in the lee of the mainmast, present, but unnoticed throughout, crept silently away, more than content with the knowledge he had gained.

*****

"Giving up your command so soon, Mr King?" The first lieutenant took the younger man by the hand and shook it warmly.

"Hardly. Thought I'd remind myself how a British ship appeared."

Caulfield beamed, clearly pleased to see him. "You did well, we made good progress." He opened his mouth to say more, then the moment passed. "Come below, and we'll fix you up."

Following Caulfield down to the gunroom King was surprised by how small *Pandora* appeared. After a week or so in the French ship her proportions seemed almost mean, while the scantlings and frames were ridiculously frail.

"Visitor for us, gentlemen." Caulfield opened the door; the only occupants of the gunroom were Fraiser and Soames, the purser. King exchanged greetings with both, and sat down at the well-remembered long table.

"So come on, laddie, tell us all about it," Fraiser urged him. "What have you been about?"

In fact King had had little time, and less opportunity, for conversation since he had last seen them, and had to pause for a moment to arrange his thoughts before he began. They listened in silence as he described the scene aboard the French ship, and nodded sympathetically when he mentioned the high number of casualties.

Fraiser shook his head. "Aye, it's a barbaric thing we do, and no mistaking."

"We had our fair share here too, of course," Caulfield said. "Stuart's never worked so hard in his life."

"An' that's saying little," Soames commented dryly. There was an awkward pause, and King felt obliged to continue his story. When he had finished, and taken a deep draught from the red wine that the steward had placed in front of him, he felt the tiredness inside begin to ebb slightly.

"No doubt you've been busy," Caulfield said, sipping his own wine. "An' I'd like to take a look at your man Crowley."

"He's sound, for an Irishman." King felt a twinge of embarrassment, remembering that Caulfield's mother was Irish. "I mean, for a man found in a French ship with possible Nationalist ideals, and..."

"I know what you mean." The first lieutenant smiled. For a moment he considered switching the conversation to Pigot; there were a number of questions that had been burning inside him for the last week, but little would be gained in the present company. Instead King asked a question that had been very much on his mind.

"What happens now?"

Fraiser shook his head. "Cannot rightly say. We won't be stayin' here long, that's for sure, Portuguese will give us harbour space, but we can't expect more, not with Spain nudging at their shoulder every moment. They'll want us gone as soon as feasible and, if my guess is correct, so will Jervis."

"There's a convoy waiting to sail," Caulfield agreed. "And he's not the type to waste time when the enemy's at sea."

"On to Gib, then?"

"Aye. Round St Vincent, then through the strait. Not got much for us there, but the master shipwright's square enough, and we're likely to pick up a few more men."

"What about your lot?" Caulfield asked him. "Need some hands no doubt?"

"I'll take any you can spare, and marines. We've several hundred French soldiers on board an' most of them are pretty fagged with pumping."

Both men nodded. "Captain will be aware of that. He's with the admiral now. Probably give you a fresh draft from another ship. An' I dare say we could find a few more topmen, now we've sorted most of the damage aloft."

"How are your provisions?" Soames had an eager, but ingratiating look upon his bullfrog face and King felt himself stiffen. Their victuals were reasonably good, having been intended to keep the large crew plus several hundred soldiers alive for three months. He had plenty of the staples: beef, pork and bread, but more importantly an excellent supply of wine and spirits, along with tobacco, chocolate, tea, coffee and spices.

"Fair," King said, his voice intentionally flat. "We'll see Gibraltar all right, that's certain."

The provisions, along with other stores, armament and supplies, would all be minuted as part of the prize when the ship was condemned. Every man on board had earned their share, and King had no intention of letting Soames get his greedy hands on them until then.

Caulfield reached for his watch and looked at it significantly.

"Better get you back, young man," he said. "We'll keep you up with events this side. Belike we'll know more when Sir Richard makes his return."

"Aye," said Fraiser, draining his glass. "That's a conversation I'd pay a fair price to hear."

Caulfield walked with him to the entry port where a cutter filled with stores and men awaited him. King turned to go, but there was an odd look in Caulfield's eye that made him pause.

"We've not had much chance to talk, not since the first action." Both men knew he was referring to Pigot's death. King waited; he had nothing to say.

"You'll have left your report?"

"Aye, with the captain's secretary."

Caulfield nodded. He liked King, and wanted so much to help him, although the right words would not form.

"There'll be a court of enquiry; you know that, don't you?"

King nodded.

"With luck you won't be called, but if so, just say as little as you need."

It was good advice, whatever the circumstances, although King wondered quite why he was being treated to it at that moment. The ship's bell rang, and the men in the cutter below were making less than subtle noises. Caulfield slapped King on the shoulder, and bid him farewell.

*****

Grey and Calder were there to meet Banks as he climbed through *Victory's* starboard entry port.

"I trust I find you well?" Calder, the captain of the fleet, ran his eyes over his junior's uniform as if eager to find something of which to disapprove.

"Very well thank you, sir, and yourself?"

"Fair enough, fair enough."

The guard of honour had finished paying their respects and Banks found himself being hustled away before he had had a chance to salute them.

"Captain Grey, I'm sure you have pressing matters that concern you with the ship."

"Indeed so, good to see you again, Sir Richard, I wish you joy of your prize."

Banks shook hands with *Victory's* captain, conscious of Calder twitching impatiently behind him.

"Admiral's waiting for you in his quarters; we need to catch the afternoon tide, so you will have to be brief."

Banks, rushing along the deck of the flagship, experienced the very reverse of King's earlier emotions. Compared with his frigate, *Victory* was a complete contrast. Built almost fifty years before, she had the dimensions and timbers of a different age. Solid, secure, and maintained to the very peak of excellence, it was hard to imagine such a ship being bothered by any form of weather or enemy.

At the entrance to the admiral's quarters a very superior marine, freshly pipe-clayed leather and with a powdered wig, snapped to attention and announced the pair, as Calder breezed straight through.

"We're due to be joined by Vice Admiral Waldergrave with five from the Channel fleet," he told Banks in a disdainful voice. "But before we can meet, we are bound to accompany a convoy out directly."

Banks said nothing, although the schoolboy inside felt he should apologise for his sudden arrival. Presumably Calder considered his appearance, together with a powerful French prize, had been intended as yet another obstacle to cause him nuisance.

Jervis was sitting at his desk as they swept into the great cabin. Now decidedly aged, he still bore an active light in his eyes, and even though his gout made standing a slow affair, there was no mistaking the warmth and energy in the firm hand he extended towards Banks.

"You've brought company with you," he said, after they had exchanged pleasantries.

"Yes, sir. I fell in with a French frigate shortly after sighting the invasion fleet."

Jervis nodded. "Invasion fleet, eh? You'll have a story to tell."

"If I may interrupt, Sir John..." Calder was positively bending forward with impatience. "The commodore will be wanting to proceed, with luck we may catch the afternoon tide."

"Pah! The commodore will not be ready this side of Christmas." The admiral directed a particularly fierce glare, causing Calder to take a step back. "Sir Richard has come a long way and will be staying for dinner; you may wish to advise my steward of that on your way out."

Never was a knight of the realm and captain of the fleet dismissed in such a way, yet Banks was not in the least surprised. Sir John was a fair but hard man who knew his own mind and spoke it. Also regarded as one who did not suffer fools, it was quite clear he fitted Calder in this category. Banks found himself swallowing dryly as the admiral turned his attention back to him.

"Take a glass of wine with me, sir, and tell me your story." He indicated an upright chair, set opposite his desk.

"I have my journals here." Banks patted the canvas-covered parcel, but Jervis waved it away.

"All in good time; first, from your own mouth, sir, and in order. Leave nothing out, I want to know everything."

*****

Guppy was waiting for the first lieutenant when he returned from seeing King off the ship. The sight of the master at arms always made Caulfield remember his own predecessor and it was with forced civility that he showed the man through to the now empty gunroom. Caulfield knew Guppy to be a bully and a coward, both rare attributes in his particular station and equally likely to influence Caulfield's impression of the man for the worse. He also suspected him of other, far more sinister habits, but then Caulfield tended to make allowances when dealing with people he especially disliked.

"Is somethin' I was meanin' to bring up 'afore now, only, what with the prize, I realise 'ow busy you was, sir."

Guppy normally spoke to anyone in authority in an obsequious, fawning manner that aggravated all the more when his treatment of those junior to him was known. Sitting across the gunroom table, Caulfield made no response, his face remaining totally impassive. Whatever mischief the master at arms might be making there would be no encouragement from him.

"It was about the firs' lieutenant, sir. I mean, Mr Pigot."

That came as no surprise, Pigot and Guppy had worked closely together; there was nothing unusual in that, considering their positions and responsibilities, although Caulfield had managed very well with the minimum of contact with the master at arms.

"An' it was more how he came to die."

This was more serious. It was Caulfield's job to find out all he could about the incident, and Guppy might well have important information.

"It weren't no accident, I mean, he didn't get hit by the Frenchies, sir. It were someone on board this ship."

There was no revelation in that; most of the crew were well aware how Pigot had met his end. Some, Caulfield suspected, knew more and it was possible that Guppy was one.

"I'd like to tell you what I know, but you have to consider my position, sir." He smiled ingratiatingly, displaying an incomplete collection of tortoiseshell teeth. Caulfield shook his head.

"I don't understand."

"Well, I wouldn't be popular, like, 'specially if people were knowing it were me what told."

Caulfield sat back in his seat. "You are the master at arms, you are charged with the security and safety of this ship. If you cannot protect yourself, I fail to mark how you carry out your duties."

Guppy's face grew white and for a moment Caulfield thought he might be about to lose his temper. Then the sickly smile returned once more.

"It were the ship I was thinkin' 'bout. Her, an' the good of the people."

"Rubbish, the only thing on your mind was your skin. Now, what do you have to tell me?"

For a moment the smile vanished and Guppy's gaze lowered. "I was hopin' for an exchange, sir. When we reach Gib, if that were agreeable."

It was certainly agreeable from Caulfield's point of view, but the man's bargaining was starting to irritate him.

"Right now I'm not interested in exchanges, Guppy. If you have information about Mr Pigot's death, I want to hear it, but I'll make no trades with you, are you clear on that?"

The eyes rose up once more and looked directly into Caulfield's. "I've a mind I should be speakin' with the Fleet," he said in a totally different voice. "There's information I have that other officers would want to hear, even if you don't."

Caulfield fought to control his composure. In his own mind there was little doubt that King had dealt with Pigot. He could not condone the action, but the lad had more than enough reason, if not for himself, then for the men he served with. Pigot; never was a name more aptly given; he was an animal, and one whose particular brand of evil fed upon the misery it could make of other men's lives. Given time it would doubtless have infested the entire ship. King had done well to be rid of him, and yet the evil lived on and now, in the person of Guppy, would probably see a promising young officer disrated and maybe even shot.

"You can speak to the Fleet," Caulfield said, slowly. "There'll be an official enquiry, it may even be being planned as we speak. You will have your chance then. Your chance to give them all the details. A man may well die for what you say, but whatever happens, remember this: There is no privacy in the court martial, every word will be reported, every name shall be known. Be sure you will spend the rest of your life serving in a navy where people have marked you down."

Guppy started back, at first uncomprehending, then a small glimmer of understanding began to burn about his face. Caulfield considered extending the threat, mentioning likely crimes that Guppy may have committed in the past. No man could serve as a master at arms without creating a few enemies, and Guppy would have more than his share. Besides, Caulfield had seen the way he watched men, the way he chose favourites amongst the younger hands, and generally abused his position. There would be many who would gladly stand against him. There had been other times when Caulfield had noted the irony of the lower deck accepting illegal ways without protest, yet rising up in anger when natural justice had conflicted with written law.

"Go and think on what I say," Caulfield told him softly.

Guppy blinked, his mind reeling from the implications that were still unfurling before him. He rose from the table and turned to go, then stopped and looked Caulfield directly in the eye.

"Don't you even want to know who done it?" he asked.

Caulfield held his glare for a second, then relaxed into a half smile. "I already know," he said.

CHAPTER TEN

The right hand of Admiral Sir John Jervis KB struck the desk with enough force to rattle the crystal and silver inkwell.

"You're tellin' me that an officer was killed on board your ship, killed, like as not, by the hand of one of your people, and you have done nothing about it?"

Banks swallowed. He could repeat the fact that he had ordered his officers to carry out their own investigation, he could remind the admiral that *Pandora* had been in action, and immediately afterwards had been weighed down with a prize. He could cite a thousand different reasons, but there was a good deal of similarity between his father and Sir John when in a rage and in his father's case he had learnt to say nothing until the anger abated.

"Damn it all, the man is still amongst you; there should be a court of enquiry, maybe even a court martial. And the sooner the better."

There was a slight twitter from Calder who, unable to remain out of the room for long, had sneaked back while Banks had been relating his tale.

"All right, Calder, I'm not suggesting we do it here." His eyes swept back to Banks and held him in their glare. "But at Gibraltar, and as soon as you arrive. There can be no more shilly-shally, do you hear me?"

131

Jervis sat back in his chair and sighed. The lid had been knocked from his inkwell, a present from his wife, Martha. Silently and with care he replaced it.

"So be it," Sir John paused, and looked Banks in the eyes once more. "Now on to more important things. You are a King's officer; I shall not dress this up for you. We have received intelligence reports of a large Franco Spanish force that sailed from Toulon just a few weeks back. We know that Villeneuve took the French ships through the straits alone, and believe the Dons went in to Carthagena for stores or repairs. They are there now, ready to sail and of a force that all but doubles ours. They may try and meet up with the French, in which case we are looking towards a spring invasion." He smiled suddenly, and Banks was aware of a strength of character he had rarely met before. "So you can understand, and maybe forgive, an old man's impatience?"

"Of course, Sir John."

"There are no marines available at present, but we have taken on men of the sixty-ninth regiment who are doing admirably well. Calder, you will organise a draft to accompany Sir Richard's prize." The captain of the fleet nodded gravely. "But you will be needing another officer; is your second up to handling the prize?"

"Mr King? Yes, sir. Although he only carries my acting warrant."

"Has he passed his board?"

"Yes, sir."

"Does his duty? Pleases you?"

"Yes, sir."

"Then we had better see him made." His eyes flashed to Calder who, once more, nodded in agreement.

"Once you make Gib do what you can to get *Pandora* ready for sea. There won't be time for a refit, just attend to the important matters, and that damned court of enquiry. Then return, and make sure you bring the soldiers with you. Commodore Nelson will be passin' through the straits at any time. If you can join with him, so much the better, if not call here for news of a rendezvous, though with luck we will meet before then."

Jervis suddenly looked very tired, and Banks felt his heart go out to him. Responsibility for the fleet rested with this one elderly man. And more than that, he had to negotiate with a friendly neutral, one who might turn, or be invaded at any moment, as well as anticipate the Navies of two major powers. All this with minimal backup, and communications to and from the Admiralty taking several weeks. "You had better return to your ship and prepare to leave. We too will be under way shortly."

The admiral's eyes were closed now, and he appeared to be asleep. Calder nodded and turned to go; Banks stood up silently and went to follow him. Without opening his eyes, Jervis spoke once more.

"It was a good effort, Sir Richard."

Banks stopped, momentarily taken aback.

"To take that frigate, with a ship the size of *Pandora*, a damned good effort, sir." He opened his eyes and smiled once more. "Tell me, are you a married man?"

"No, sir."

"That is good. Marriage is a wonderful thing, but not for young officers. I expect you to go far, Sir Richard, but only if you keep yourself unencumbered."

Calder was gone now, and Banks felt that he should follow. "Thank you, sir," he said softly, and left.

*****

King returned to the prize to find *Pandora's* marines handing over to the soldiers. The decks were cluttered with red and blue coats, with the white helmets of the guards looking strangely at odds with the leather shakos of the marines. An army lieutenant approached him and saluted hesitantly. Even though he had removed the white collar flashes, King was still wearing his midshipman's coat, which lacked the white lapels of a full naval lieutenant's uniform.

"You are the officer in charge, sir?" the man said. Although a member of a Welsh regiment, the only accent he possessed was that of an upper class Englishman.

"Thomas King, lieutenant in command," King replied in as stiff a voice as he could muster. The prejudice he held had nothing to do with the fellow being in the army, he had had remarkably little contact with proper land solders. But for all his life King had lived under the control of the aristocracy; control that had rarely been blessed by intelligence, and seen him placed in awkward and dangerous situations on more than one occasion. This particular example was of inferior rank and King was determined not to be lorded over.

"Alexis John Horatio Stafford at your service, sir. My men will be accommodated within the hour, you are free to remove your marines at any time."

"Very good." King looked about for Martin, who was nowhere to be seen. He turned and questioned a corporal standing near.

"Mr Martin is below, speaking with my captain," the lieutenant interrupted, adding in a more conversational tone, "They were at Eton together, don't you know?"

King might have guessed as much. He had been looking forward to being free of the stuffy marine lieutenant although now, it seemed, he had only exchanged him for two like-minded prigs.

"Make sure your men are fully conversant with the exercise arrangements of the prisoners," he said. The lieutenant raised an eyebrow.

"Exercise? "You want to give the prisoners facilities to roam? Damn it, sir, they are Frenchmen!"

"I want the prisoners to reach Gibraltar in as good a condition as possible. That will entail allowing a proportion above decks on a regular basis. I am also keen to see that this ship remains afloat; hands are needed to man the pumps at all hours and I would rather they be French ones. If your men are not capable of seeing to this in a competent manner, I will request my marines to be retained. And you and I, sir, are not equal in rank; you will address me properly at all times. That is the way we do things in the Navy, don't you know?"

His anger was partly fuelled by the man's impertinence at questioning an order, and partially by the tone and timbre of his voice, although King assured himself that it was also the idea of keeping the French soldiers penned up for long periods, long periods when their confined state might lead them to rash plans for retaking the ship; that was the real justification behind his outburst. The lieutenant saluted smartly and turned away, the nearest he could get to snubbing King in return. King was in no way put out; he had made his point and would continue to do so for as long as was necessary.

In the short time that they had been at anchor, Everit, the carpenter from *Pandora*, had brought a team of men across to inspect the French ship. King saw him now as he made his way back to the great cabin.

"Ship's in a reasonable state, sir," he said, knuckling his fore-head. "Frame an' fabric are sound, an' the Frenchies 've made some steps with repairs." There was only a hint of disdain in Everit's voice, and King guessed that he was quite impressed. "I've taken the liberty of settin' my men to work in the great cabin, sir. Can't do much 'bout that quarter-gallery, of course, but the rest's a bit more habitable."

King looked past the man and was pleasantly surprised. The major shot holes had been plugged, and deadlights set up at the shattered stern windows. These were folded back now, allowing bright sunlight into the room, revealing scrubbed paintwork and fresh canvas flooring. Shuttering had been secured across the gaping hole left where the quarter-gallery had been, and furniture brought up from wherever it had been stowed before the action. Crowley was standing at the table that almost ran the entire length of the stern. There were three large silver candlesticks, along with other expensive items of table decoration. To one side a smaller table held several dozen crystal glasses that sparkled in the bright sun. Crowley, solemnly laying out places for a meal, was also watching him surreptitiously, clearly trying to gauge his reaction to the changes.

"That's good work, Everit," King told him. "I wouldn't have believed you could have done so much in a few hours. The carpenter gave a rare smile.

"Amazin' how the hands'll work when it's in their interest, sir."

Of course, *Aiguille* was to be condemned at the prize court, and any sum she made would be divided amongst the crew. The carpenter's mates would share one eighth with other junior warrant officers, so it was well worth their while making the ship appear as sound as possible. King finally turned to Crowley.

"Expecting company, are we?"

The Irishman looked up. "Layin' out the dinner, sir. Thought it would be a shame to waste all this good silver and china when we've fresh officers aboard."

It was probably right that he, as lieutenant in command, should welcome the new men with a meal, although King did not relish the prospect.

"And have you found a man to cook for us?" King asked, temporising.

"Oh there's no shortage amongst the French, sir," he said. "But then I'm a skilled man myself, an' I'll not disappoint you with made up meals. We've beef an' kidneys a boiling in the galley an' six geese ready for the spit."

King supposed that he should have become used to Crowley's knack of filling the right hole at the right time, but just occasionally he hoped the man might make a mistake, if only to reveal himself human. The trust that had grown up between them was strong now; it was hard to remember the rough, supposed Nationalist he had first met barely a week ago.

"You're taking a lot on yourself," he said, with a faint smile. "Doesn't bother you, cookin' for all these Englishmen?"

Crowley's face was quite impassive. "Why should it do that, sir?" He looked up and for a moment the smile was returned. "I always believe in keepin' my enemies where I can sees them."

A tap at the door heralded the arrival of Dorsey, strangely in uniform after the slop clothes they had all worn for the last few days.

"Boat from the flag brought this, sir." There was something else about the lad other than the blue coat. He was regarding him in a reserved, contemplative way. Maybe this was bad news; had he been relieved of his command after all? King snatched the thick, waxed envelope from him and opened it. A single sheet of parchment was inside, nothing more. There was a seal to the left-hand side, and his name came out to greet him, written bold in a flowing hand. He took a quick breath. Below there came the signature of Sir John Jervis, then that of Evan Nepean; presumably the admiral kept a stock of these blank, so they could be issued at the appropriate moment.

Slowly realisation dawned on him; he had been made, he was now officially commissioned as an officer. He felt the blood rush to his head. There would be no doubts now; unless he was broken or retired, he would receive half pay for the rest of his life. He looked to the bottom left and noted that he had been given seniority from the day of the action, a nice touch.

"I'm made," he said in a quiet voice, although all those about him were listening intently. Dorsey was smiling and wishing him joy of his commission, and even old Everit's face cracked slightly as he knuckled his forehead, then cautiously offered him his horny hand. King felt the happiness erupt from within until it seemed to fill his very veins. There would never be a better time that this, never, not even if he rose to be admiral of the fleet. This moment was unique and would stay with him always. He felt the first warning signs of tears, and hurriedly brought himself back to matters in hand. Everit and his crew were all but done, and Crowley was quite right, there must be a welcoming dinner. He walked round the large table and stood looking out at the fleet through the broken stern windows.

"So, you're a King's man, proper now, are you?"

The voice of Crowley interrupted his thoughts. He turned to him.

"Is that a problem?"

Crowley smiled and offered his hand, which King gladly accepted. "I'm happy for you."

*****

"You see the thing with heights is they never seem so bad from below."

Bennet nodded at this piece of wisdom, although to him the climb up to the foretopsail yard still seemed daunting, even when viewed from the stability of the forecastle.

"Wind's comin' off our larboard quarter," Ford continued. "So when they gives the word, we make for the larboard shrouds, that's the weather side at present."

"I got it," Bennet confirmed, but the doubts remained. In all the time he had been on board *Pandora* he had not gone aloft. Despite the fact he was a landsman, and completely unskilled, the Navy needed men, and for him to fall and die, or worse, be injured and take up space and medical supervision, would be a waste. First he had been trained in knots and splices, proved to be a steady tackle-man on the great guns and passed several watches with the afterguard. If he never excelled at anything else, at least he was now earning his space. More importantly Bennet had also shown himself capable both of taking instruction, and learning from it. Now he could be considered worth passing forward for the next challenge; for if he could be trained up as a topman, as Ford, his divisional midshipman, and the boatswain thought, he would really have arrived.

To go aloft in the gentle warmth of a Portuguese breeze with the ship just gathering way was almost ideal conditions, as Bennet, who still viewed the prospect cautiously, was well aware. There could never be a better time, and if he were to fail, it may as well be now as ever.

Forward, the men were catting the first anchor; at any moment Banks would order sail. The rest of the topmen stood in a group separate, aloof, from the forecastle hands and waisters. They were the elite, the best seamen in the ship. They were the ones who went up in all weathers, wrestled with unhandy masses of damp canvas, fought the elements that tried to knock them from their perilous perch, and performed all manner of tricks that would impress a circus performer. And all as many times as was necessary to secure the safety of the ship. In the British Navy shipboard accident was the second most likely cause of death, and even though it was these men who were the ones most prone to meet it, they remained determinedly undaunted by the risks they took. It was nothing to see a man walk the length of a yard, simply to avoid the slow and ponderous progress along the footrope, and to descend to the deck by any means other than a roughly tarred backstay was considered odd in the extreme. Off watch they would climb for recreation, competing with each other in all types of death defying tricks; a practice that had become known as skylarking. Even as a trainee, standing with the topmen and about to go aloft for the first time, Bennet was conscious of their sense of pride and wallowed unashamedly in its reflection.

Movement on the quarterdeck caught the men's attention long before the high-pitched whistles and shouts sent the first man to the shrouds. It was Cobb, one of the midshipmen, who held it a point of honour to lead the men aloft, even though he would remain on the top, while they went out along the yard.

"Come on, that's us," Ford told him, then made for the weather shrouds.

Bennet was one step behind, and swung himself out over the side as he clambered above the forecastle channels, and up onto the shrouds. The ratlines, untarred rope that acted as rungs across the shrouds, were slack and moved alarmingly as he placed his feet upon them.

"Three an' one," Ford muttered to Bennet's left. Bennet nodded, he knew the rule: keep one hand and two feet or one foot and two hands secured at all times. Later when, if, he became proficient, he could indulge in the scampering antics that were now going on about him as the men swarmed up.

"Keep your eyes to the top, the only reason you wants to look down is to see how far you've been. Measure it to the top, an' you won't need to look anywheres else."

They were getting closer to the foretop now; a proper platform, made from reassuringly heavy chunks of wood that seemed almost like an oasis of solidity in a floating world.

"You can go through the lubber's hole first seven times; after that it's the futtocks for always."

Bennet watched as the other men clambered up the futtock shrouds, hanging back, almost horizontally, as they did, their entire body weight hanging on their fingers and toes. He gratefully made for the lubber's hole and pulled himself through.

"First time up?" the midshipman asked as he emerged on the foretop.

"He's for the foretops'l yard, Mr Cobb," Ford answered for him. "Come on, they'll be startin' without us!"

They were. In fact the foretopsail yard was already fully manned, with two leading hands sitting astride the yardarms as Ford and Bennet began to clamber up the topmast shrouds.

"Tops'l will fall any moment. Might cause a bit of a draught, be ready for it."

Bennet nodded, the climbing had taken much of the wind from his body, and his hands and the soles of his feet were starting to complain.

Sure enough the canvas was released in short jerks, then the entire yard moved round as the hands below manned the braces, pulling the sail into the wind. They had reached the foretopsail yard now, but Ford took Bennet onto the crosstrees to get out of the way of the other topmen, some of whom were now starting to clamber back in from the yard. There was a shout and a roar of laughter as Dickens, one of the nimblest, hitched onto an unsecured brace, letting himself down to the deck like a bead on a string, much to the annoyance of the forecastle men who had to hold him.

"Come on, I'll takes you out to the first quarter," Ford told him, when the yard was empty, and it was at this point that Bennet looked down for the footrope, and the world began to swim.

It was not possible, it could not be happening. There were all the features he had come to know about the ship: the grating, hatches, gangways, fife rails. All the clutter of a ship of war yet small, oh how small, and he was suspended above them with only his hands to hold him. He let out a gasp, and Ford immediately turned back.

"Hey now. Fix your eyes on me, don't worry about what's going on below!"

Bennet was rigid with fear. He knew that only by relaxing for a moment he would die. It was as if a great magnet was pulling him down. Pulling him down, sucking him from where he stood. Maybe it would be better to give in to it; anything was preferable to this terror. He felt a strong and surprisingly large hand over his, clamping him to the shroud that was only just in his grasp.

"Grip tight, hold. Let me feel you hang onto that line."

Slowly Bennet found his hand was obeying, and his fingers fixed themselves to the thin rope. "Now the other, next to it."

He moved his left hand and took the line also.

"Firm grip?"

"Yes."

"There, now you can't fall, see? Can't fall 'cause you're locked on. Got it?"

Bennet nodded.

"So, if you can't fall, you've nothin' to worry about."

It all sounded absurdly simple and yet, with his fingers tight about the line Bennet felt far better, so much so that Ford could remove his hand and leave him standing on his own.

"Now, the horse is here, that's the foot rope. No, don't look, find it with your feet; reach out, feel."

The only thing that was keeping him up was Ford's voice, and it was quite natural for Bennet to obey without question. He allowed himself to stretch one bare foot out into the air, and came unexpectedly into contact with a taught line. "You can rest on that, it's safe. Put your weight on it."

He did, having to shift his body out slightly in order to do so. Then it seemed natural to lean against the yard, rest his belly on that firm, warm, smooth, timber.

"That's it, keep your weight forward, and you're sure as a rock. Then step along, move your other foot on the horse."

Once more he obeyed, now resting both feet on the footrope, while his body leant over the yard, which his hands also gripped. Beneath him the foretopsail had filled with wind, and was now being pulled taught as the hands sheeted it home.

"Right, move on. Watch out for the slings and stirrups; we'll go to the yardarm and back."

They did, slowly at first, but gradually Bennet grew more confident until he was edging himself away from the mast in short but certain steps. The yard grew slightly thinner as he reached the second and third quarter and the square wooden pole became round and easier to grip.

"That's far enough, now rest forward." Bennet turned to his right to see Ford bent over the yard, his body seemingly balanced about his stomach. It would mean looking down, and Bennet geared himself for the challenge, although as soon as he bent forward it was not the solid deck that met his eyes but deep, clear water. Deep, clear water. The sail was taught and he could look past it easily, while the height allowed him to see almost to the bottom. Deep, clear water. Soft, forgiving. He could fall now and it would be all right, although strangely he felt quite safe. Quite safe and, probably for the first time in his life, totally in charge. Below him the grey wash of a school of small fish could be seen as it magically flew beneath the surface. Changing direction as one, they appeared as a single large animal rather than many small.

"All right are you?" He turned to Ford and grinned.

He was fine.

"Reach down to the sail, can you feel the earring?"

Bennet felt the small rope and nodded.

"An' below that there's the reefband, those are reefpoints that hang down. Next time you feel one of them it's likely to be blowin' some."

Bennet fingered the short lengths of sennet. Less than a month ago he had barely seen the sea, let alone a ship on it, and yet now all these details were starting to appear quite natural to him.

"Ready to go down now?" Ford asked.

"Aye, reckon so."

"Take it by the shrouds, if you likes. You done all right for a newcomer."

Bennet shook his head. He had gone through the lubbers' hole, and had a bit of a wild time before he got onto the yard, and yet here he was now, far more solid aloft than he had ever expected to be. None of it would have been possible without Ford, and he wanted to prove himself to the man. Show him that he had been worth bothering about.

"Take it down a back stay, if you likes," he said.

Ford's eyes rose in surprise, but he smiled readily. "Aye, if you've a mind."

Bennet led them back to the mast, then Ford selected a backstay.

"You got to take it slow. Speed up later if you wants, but watch yourself first time. Lines can burn, and if you go too fast you finish with one hell of a bump."

Bennet took hold of the line that was thick and iron tight.

"Want me to show you how?"

"No, I'll be right." He had seen too many topmen descend not to know what to do, and however confident he now felt, he had no intention of allowing Ford to leave him alone.

"Swing your leg about, and hold fast. Gravity does the rest."

Bennet braced himself, then did exactly as he was told. Ford was right, in no time he was travelling down the rope, the rope that had appeared smooth, yet now turned out to be about as slick as a rat-tailed file. He closed his hands about the stay, and felt a stab of pain as the rope burnt. Panicking for a split second, he remembered his legs and closed them about the line. His duck trousers puckered slightly, but there was no doubt that he was slowing. Then the deck was suddenly very close, and instinctively he released his grip, and fell the last few yards, landing feet flat on the deck, and staggering forward a pace.

Jameson was there, eyes wide as he grinned at him.

"You done all right?"

"Aye, he done all right," Ford told them, as he too landed on the deck. "Not as fast as your first time down," he said, punching Jameson playfully on the arm. When a boy Jameson had completed his first trip aloft by falling from a topsail yard.

Peters, the boatswain, approached them, walking stiffly and with a grim expression on his face.

"Al'ays take it as fast as that down a backstay an' one time you'll come a right cropper." The elderly man reached out for Bennet's hands and turned them palm up. There was a faint run of blood just appearing through the heavy coating of tar. "Hands grow thick with use, but you'll never make 'em fire proof. Take it slower, lad."

"Aye, sir. I got carried away."

The officer regarded Bennet for a moment, his deeply tanned grey face softened slightly and a smile was dangerously close. "You're rated to the foretop from now on, so better keep an eye on 'im, Ford. But like I says, take it slower next time or you'll end up on the deck like so much puddin'."

CHAPTER ELEVEN

By morning they were off Cape St Vincent, with clear weather and a steady wind that came across their starboard quarter, giving both ships five knots, a creditable speed considering *Aiguille* was still running under a jury rig. By noon they had less than two hundred miles to go, and King was starting to regret his invitation for dinner at three. He had met with Captain Llewelyn on two occasions, and liked him less each time. Despite the surname, he too was as English as roast beef and had all of the prim, indifference of his second in command. *Pandora* had sent a boat across that morning. Apparently Martin had left some vital piece of equipment on board, and prevailed upon Caulfield to retrieve it for him. King had been sorely tempted to use the opportunity to invite a few of his shipmates to dine. Surely Banks would have no objection to some of the junior officers, and perhaps even Fraiser or Caulfield joining him. Eventually he decided against it; he was not certain of the etiquette involved, and a written request was always more bald and unforgiving. Instead he arranged for Manning to help him share the burden of the two stiff necks; together they might get the whole thing over as painlessly as possible.

During their brief stay at Tagus a fresh spar had been obtained to stand for the mizzen. They had rigged a form of lateen sail on this, using a spare maintop yard from *Pandora*, which had allowed staysails to be set and for a more balanced rig in general. Now the ship sailed far more sweetly with barely a trace of gripe.

King looked back at *Pandora* two cables behind them. The officers had finished their noon sights and the quarterdeck was clearing, presumably they would be issuing spirits and serving dinner before long. His eyes flowed easily over the frigate, noting the extra work that had been carried out, and the newly set foretopsail. The ship still looked slightly ungainly with her foreshortened jib boom, but that would be set to rights at Gibraltar. Passing from the bowsprit, his eyes fell upon a figure standing, very much as before, at the beakhead. The pleasant feeling that came from being in un-accustomed sunshine left him, and he found himself looking more intently. It was the same man as before, a lieutenant; the white facings of the lapels were quite distinct, and definitely not Caulfield, the build was different. There had been no talk of another lieutenant being taken on. He looked closer, there was something in the man's stance that did strike a chord, but he could not quite place him. The deck glass was in the binnacle, he could turn and collect it in a matter of seconds, but King had no intention of letting the vision slip away as before. He was standing quite still; the more King watched him, the more certain he was that he knew the man. A sound from forward made him start. The guards were being relieved at their posts; soon a contingent of Frenchmen would be brought up to stand for a while in the midday sun. He heard the bellow of Stafford as he berated some private, but still King watched the mysterious lieutenant, and still he remained motionless.

"Surgeon reports two fresh cases of the flux, sir." Dorsey's voice cut into his thoughts, forcing King to turn away and answer.

"Very good. Mr Manning has my permission to extend the sick bay, should he so desire."

Their winter excursion had brought out a good deal of heavy colds and influenza amongst the French. To these had been added a more general gastric condition that appeared to have much to do with the preserved beef they carried. Manning was more than capable of looking after the patients while the sickness ran its course. He turned his attention back to the mysterious lieutenant and with little surprise noted that he had disappeared once more.

*****

"The last time I was at Gib was with the *Benevolence*, back in ninety-two." Johnston was sitting back on his form after supper, and watching while Jameson, the current mess cook, collected up

146

the platters. "We had a master at arms with us called Simms, rum looking blighter with a broken nose."

"An' a scar down one cheek?" Flint interrupted.

"Aye, that's him," Johnston nodded. "Came from 'ampshire, as I recall." However large the Navy might grow it remained an intimate club and there were always shared acquaintances. "Anyways, he had this bird, big black thing it were, called it Jake. Used to follow him round the ship, made the first luff's life a proper misery it did."

The men were relaxing after dinner. The morning's warmth had put them in an affable frame of mind. Those who messed to either side had noticed Johnston start a story, and were now silent in the hope it was one they hadn't heard before, or elsewhere.

"After a while we in the barky took to it, rather as a mascot; one of the lads even taught it to speak a few words. Said its name, and a lot of rude things - it had a dreadful mind, that bird. Then it started shouting out the 'all's well' at the turn of the glass, and copying the bosun's mates when they calls... which were a mite confusing," he added as an aside. The men round the mess table nodded in silence, true or false, they liked a tale and Johnston was known for them.

"Anyways, we were in Gib for seven week all told, and by the second week cap' started grantin' shore leave." He turned to the boy, Billy. "They do more often, at Gib, 'cause there's nowhere to run, see?" The boy nodded seriously, and Johnston continued.

"Anyways, the port admiral were a bit of a tartar, and it was down to him that we were there so long. We'd been out of England for nigh on two year, and what with being only a couple of weeks from home, well we were fairly pricked." He paused to swallow from his blackjack, enjoying the moment as much as any of them.

"He kept dogs, the port admiral, and the one we all knew was called Henry. Bloody silly name for a dog, if you ask me, an' a bloody silly dog too. He was small, but snappy like, the kind that used to nip at your ankles when you went about. 'Course, being the port admiral's dog, there weren't much you could do. One of our reefers took a kick at him once, and got into all sorts of trouble.

"So, this bird must have taken a disliking to Henry, for it took to picking on him. Kept flying overhead, just missing like, and the port admiral would get right upset; bellowing at his dog and swearing worse than the bird, he did. 'Course, he 'ad no idea who it belonged to and we thought it fine."

Men at the next mess shuffled impatiently as Johnston opened his clasp knife and cut himself a chunk of Warwickshire cheese. Now that he had his audience he was in no great rush to finish the story.

"After a bit the bird got fed up and 'ad other ideas. He started calling the dog itself. True lifelike it were, just as if it were his master. Then one day he really got the grip. We 'ad liberty an' was walking as a group along the quay, Simms with his bird flappin' about, and we all looking forward to a bit of a cruise, when the bloody dog appears again."

He took another bite of cheese, pleased with the attention he was being given.

"Straight'ways, Jake's up an' off, callin' 'Henry, Henry!' Well, we falls about, I can tell you, and the dog went fair simple. Then the bird lands and calls out again. Soon as he sees it on the ground, the dog's off and after him. Gets about a yard away an' the bird takes off and flies a bit more. We watch this, laughing like. Then we realises what the bird's up to."

The sea of blank faces was extremely gratifying, and Johnston treated himself to yet more cheese.

"You see, he's drawing the dog along the quay, landing everso often, calling his name, and taking off again. Afore we knows it, the bird's at the edge and there's the daft dog haring after it, all spit and grizzle. 'Course you can guess what happens."

Some smiled appreciatively but the boy, Billy, shook his head. "No," he said.

Johnston sighed. "Dog tries to get the bird, bird flies up, dog falls off the quay, and that's the end of it."

The men were laughing now, much the happier for hearing the end of the story.

"So what came of the dog?" the boy asked.

"Drowned, far as I can remember, sure as hell we weren't gonna save him."

"Yes, but what about the bird?" Billy again.

"Bird weren't no help," Johnston told him. "See, it couldn't swim." Johnston's voice was completely flat, although he began to rub at his face to hide his expression.

*****

Crowley had certainly done them proud; the great cabin was spotlessly clean, and positively shone with the reflected light from a dozen good wax candles that sat in heavy, squat silver candlesticks. A great white damask tablecloth spread over the main dining table, where places were neatly laid for every guest, with silver trivets set along the centre. Fresh number one sailcloth covered much of the splintered wood Everit had been unable to repair, and even the eighteen-pounders, also concealed and bedecked by strings of coloured signal flags, had lost much of their belligerent appearance. A rich smell of cooking hung in the warm air, and King would have felt in reasonable spirits, were it not for the prospect of sharing the next few hours with Captain Llewelyn, Lieutenants Stafford and Webb and three French officers.

A tap at the door heralded the arrival of Manning, looking strangely formal in a long black borrowed coat that was slightly too wide for his shoulders. King smiled at his discomfort, and drew a little consolation from the knowledge that the surgeon's mate was equally against the afternoon's entertainment.

"Are our guests assembling?" King asked. Manning nodded.

"Aye, the lobsters are in the coach laying siege to the brandy."

"Brandy, at three?"

Manning grinned. "You're starting to sound like Mr Fraiser."

"Aye, but they haven't eaten yet."

"What of *Lieutenant* Fonquet?" The young man who had met King on boarding the ship was one of the few senior officers left from the French crew, Segond having died on the evening following the action.

"He's there as well, along with the two French army officers; babbling away like monkeys, they were."

King sighed again. "I suppose we'd better join them?"

Together they walked out of the great cabin and into the coach, the small outer room where the guests were assembling. Despite the language barrier everyone seemed to be talking at once; a heavy scent of spirit filled the air and it was hard to remember that so recently a bloody battle had been fought between what now appeared to be the best of friends. He caught sight of Dobson, the seaman he had found drunk the first evening. Now smartly dressed in some sort of red uniform coat, he held a large silver tray with two half-filled decanters, and was circulating amongst the officers with all the aplomb of a London butler.

"Ah, Mr King," Webb boomed on seeing him, "hope you won't be filling us up with any of those made meals; can't stand that foreign rubbish."

King made some neutral comment and passed on as fast as he could. Fonquet was standing alone; his face, clearly flushed, carried a slightly stupid smile.

"Captain, you have joined us at last!"

King gave a reserved smile in return, then drew back suddenly worried that the man might try to kiss him. "Are your quarters to your liking, *Lieutenant*?" he asked hurriedly, holding his hand up to Dobson who was pressing a full glass of brandy on him.

"My quarters?" the *lieutenant* mused. "Ah, you mean *la fosse au cables*: Yes, it is fine; we are all very, very warm together, thank you." He gave King a brief smile. "And thank you for the trust you have shown to us. It is most..." He struggled for the word, and King found himself edging away towards Manning, who was talking to Captain Llewelyn.

Crowley appeared as if by magic, and announced the meal, allowing King to return to the great cabin. They entered in one loud, long, swaying line, each gasping in surprise at Crowley's work before walking with single-minded assurance to the wrong chair.

King had decided against a grace, not wishing to offend the French who would doubtless be of some papist persuasion and Crowley, supported by the flushed and clumsy Dobson, appeared immediately with the first course of deep green pea soup.

Pea soup, although one of the few good dishes a ship could offer, was not one of King's favourites, and he sipped at his with caution. This was no simple mixture of dried peas and brackish water however; Crowley had clearly done something special. Twice King found small gobbets of pork, and there was a mildly herbal flavour that was slightly tart, yet very appetizing.

The wine was flowing now; Crowley had put out nine bottles of some obscure claret that meant nothing to King and all appeared to have been opened simultaneously. King sipped at his, enjoying the subtle combination of flavours while the French army officers on either side leaned back in their chairs to make sure that every drop was safely deposited. For a second he caught Manning's eye. The surgeon's mate appeared to be making heavy weather of Fonquet's conversation, and pulled a face at King.

Dobson staggered in under the weight of three geese that all but made their last flight onto King's lap. Three more were deposited in front of Captain Llewelyn and both men stood to carve when Dorsey appeared at the cabin door.

"Beggin' your pardon, sir. But the bosun's having a problem with the foretop."

"The foretop?" King looked about the assembled company, who had been surprised into silence by Dorsey's arrival. Apart from Fonquet, who was currently smiling benignly at nothing, there wasn't a seaman amongst them. He replaced the carving knife and fork with every sign of reluctance. "Gentlemen, you will have to excuse me, I'm afraid matters pertaining to the ship demand my attention."

A series of disappointed groans followed, although most were addressed to the three geese that had yet to be carved. Manning was looking more concerned, and King shrugged. "It's the foretop," he said, and made for the door.

"Foretop?" Fonquet mouthed the word experimentally. *"Hauberks de misaine*? But there is nothing that could be so very wrong there, surely?"

Manning sighed. "No, I'm certain everything will be fine."

"But the foretop?"

"It is something we say, in England. An expression, if you like. It means that someone has been prudent enough to arrange a diversion."

Fonquet opened his mouth to ask more, but a plateful of roast goose was placed in front of him, and the matter dropped.

*****

Gibraltar was all they could have wished for; a safe haven for rest and repair under the imposing but oddly reassuring bulk of the rock, with shore batteries, a garrison and the British flag to shelter them. King was to return to *Pandora* as soon as the last of the prisoners had been transferred. Before he left he took a final tour about his command. Now almost emptied *Aiguille* was still showing signs of her recent battle, and without her countrymen it was as if she had reached the last stage of defeat. The tricolour had been lowered, and soon she would be passed over to British dockyard hands. The prize court normally met within the week, and everyone was quite certain that the Admiralty would buy her in. She might stay a month or two to be patched up, before making for England under a scratch crew. There she would be welcomed by an

Admiralty short of heavy frigates, and detailed to a crown dockyard. Within a year she would emerge again, freshly set up and with a proud new flag flying from her gaff, to be set against those who had built her with only her name (which was rarely changed) left to betray her roots.

King walked slowly to the entry port. What dunnage he had taken was all back in *Pandora*, and now there was nothing to keep him. Four soldiers were drawing the charges from the two carronades, and a party of waisters from *Pandora* were starting to add fresh paint to what repairs had been effected, tarting up the prize to get the maximum return from the court. And Crowley was there, looking strangely alone on the larboard gangway, dressed in fresh slops and carrying a small canvas ditty bag.

"Shouldn't you have gone with the others?" King asked. He had almost said prisoners but the word sounded insulting.

"That's a question for future debate," Crowley snorted. "Could be I'll hate myself for it later, but I'll be staying awhile."

King raised an eyebrow. "Pledged yourself to the King, have you?"

Crowley shook his head. "For the King, no."

It was common enough to offer prisoners the chance to volunteer; the loyalty oath would only be required should they advance beyond junior warrant rank. In a navy that counted French and Spanish amongst its people, King supposed he should not be surprised; the man had made it clear he owed allegiance to no one.

"And you needn't be thinking it's you I'm following. I'd join up with the devil himself, if he gave me a suitable berth."

But King already knew him well enough to be pleased. In the few days they had served together he had come to rely on Crowley, and the idea of him being incarcerated in a Mediterranean prison was appalling. "Right, we'd better be getting on then." They both made towards the entry port as King continued. "I'll see you rated able, that's if you've a mind to serve in *Pandora*."

"That's my intention," Crowley said seriously.

"I'm glad to hear it." Certainly the future seemed far brighter with Crowley around. "I wouldn't trust you anywhere else."

*****

The pot house was towards the top of the rock and, even at this early hour, had customers.

"Well, we've been across most of Gibraltar," Bennet grumbled. "I only hopes this place fits your tales."

Flint shrugged. He was also tired; like most sailors he had little stamina for walking and secretly was rather disappointed with the tavern. The last time he had been on the rock it had been the focal point for all shore leave. It was run, as the best always were, by Spaniards and had the finest wine, the best entertainment and the cleanest women he had ever encountered. Now though, admittedly at an hour that most civilians would hardly recognise, the place seemed decidedly seedy. At the next table two sailors were fast asleep; their hands lying palm down by their heads, while across the room another group were staring stupidly at their full glasses as if uncertain as to their actual purpose. Two guitars lay unattended at the far end of the room, and next to the bar a parrot slept in its covered cage.

A man, bareheaded and with a skin that would not have looked out of place on a tortoise, approached them. "What is your pleasure, gentlemen?" His smile was functional, and it was not the welcome the sailors expected and craved.

"Wine: your best." Bennet spoke. He still had his bounty money - two guineas for a landsman - in his pocket, and was determined to show his messmates that he was a man who knew how to enjoy himself.

"Very good," he paused, eyeing each man professionally. "Perhaps you would like some company?"

All eyes turned to Flint, of the group the most experienced, and the one who had first proposed this highly unofficial outing.

"We will see them," he said. The man nodded, and clicked his short dark fingers. Three young girls, one still yawning, were soon presented to the men. Flint nodded, it was better that he had expected and soon the women were sitting at their table and drinking their wine as if they were the old friends that the sailors had so much wanted. The women laughed at one of Bennet's jokes and the men began to feel warm inside. They might cry out for the touch of female flesh, and afterwards brag about their wild conquests ashore, but this was as much in every man's mind as any lustful encounter: The company of women, the flash of their eyes; the fact that they recognised their sexuality, and treated them as men; this was the real pleasure of shore leave.

*****

Pandora had been secured to a jetty that ran from the end of the new mole. With most of her stores removed or shifted toward the stern, her bow had been raised by several strakes and the lack of jib boom, removed to repair the bowsprit, added to her vaguely alarming aspect. Everit, assisted by his own men and a team from the shipwright's office, had rigged a platform about the damage to her bow, and was currently engaged in removing the half-timbers. Banks stood with Caulfield and Fraiser, who had just returned from the master shipwright's office.

"There's no problem with timber, they've quite a bit laid by, and we could do the job with our own spare if called to." Caulfield was feeling slightly disorientated, a symptom not unknown to him when first standing on solid ground after a spell at sea. "And they're all right for spars and cordage, there's two that would serve for the jib boom, and they could even find a fresh bowsprit if needs be."

Banks remained silent. He would prefer it if the bowsprit could be left alone, if only for the time that would be taken replacing it.

"Main problem seems to be manpower. They're very short at present. The dear knows how they're going to deal with *Aiguille*."

With topmasts and spars down the prize was moored about three hundred yards away. Following the most basic repairs to her hull she had been washed out and buoyed. An awning was now rigged over her quarterdeck, and she was fast acquiring the look of a hulk. The prize court would be meeting at the end of the week. In theory it should take little consideration of her outward appearance, although Banks doubted that any committee that comprised of as many tradesmen as naval officers could be persuaded to see beyond her seemingly decrepit looks and pay top dollar for the ship. It was of little concern to him, although he knew from experience that his men would serve that much more willingly with money, or even the memory of it, in their pockets. Thinking of the prize court naturally led him on to the court of enquiry, due to meet the following Monday. He had written his own report and seen those submitted by his juniors and was well aware that no solid conclusion could be drawn from them.

"We can do much of the work ourselves of course; I've already started the bosun on a full inventory." Caulfield was still reporting on the ship, unaware of his captain's lack of attention.

"Very good, make it so," he said, briskly. "Work tide and tide if you have to, but we need *Pandora* ready for sea without delay. Oh, and ask Martin to rig a piquet line forward of the jetty. No man to pass beyond without written instructions from an officer." He had already noted a group of interested women on the quay. Unless something was done there would be liquor on board within the hour and by nightfall those of the crew who weren't drunk would have run. *Pandora's* marines might not stop all the crew from leaving, but at least they would act as a deterrent.

Caulfield touched his hat automatically. "Three have gone abroad already, sir. Bosun sent them to collect some cordage, and they've not come back."

"Runners?"

"No, sir. Good men, we'll see them back by nightfall, and I'll make sure they don't get another chance."

"Very good." For three men to wander was hardly surprising considering the pleasures that lay barely feet away from them.

A thought occurred to Banks. "Better tell the men that shore leave will be granted to any department that finish their tasks before we are fully ready to sail." That was hard on the carpenter's crew, who would have the most to do, but he knew of no greater encouragement for men to work than the chance to be let out on a foreign shore afterwards. "And Mr Caulfield, you may also inform them that I will personally advance the prize money if *Aiguille* is condemned at a reasonable rate."

Caulfield grinned, suddenly aware of an unforeseen advantage in having a wealthy captain. "They'll appreciate that, sir."

Money in their pockets was also a requirement of any Jack ashore; now he could do no more in the way of motivation. "I have to call on the governor at noon." Banks took a final look at his ship. "I don't expect to be back before four, see what can be achieved in that time."

Both men touched their hats, and Banks broke away, walking, uncertainly at first, along the firm wooden decking and on to the rough stone road.

Gibraltar was as he had remembered, and he loved her for it. The warmth of the Mediterranean sun reflected from the stone, whitewashed houses, opening up the windows and bringing forth a mixture of cooking smells ranging from boiled British mutton through simple paella to even more exotic cuisine. A short haired dog appeared to walk with him a while, before darting off without warning when something else took his fancy, and an unknown lieutenant saluted him in a casual, almost friendly manner, that would certainly not be approved of in any home port. It was an hour before his appointment and there were a number of calls he should make: to his agent and banker for one. But Banks felt in no need to hurry, he was enjoying being free of the ship, if only for a short time. He turned off the main street on impulse, and began to climb one of the many narrow lanes that led into the residential side of the town. It was quieter here, and more in keeping with his frame of mind. Soon there were no other naval personnel in sight, and the few English faces he did see belonged to local workmen. He walked on until the open doorway of a coffee house beckoned, and once inside he was grateful as much for the gentle darkness as the cooler, slightly scented, air. A girl with jet-black hair that billowed over her shoulders, emphasising the vast expanse of bared chest that Banks found slightly shocking, smiled at him. His eyes adjusted to the light, adding ten years to her age.

"Wine for you, captain?"

Banks was wearing full dress uniform, although he suspected that all naval customers were addressed in this way.

"Sherry, if you please."

"A bottle, yes?" She smiled professionally. There were many men of his acquaintance who would think nothing of downing a whole bottle of sherry before noon as an aperitif to more serious drinking, but the idea appalled him and he shook his head emphatically.

"No, a glass, thank you."

He sat down at one of the wooden benches. There was no one else in the room, apart from the woman who seemed intent on revealing as much of herself to him as was possible while uncorking a bottle and filling a glass.

"You like a room, yes?" she murmured, placing his drink in front of him and pressing her bare arm against his shoulder. Once more he shook his head. The last thing he needed was the company of women; despite any other complication the risk of gleet or pox, together with their foul cures, was cause enough to turn the woman away. The hands had a good saying for it: one night with Venus and six with Mercury; not for him, not on such a casual basis. "Maybe later, eh?" She regarded him with a mixture of disappointment and contempt. He reached into his pocket and pulled out a silver coin. She took it without a word, and left.

It was the beginning of February. With luck he would see *Pandora* repaired and at sea by the middle of the month. That was assuming the court of enquiry presented no problems. He took a sip of his drink as the consequences of a bad result followed by a worse court martial presented themselves. The sherry was pleasantly cold, and the strong flavour was enough to put his thoughts onto a safer track. Jervis had been adamant that he expected the Spanish to sail from Carthagena before then and rumours were rife of French fleets already at sea; some said a squadron was even now coming down from Toulon. This spring was bound to see a major fleet action somewhere on the Atlantic and with the Dutch making aggressive noises they would be lucky to avoid another major confrontation on the North Sea. Either, if poorly handled, could mean the end of the British Navy's dominance and when that had gone there would be nothing to stop a full-scale invasion.

France was certainly ready for it and was even practiced in the art. In addition she now possessed the leaders - Bonaparte, for one; so recently successful in his Italian campaign, who could carry it off.

The drink had restored his previous feeling of well-being, and he finished the glass. The woman had gone; perhaps he had insulted her in some way. He cleared his throat and heard movement from the room behind. Certainly this was not the time to be in port; ships like *Pandora* were in short supply and likely to be extremely busy. He looked at his watch, still more than half an hour until he was due to meet with the governor; enough time for another sherry. The noise had stopped now, but the woman had yet to appear. Maybe it would be better to find somewhere else, somewhere a little more popular, where they would pay the right sort of attention to their customers. He stood up, dragging the bench back noisily with his knees. There was still no reaction, so he walked out of the room and into the sunlight. It took him a second or two to adjust to his surroundings; he must have walked further than he had thought; the lane was deserted, and the houses seemed far meaner than he had remembered. Gibraltar held one advantage in that it was very hard to get lost. Small in area and usually well populated, the simple act of walking downhill was normally sufficient to find the harbour. Deciding against looking for further refreshment, Banks turned and began to retrace his steps, his mind still dwelling on his ship and the possibilities ahead. He hardly noticed the three men who came up the hill towards him.

Well-built and carrying heavy staves, they appeared decidedly unsavoury. Banks had no intention of interfering with them and made to walk past. They had other ideas and silently blocked his path, holding their staves across their waists, their faces set in grim determination. Banks had been captain of a ship for too long, there had been no such confrontations for several years and he had to restrain the instinctive reaction to bellow an order at the men. Instead he turned and was mildly surprised to find two more of the same behind him. He looked about in desperation but, as if by arrangement, the street was otherwise empty.

His hand went to the hilt of his sword; the men in front took a pace towards him, raising their staves to shoulder height. Banks had very little space to draw his weapon, and even then, surrounded as he was, there would be no room to wield it effectively. He could reach into his pocket and bring out his purse; it was well filled with gold sovereigns that might buy him the time or space to run. Certainly he could afford the expense, but the idea of running from a fight, however high the odds, went against his instincts.

Movement from behind alerted him, and catching the sight of a shadow moving quickly made him dodge to one side, missing a blow aimed for his head that would have certainly knocked him senseless. He ducked down, and sprang forward, drawing his blade as he did, and hitting one in the face with the hilt. These were clearly desperate men, possibly deserters from the Navy or Army; how such men could survive on a small rock was a mystery. His sword was safely in his hand now, and he hedged his way to the side of the lane, feeling the smooth stone wall of a house at his back. The men grouped in front of him were clearly about to move in.

"British officer!" he bellowed. Then, in desperation, *"Pandora!"*

The ship was easily a mile away, and he himself had given orders forbidding shore leave. The men moved towards him uncertainly, then there came a shuffle from up the road. Banks shouted again, and was rewarded by the sight of three seamen thundering down the lane, their unaccustomed shoes clattering on the hard ground. The men turned also, although they made no movement to run, clearly confident of handling themselves in a scrap, possibly even relishing the prospect.

The first seaman launched himself onto one of the thugs, knocking the larger man to the ground where he rolled into the gutter. His mate, a far younger lad, tried the same on another, but lacked the momentum. Instead the two locked together until the lad freed himself and landed a credible punch that knocked the stave from the man's hand. Banks saw his opportunity and waded in, bringing the hilt of his sword down on one greasy head, before righting the blade, and holding it to the throat of a sallow man with bad teeth and a runny nose, who backed away as if drawn by a string. The man dropped his stave, and fell against the opposite wall, the blade still resting against his flesh.

The third seaman had been hit and fell to the ground, with his assailant standing over him. One of his mates turned to help, but Banks got there first, swinging his blade, and catching the attacker across the forearm. The man screamed as a jet of blood shot out to show where the fine edge had cut deep into him. The stave fell to the ground and the man held his wound with his other hand, the blood bubbling up between his grubby fingers. Another turned to run when a seaman's fist caught him on the jaw, sending him backwards and to the ground.

Three of the attackers were now tumbling away down the hill, with the young lad roaring behind them. Another lay cold on the road, with the fifth moaning softly as he held his damaged arm. Banks bellowed for the lad to return. He looked back and caught the eye of the first seaman and grinned.

"Thank you, Flint. Thank you very much indeed."

Flint nodded, and knuckled his forehead.

Bennet, the third seaman, was looking slightly abashed, as was Jameson, returning up the hill and panting slightly, but Flint had all the calm authority of a ship's corporal.

"I expect your party was detailed ashore?" Banks asked, breathing heavily.

"That's right, sir." Flint readily agreed. "Bosun sent us to order cordage. We heard you shouting, and thought there could be trouble. Difficult area, this. Not one I'd care to go to without company, and unless I was on official ship's business," he said with emphasis. "Place is nothing but pots houses and knocking shops."

Banks nodded and smiled. "I shall bear that in mind for the future, Flint. I assume you have completed your tasks ashore?"

"Oh, yes, sir." The smell of alcohol was unmistakable.

"Then you had better repair to the ship. If anyone asks about your absence, you may refer them to me."

"Thank you, sir." There was no surprise in his voice, it was natural justice, the kind the lower deck understood and appreciated. "And what would you have us do with these two?"

Banks considered the men; well built, and clearly willing to fight, providing the odds were on their side. "Present them to the first lieutenant with my compliments. Let them be read in, make sure they get a thorough scrape. I expect to see them both at Thursday's muster."

"Very good, sir." Flint reached down to the comatose assailant and swung him up; Bennet caught hold, and together they lugged his insensate body down the street. The second man stumbled himself upright after a kick from Jameson.

Banks watched them go, then delved into his jacket pocket. It was ten minutes to twelve; if he didn't move himself he would be late for his appointment with the governor. He replaced the watch into his pocket, brushed his uniform down as best he could, and began to follow his men down the lane.

CHAPTER TWELVE

A captain had been appointed from the port admiral's office. His name was Andrews, and he was a heavy, comfortable man of late middle age who wore a hard horsehair wig and took snuff. Banks greeted him at the starboard entry port after representatives of the ship's company had paid their respects.

"I regret having to put upon you, sir," he said as he led the way to the great cabin.

"Not at all, Sir Richard, not at all. I have no great pressing duties; since *Liverpool* was condemned there's been precious little for an old dog like me. Besides..." he grew confidential and Banks caught the hint of morning sherry, "if my time here can have you and your saucy little ship back to sea the sooner, then it will be well spent."

Caulfield was introduced and together they stepped into the captain's apartment, now swept clear of all personal furniture for the occasion. The coach was laid out like a waiting room, with mess benches placed in lines. Beyond that the dining table had been taken up and laid widthways in front of the stern windows.

"It seemed better to request a president from outside the ship," Banks continued as they took their seats. "I have no doubts about any of my men of course..." he paused, not knowing if he had said too much, but Andrews was an experienced officer, and understood entirely.

"But a dispassionate eye is the more reliable," he nodded. "Of course and, the dear prevent, should we need for a court martial, you'll have another's testimony to refer to."

Banks smiled; the captain was far more in touch than he appeared. Andrews sat down heavily and proceeded to bring out the numerous reports that had been assembled from the officers. These he lay before him in two neat piles. Banks and Caulfield, seated to either side of him, tried to define his criteria for division without success.

Davies, the captain's secretary, seated himself at the far side of the table.

"Will your sailing master be joining us?" Andrews asked Banks rather pointedly.

"Yes, of course," he raised his voice, "Send for Mr Fraiser, if you please."

The call was repeated by the marine sentry, but Fraiser did not appear.

Banks shifted uneasily in his seat. This was a bad start, and he was surprised that Fraiser should let him down on such an occasion. Banks turned to Andrews and was about to apologise when the master made his entrance, obviously hurried, his face bright red, and jerking his coat into position as he came through the door. Still slightly breathless, he presented his apologies to the two captains sincerely enough, and Banks felt it would take very little effort on their part to get him to bow.

"Take a seat, man," Andrews instructed, before picking up a sheet of paper he had brought with him, and reading in a firm stentorious voice, "Court of enquiry into the death of Lieutenant William Henry Pigot, being held on board His Majesty's ship *Pandora* on this seventh day of February, 1797. Those present..." he looked pointedly at the secretary, hastily scribbling at the other end of the table, and received an acknowledgment.

"Gentlemen, I have read the testimonies submitted by the officers of *Pandora*, and propose to follow these up with interviews. But before I speak to any man individually I have a few general questions to ask." He peered at his notes for a second, then continued in the same firm voice. "The first thing that concerns me is when Mr Pigot fell, and who attended to him."

Caulfield cleared his throat. "Do you mean the surgeon, sir?"

"No, I have his report. Who actually went to his aid?"

"The nearest was a volunteer, a boy; Rose. He is acting as midshipman."

"And the first officer?"

"That was Mr King. He was senior midshipman at the time, sir." Caulfield said the words with care, wondering if Andrews was unusually astute; he certainly seemed to have gone straight to the point.

"So by that we can assume that Mr King and Mr Rose were the two most responsible men closest to Mr Pigot when he received the fatal shot?"

It seemed an obvious assumption, and yet no one felt inclined to agree.

Caulfield spoke: "If I might make an observation, sir."

"Of course."

"There were upwards of fifty men on that part of the deck during the action, any of which would have had a perfect opportunity..." He stumbled, his throat had gone very dry and he tried to clear it. "Any of which could have seen Mr Pigot fall."

"So I understand." Andrews nodded sagely, although Caulfield thought he caught a note of deeper significance in his voice.

"I observe that the action took place during darkness, and yet there is no report of the sight of a flash, and none of the hands will admit to knowing anything else of the incident, am I right?"

"That is correct, sir."

Andrews sat back in his chair. "Gentlemen, I wonder if we might speak frankly for a moment?" He held up the palm of his hand to the secretary who, taking the hint, placed his pen on the table, sat back and folded his arms.

"I know very little of the late Lieutenant Pigot, our paths did not cross, and neither have any stories about him come my way. However, I do believe he has a brother?"

"Yes sir, a post captain. He has the *Hermione*."

"That's right, a frigate, currently in the West Indies, I believe. Captain Pigot has made rather a name for himself, and it is not the kind of reputation most officers seek." Andrews was careful not to meet anyone's eyes as he spoke, and Banks inwardly decided that despite his rather easy, self-indulgent appearance, the senior captain had a sharp mind and there was little wrong with his intuition either.

"I should also say that I do note a certain detachment in these reports." He tapped the papers in front of him. "Some captains are favourites amongst the men, but there are very few first officers who are so fortunate. And it is against their duty to be so. However, if Mr Pigot was something of an exception in either way, I hope you would tell me." He reached into his waistcoat and withdrew an ivory snuff box. "Unofficially, of course."

There was silence as Andrews took his snuff, then he closed the box, and looked directly at Caulfield. "Your opinion of him, sir?"

Caulfield opened his mouth, but said nothing. It was not a situation he had prepared himself for, and he was quite at a loss.

"If I might interject?" Despite his late arrival Fraiser was more composed now, and as he began to speak his words fell with the solemn authority of a bishop.

"Mr Pigot was an unfortunate man. His manner was unnecessarily harsh, and he often spoke or acted more for his own gratification than the good of the service. In the short time he was in this ship the morale and efficiency of the people deteriorated to the extent that the junior officers were starting to report mutterings."

Caulfield considered Fraiser. There was certainly something different about the man; he seemed charged with an inner energy; quite at odds with the slow, careful officer he was accustomed to.

"*Pandora* was a fresh ship sailing with a fresh crew, was she not?"

It was a good point. "Yes, sir."

"And since the regrettable death of the first officer, how have things altered?"

"The ship has become more efficient by ten fold, sir. And the people far happier."

Andrews smiled. "Tell me, Mr Fraiser. In your experience, is it not usual for there to be a fall in morale, and possibly general capabilities, when a ship leaves harbour on the first occasion?"

"Yes, sir."

"And in the hands of competent officers, that poor state of affairs is usually corrected, as the humour of the men is gradually improved."

"Indeed, sir." He opened his mouth to say more, before closing it, and sitting back.

"Very good, I thank you for your comments, Mr Fraiser. Can I turn once more to you, Mr Caulfield?"

Caulfield cleared his throat again. "I... I have to agree with Mr Fraiser, sir. I observe how what I say may be regarded, but Mr Pigot was unusually vindictive in his actions."

Andrews pursed his lips. "I see no record of excessive punishments in the log?"

"No, sir. There was little, official that is. His methods were of a more subtle nature. He had a way with the men..." Again he faltered.

"I think Mr Caulfield means Mr Pigot indulged in strange fancies," Fraiser continued.

Andrews cleared his throat. "Did he have an unnatural liking? Certain 'favourites' perchance?"

"No, sir. Not in that way."

"Then how, pray, was his behaviour strange?"

"His actions were irrational, his punishments cruel and deeply wounding. This was not an unfortunate affliction; it was one he determinedly developed. He enjoyed exercising his control, he enjoyed humiliating people."

"You're saying he was an evil bastard?"

"Yes, sir."

"I think I had guessed as much, but I do not see how that can affect the case in any way. If all the evil bastards were taken out, the British Navy would be much the smaller for it." A ripple of awkward laughter played about the room. Andrews let it die before continuing. "Smaller, but, may I say, not better." The silence that followed said more than the laughter that had preceded it.

"Sir Richard, we have yet to hear from you."

Banks shuffled uneasily. This was a novel approach, asking officers to comment on their fellows and not one he totally approved of, although he did concede that Andrews was obtaining results.

"I had little time to get to know Mr Pigot of course, but I may say that we did have altercations. On the night of his death he was to discipline Mr King for reporting a sighting."

"A sighting? Was it made in folly, or jest?"

"No, sir. He had correctly reported the French invasion fleet. The log has it."

"Yes, I recall. There was a heavy fog."

For some time there had been the gentle hum of conversation from the coach, and now the noise grew suddenly louder. Andrews looked up sharply and shouted for silence in a surprisingly deep, harsh voice that also brought every man at the table to attention. The noise stopped at once and Andrews bowed slightly to Banks.

"Forgive me, Captain, I am not accustomed to being a guest in another's ship. You were saying, about the incident in which Mr Pigot was to discipline Mr King?"

"At the time he was under the impression that Mr King's sighting was false, and had needlessly taken *Pandora* from her proper course."

"That would seem harsh," Andrews mused. "Not normally a situation where punishment is required, although obviously we are viewing the incident with the benefit of hindsight." He sat forward in his chair. "Mr King, his name has cropped up before?" Andrews felt for the reports, looking for King's amongst them.

"He has recently been confirmed as lieutenant," Caulfield said, a trifle hastily.

"Has he?" Andrews' eyebrows rose. "So you might say that he benefited from Mr Pigot's death?"

The fact had not occurred to any of them before. Andrews continued. "And wasn't he the junior officer who attended to Mr Pigot; the one who would have been closest to him when he fell?"

"Yes," Banks confirmed in a dry voice. "That was King."

"And he was to be punished that night?" Andrews added in an undertone.

Caulfield felt the strength ebb from his body. He wanted to act, to say something of real significance. To proclaim Pigot for the animal he had been, and yet so far he had said little to help his friend, while Banks appeared determined to lead the young man to court martial and execution.

"Mr King would seem to be a principle in this matter." Andrews' manner had changed and was now very brisk and horribly businesslike. "In fact I am surprised that you gentlemen have not questioned him the sooner. May I suggest that we return to open court, and call him as a witness without delay?"

*****

King appeared wearing his old midshipman's jacket with the white collar patches removed. There had been little time to commission a new uniform from a tailor in Gibraltar, and Caulfield's build was far heavier, and totally excluded him as a lender. The gunroom servants had spent some time with a flat iron and brush trying to tempt what remaining nap the cloth held into order, but the result was not impressive, and as he stood in front of the group of officers he felt dowdy and unkempt.

"Please, take a seat, Mr King." A chair was brought by one of the sentries. King sat down and heard the unmistakable whisper of good luck. He turned back and saw that the marine was Collins, one of the cockpit servants. Rather than encourage, the incident made him feel more flustered than ever.

"I understand that you have recently been made lieutenant?" Andrews was looking at him not unkindly.

"Yes, sir. Admiral Jervis was kind enough to grant my commission."

"Then let me add my congratulations."

King mumbled his thanks. Andrews' eyes fell to the table for a second or two, and when he looked up again they held a very different light.

"Mr King, you were stationed on the main deck during the action in which Mr Pigot died?" Andrews' voice was also far firmer, and King felt his pulse begin to race.

"Yes, sir."

"And on seeing him fall you went to his aid. Did he say anything to you?"

"No, sir. No, Mr Pigot appeared to be dead, sir. His head had been hit..." The image of Stuart's grisly specimen came suddenly to his mind. The head would still be on board, if any of them wanted to see it. The thought stayed with him, making him falter. He opened his mouth and closed it again, its job undone. Andrews raised an eyebrow.

"Mr King, have you been in action previously?"

"Yes, sir."

"Can you elaborate?"

"I was in *Vigilant*."

"Indeed?" Andrews raised one eyebrow. "A gallant action. What part did you take?"

"I was acting lieutenant, sir, in charge of the explosion vessel."

"Very credible, Mr King. Clearly, then, you are used to the confusion of battle and, can I say, the debris it can produce."

Banks leant forward. "Mr King was recently prize master of the *Aiguille* frigate, sir. We fought her until she struck; he took charge of the vessel. She had over four hundred soldiers in addition to her crew; a great many were casualties."

Andrews nodded. "Thank you, Sir Richard. Again, I may say you appear a very capable young man, and clearly not one afraid to take control when the situation demands it. So tell me why, sir, why do you blanch when the subject of the death of Lieutenant Pigot is brought up?"

King hesitated. How much had already been said? Should he mention the head that Stuart still kept in spirits?

"The man was no friend to you, no friend to anyone aboard this ship as far as I can tell. Yet when I speak of him you stammer like a child."

There was nothing he could say. Andrews reached forward and collected the small, distorted ball that sat on the table.

"Do you own a pistol that would shoot a ball of this size?"

Caulfield stirred awkwardly in his seat.

King looked at the ball. "Yes, sir."

Andrews nodded. "And does your pistol have a rifled barrel?"

"Yes sir."

Andrews dropped the ball onto the tabletop; it fell with a resounding report that echoed about the great cabin.

"And were you carrying that pistol on the night of the action?"

"No, sir."

"Did you not place it in your waistband, knowing you were to be in action, and hoping for a chance to see your greatest enemy dead?"

"No, sir."

"And when your ship did indeed go into action, did you not find the ideal opportunity to do your work, confident that no man could be certain that Mr Pigot had died at your hands?"

"No, sir." His voice had risen in pitch until it was very nearly a scream.

"Confident that, even if you were observed in your wickedness, Mr Pigot was held in such low esteem that your actions would go unreported?

"No, sir."

Andrews sat back, sighed and continued in a softer tone. "Or, perhaps, did you only intend to threaten Mr Pigot. Maybe show him you had the pistol? Plead with him to extend a little mercy to you and your shipmates? Perhaps he had gone to strike you and the piece had gone off? That would not be murder and the court would be understanding. Is that what happened?"

Caulfield opened his eyes, which had been closed for some time, to see King obviously confused. The boy went to speak and for several seconds the room hung in expectation.

"I say again, you may have had just cause, and a shipboard accident is easily understood, easily explained and by some may not be regarded as a crime at all. Tell me, laddie, is that what happened?"

King shook his head. "No, sir." The room exhaled as one. "No, I did not kill Mr Pigot. I was not carrying my pistol during the action. As far as I know it had been cleared away with the rest of the cockpit items." He sensed the eyes upon him and felt very small, very vulnerable. "I'm sorry, sir, but it was not me."

Andrews smiled unexpectedly. "No, son. I don't believe it was. And I, for one, am very glad."

The tension in the room eased, and the air itself seemed suddenly lighter. The noise of a loud and generous sneeze came from next door, forcing Caulfield to bite his tongue to control the hysterical laughter that he felt was very close. Fraiser was talking now and he steeled himself to listen.

"If I may say a word, sir. I have information that might be of interest to this court."

Andrews bowed his head. "Then speak away, man. Do you wish for this to be in open court?"

"No, sir. I feel this should be between ourselves for the time being."

Again Davies gratefully laid down his pen.

"Just before we convened I was alerted to an important matter by Mr Lewis, one of the master's mates. He had a man in his division who wanted to come forward and admit to the shooting of Mr Pigot."

The silence was complete, even the noises of the nearby port seemed to hang suspended.

"I sent for him, of course, sir, and desired that he should await the court in the captain's coach. I had to ask Mr Lewis a few further questions as you might understand, and then I came straight here. It was when I arrived that I noticed a group of men and a boy awaiting outside in the coach. There were eight, and all of the same mess, sir."

Andrews snorted. "You think that the actual murderer is one of the mess, and his fellows are standing by him?"

"Yes, sir."

"May I say that is not unusual behaviour on behalf of the lower deck. Somewhat sentimental, maybe, but loyal and speaks well of them and the ship. We will have to interview each, of course, but it should be little trouble to determine the culprit."

"Yes, sir."

"We will start by seeing them as a body." Andrews inclined his head towards Banks. "With your permission, sir?"

"Call the men in from the coach."

The marine repeated the order, stamping the butt of his musket onto the deck. The door opened and Flint's face appeared. He strode in confidently, with the rest of his mess in tow. The last was Billy, who swept the room with his wide, brown, doe eyes, totally void of any possible murderous intent. Wright blended in with the rest and no one paid him any particular attention. They stood in a row facing the officers, as Collins, the marine, clumped his musket again.

"Get back, you lot, and wait your turn."

"What is it, Sentry?"

"There's more out here, sir, but we can't rightly take them all at once."

Andrews stood up, and tried to look over the heads of the men in front of him.

"Stand aside there," Banks barked. "And open up those doors."

Dutifully Flint's mess separated, while Collins opened the double doors that made the coach and great cabin into one room. From there it could be seen there were upwards of thirty men crammed into the benches.

Andrews snorted and regarded Flint's mess. "Very good, you may go now, and please close those doors."

The seamen turned and swaggered from the room, leaving behind an air of wonder. When they had gone Andrews helped himself to more snuff.

"Well, I must congratulate you, Captain. You certainly have a tight set of people."

"Sir, you must not think this was any of my doing."

"No, no, my dear sir. The very opposite. However, that little demonstration has told me more about our late lamented Mr Pigot than any number of reports and opinions could ever."

He reached forward and idly picked up the ball that lay on the table. He held it to the light, and passed it from hand to hand.

"There are many things that we are discovering in this war." His voice was slow and meditative, and Davies, the secretary, seemed unsure whether or not he should be taking notes. "Some fellow keeps pestering the Admiralty with an idea for rockets, and another who wants to send dolphins into battle with charges attached to theirselves. I know the French have been experimenting with balloons, and there was that time they tried to mount a furnace inside a brig to fire red-hot shot; infernal thing burnt to a cinder, as I collect. Tell me gentlemen, is it so ridiculous that they should be using rifles, of a power and range unknown until now?"

There was no answer, and for several seconds Andrews continued playing with the ball. It dropped onto the desk, and he snapped back almost at the same instance. He drew his chair back and turned to Banks.

"Captain, it was conscientious of you to invite me here, but I see no further reason to remain."

He picked up the reports in front of him and knocked them together. Then, with a swift but firm hand, ripped them in two.

"Gentleman, it is my opinion that Lieutenant Pigot died as the result of enemy action. His death is most lamentable and naturally his family will be provided for in the usual manner."

Andrews turned to go, his movements were brisk and businesslike, and Banks had to fairly run to catch up with him as he left the cabin.

Outside the coach was still filled with muttering seamen, one leant forward and dragged Billy out of the way as the two captains swept out and along to the main companionway.

The sun was out to meet them as they emerged onto the quarterdeck. Andrews turned to Banks and smiled. "You have a fine ship; one that will be ready for sea before long, I believe."

"Yes, sir, three days at the most."

"Then I wish you joy of her, and a safe passage." He held out his hand, which Banks accepted gratefully.

"Thank you, sir, thank you for all you have done."

"I have only done my duty, sir. As you have, as many of your people have. One in particular..."

For a moment Banks was taken aback. "Forgive me, sir, I..."

Andrews barked out a quick laugh. "The fellow who settled that evil blighter Pigot's hash, what?" He slapped Banks hard on the shoulder, before turning and backing out of the entry port.

Three sidesboys rushed to the spot and hastily stood in line while a boatswain's mate appeared looking a little disappointed at not being able to pay compliments.

"Begging your pardon, sir. We had no idea the captain was leaving, not so soon, like."

"That's all right, Croxley." Banks raised his hat to the corpulent and somewhat antiquated sea officer who was now taking his place in the sternsheets of his gig. "I think Captain Andrews really rather surprised us all."

CHAPTER THIRTEEN

On the evening of the 9th of February, after a frantic day of replacing stores and taking on water, *Pandora* had been warped into the harbour and was now ready to set sail once more. The repairs were to a good standard and she now boasted a bow as strong and as watertight as any, with the minor point that the paint supplied at Gibraltar was of a slightly different hue to that of the rest of her hull. She also had several fresh sails, as well as new standing and running rigging where necessary. Banks looked at his watch; the wind was ideal for finding Jervis's fleet and he wanted to make the best of it, although it seemed Martin, the lieutenant of marines, had other ideas.

"No sight nor sound, sir," Caulfield said glumly. "Peter's been flying for nigh on two hour, and he was well aware of the circumstances."

There had been limited leave for all of the officers and most of the lower deck had spent at least one evening ashore, their conduct and return guaranteed by bondmen. Martin, it seemed, had abused the privilege; as a marine there was little required of him other than to arrange the piquet and he had hardly been seen on board *Pandora* throughout their stay. Now he was stretching the leniency still further by delaying the progress of his ship, a disciplinary offence in itself and especially annoying when they had all worked so hard to get back to sea.

"Wait, I see him!" Cobb was standing next to the taffrail with Woolsey, the new midshipman they had been given from *Liverpool*. "He's heading down main street with a package under his arm, reckon he's been visiting Lady Howe."

Banks looked at Caulfield. "Lady Howe? I had no idea she was ashore?"

Caulfield shook his head. "It's not her ladyship, sir. The men have a name for a particular woman."

"Oh." Banks started to say more, then decided against it; should Martin have delayed his ship for some immoral purpose it would not help his case one bit.

"It's not like that, sir." Caulfield was clearly reading his mind. "She runs a laundry, we get all ours done there when there's a chance. Good fresh water, she uses, and proper soap."

"Lady Howe's laundry stays cleaner for longer than anyone else's, sir," Cobb added in a confidential voice.

Martin was on the front now and gesturing to a skiff to carry him out to where *Pandora* was swinging to her single cable.

"Very good, Mr Caulfield, you may make sail."

Caulfield touched his hat and began to bellow orders. On the forecastle Rose supervised the raising of the anchor. It went without a hitch with the quartermaster shouting "up and down" just as the topsails were unbent. *Pandora* was under way when Martin's skiff bumped against the side, and he clambered up the entry port with a brown paper parcel under one arm straining to be free of its string.

"You are late aboard, Mr Martin." There was no point in disciplining the man in private when the entire ship was aware of his offence.

"I do beg your pardon, sir. I was delayed."

"We were all delayed, Mr Martin, on account of your washing!"

The marine looked abashed, and Banks wondered if the universal derision of the ship was possibly punishment enough. Disciplining a senior officer was a delicate matter at the best of times.

"Take it below, I will speak with you later."

Martin touched his hat and went toward the main companionway just as the heavens intervened, and his parcel burst open.

The laughter that accompanied his misfortune started on the quarterdeck, but quickly spread to the entire ship as the parcel's contents were revealed. Martin reached down in disgust, and picked up one of a series of women's petticoats that lay, perfectly starched and pressed, on the white strakes of the quarterdeck.

"Damn the woman!" he shouted, more red-faced than ever. "She's beavered my bloody shirts!"

"Looks like you've got the wrong parcel there," King informed him seriously.

"Bloody thief, now I haven't got a dress shirt in the ship, nor no stocks, nor handkerchiefs!"

"That's pretty fair lace, Mr Martin," Fraiser said, examining one of the petticoats. "Reckon you're the right side of the bargain. Turn any woman's head, these would."

"And one or two men's, I'll be bound!" Caulfield added.

"Right side of the bargain, be damned!" The marine stomped off the deck with the laundry under his arm. The hoots and laughter that followed might have been condemned by some as poor discipline, although Banks felt that *Pandora* had already reached a high level of efficiency, and the men could be allowed a fair joke. Besides, he had been searching for a just punishment for Martin and when one so perfectly apt was provided for him, it seemed churlish to refuse it.

Pandora sailed swiftly out of the harbour under topsails alone, then added forecourse jib and staysails until she was cutting through the water at a good nine knots, with the wind blowing crisp and steady on her quarter.

Banks stood on the quarterdeck enjoying the chill of the evening. If the previous nights were anything to go by, the fog would soon come down, and he wanted to make as much progress as possible before then. A fleet of Spanish ships had passed Gibraltar some eight days ago and the Levanter had blown almost continuously ever since. Should they be heading across the Atlantic they would be a good way off by now. But if their intention was further north, a French base, Ireland or even the Channel, they would have been taken further into the Atlantic than they would have wished. They might miss Jervis's fleet, currently cruising off Cape St Vincent, and with barely a handful of frigates available to him, Jervis would need *Pandora* to help search for them.

*****

By four bells in the first watch, ten o'clock, 'down hammocks' had been piped and the watch below was mostly asleep. The fog had come down earlier, and now the ship rode through the mist under topsails, with topmast lookouts on the main as well as the fore. Below, the ship was thick with sleep and as Manning made his way back from the repaired warrant officers' roundhouse, his mind was hardly alert. Queenie, the newly acquired goat, bought to replace the much-lamented Charlotte, was snoring deeply in her manger. The rest of the livestock; the hens, geese and piglets, were also silent, as was Sammy, their devoted keeper who shared their lives, along with their bedding and most of their food. Manning crept past and on toward the galley, where the gentle rumble of night-time conversation could be heard. From out of the darkness a figure loomed, silhouetted against the lanthorns that swung by the galley. It was wearing a commissioned officer's hat and the heavy watch coat suggested he was on duty, except Fraiser had the watch and was of a far slighter build. Manning stood to one side, blending into the shadows, as the figure passed. He watched as he stopped, and bent over the sleeping figure of Sammy. The man turned in his sleep, then opened his eyes, muttered some nonsense and reached for the warmth of one of the pigs for reassurance. Seconds later he was wide-awake and staring at the mystery figure. Sammy's eyes grew round and white in the dim light, and his mouth opened in a soundless scream. Satisfied, the figure turned and swept aft, disappearing behind the galley, leaving the simpleton mumbling in terror.

Manning stepped forward, and knelt down, taking Sammy's shoulders in his hands.

"Steady there, steady, you're safe now." The man was on the verge of shouting; just one scream would be enough to call for all hands; *Pandora* would have sufficient excitement in the next few days without half her people being roused from their sleep unnecessarily.

"Steady there!" Sammy was focusing on Manning's eyes, and gradually began to calm down and breathe normally.

"It were Mr Pigot," he said finally in a voice unnaturally loud, yet not as much as to raise the alarm. "He comes and sees me when I'm abed."

Manning continued to speak soft calming words to the man, and gradually his panic subsided. "Has he been before, Sammy?"

The man nodded. "Regular."

Manning gave a grim smile. "Well don't worry," he said. "He won't be coming again."

*****

By morning they were off Cape Trafalgar, with the wind constant, though less strong. Caulfield had added extra sail during his watch, but even with courses and topgallants, they were barely making four knots. King had the watch, and Manning approached him diffidently. He was now a full lieutenant, and had every right to be aloof to one barely of warrant rank. But the smile was the same and as soon as they began to talk it was just like when they had shared the same berth, less than three weeks before.

"You've yet to fix yourself with a uniform, then?" Manning asked. It was quite customary for lieutenants and even captains to appear on duty in slop clothing, although Manning was well aware of King's financial state, and guessed that he had nothing in reserve other than his midshipman's jacket.

"No, somehow I didn't get the time to kit out at Gib. Maybe there'll be a chance later, once we've dealt with the Dons."

"Pigot was about your size," Manning mused. "Why not take a look through his stock. Snips could alter anything for you, if there's a need."

Their late first lieutenant's clothes had been moved into the officers' storeroom when Caulfield had taken over his cabin. Usually the possessions of deceased officers were passed about amongst their fellows, almost as a form of tribute, although no one had felt the desire in Pigot's case.

"Watch her head, there!" King's attention was taken away as the helmsman allowed the ship to fall off slightly. Manning waited until the ship was back to her normal course before continuing.

"It's a strange thought; he was on board this ship treading this very deck not more than a month back. Sometimes it seems as if he was never there, and other times..." he paused, "well, like he hasn't really gone."

King eyed him cautiously. Did he know about Stuart's grisly trophy? Probably - they both worked in the same department, after all. And what else? The mystery figure on the beakhead; he was almost certain it had been Pigot, and yet the enquires he had made amongst the men had proved fruitless. It had been a delicate operation, to ask if anything untoward had been noticed in the privacy of the men's heads; some strange and rather worrying responses had been offered up, but none that shone any light on the subject. Only Sammy in the manger seemed to know what he was talking about and enthusiastically identified Pigot as being alive and well and roaming about the ship. But Sammy was a simpleton, and King had come to the conclusion that he was fast becoming like him.

"The fact is," said Manning, finally taking the plunge, "I saw him last night. Saw him, or someone who appeared mighty similar." Manning had been aimlessly watching a hand as he secured a wayward part of the Burton tackle, but turned now and studied his friend's face. He was watching for some sign of pity or contempt, the understanding look for a naive fool and the indulging of his fancies. But there was none of this in King's expression; instead he saw only relief.

*****

That night, the night of the 10th of February, the fine weather broke and a storm blew up. Below, in the homely damp warmth of the lower deck, Flint and his men had just come off watch and were rubbing themselves dry before they could clamber into their hammocks for four hours' blessed peace.

"They'll be calling for us before two bells," Calver, the topman who had replaced Carter, muttered as he untied the tight, hard parcel that was his hammock. Calver was part of the fresh draft of twenty men they had been granted at Gibraltar. His last ship had been *Liverpool*; a stately three-decker laid down nearly sixty years ago. *Liverpool* had survived numerous small encounters and one full-blown fleet action, but time and thirty years spent in the Mediterranean sun, had finally accounted for her. Calver made no secret of the contrast he felt from his old ship, with her heavy, if rotten, stanchings and flagship standard of bull, to this greenwood gunboat that he had yet to love.

"Aye," Wright agreed readily. "Were we in *Liverpool* now, we shouldn't be wet. No, we wouldn't even have need to go aloft. Ships like *Liverpool* does all their reefing theirselves."

"I've had no one like you, Sam," she tells me. "Not never." Lawlor had been regaling them with tales of his shore leave ever since his return. Most had been pleased to listen, although now the stories were getting somewhat beyond the pale.

"And were we in *Liverpool* now, I dare say the stoves would be aglow below deck." Dobson had caught the drift. "And each of us would be stepping into our nice warm bed gowns, all hot from the irons which our nice warm chamber maids ha'been using on them."

"Ah, scoff your fill, I tell you: crank she may have been, but you could hoist this little pisspot aboard the old *Liver*, an' hardly notice she were there."

The sight of King, a commissioned officer, together with the surgeon's mate, passing along the berth deck caused hushed comments from each mess. King was well liked and respected by all, but it was rare to see any officer above the rank of midshipman in a space and at a time that was almost sacrosanct as their own.

"Something afoot?" Flint looked enquiringly at Wright, who shook his head.

"Blowed if I knows; been no murmurings." The two had passed out of the berthing area now, and were climbing up the companionway. Flint stood up and walked to the centre of the deck, his exaggerated nonchalant manner attracting attention all round. Whistling noiselessly, he glanced forward, before taking a few steps up the companionway, stopping just where his head was level with the main deck. He watched as the two officers disappeared into the darkness next to the manger. One moment they were there, the next they were gone, in just the same way that Bennet had described seeing Pigot that night. Intrigued, he continued up the companionway and on towards the galley, where a gentle wisp of tobacco smoke marked three of the men who were having a night-time pipe. He moved forward; both roundhouses were open and empty, only Sammy was about, laying out the straw that would be bedding for the animals and himself. There was no sign of officers. He was starting to think he must have missed them completely, when a movement in the shadows opposite the manger caught his attention. He stepped forward; his eyes were now fully adjusted to the gloom, and could just about make out the shapes of two men as they sat hunched up against a broad oak knee.

"Is anything amiss, sir?" he asked. One of the bodies moved.

"Piss off, Flint." It was Manning, the surgeon's mate. Normally quite a civil fellow, yet his voice sounded taught and urgent.

"Very good, sir," he said, almost automatically. He watched for a second or two more before turning around and heading back for his berth.

He returned to find hammocks now lay hung from every other hook in the deckhead. Lawlor was still regaling them with exploits as Flint silently slung his own and pressed the biscuit mattress into it.

"I've not known anyone like you. Not so passionate, nor so caring," Lawlor droned on. "All the girls said the same; I made a real hit. Some even used to ask for me, special like."

Flint climbed into his bed and turned to one side. They would be on duty for sure in less than four hours; until then he was not going to waste a second of sleep worrying about the habits of officers. Lawlor was coming to the end of his tale, his voice growing low and deep; soon he too would be dozing.

"And you know the nicest thing one of them said?" he asked, to no response. "Sam, you're so good at this, we should pay you. We should pay you, now weren't that sweet?"

Calver had been quite right; within the hour the call went out for men to shorten sail, and Flint and his mess rolled out of their hammocks, still rosy with sleep, and trudged up to the howling storm that now appeared at its worst.

"Double reef in the fore tops'ls," Calver muttered, disgusted. "If we was in *Liverpool* now, we'd be safely snugged," he said, as he made for the weather shrouds.

"If we was in Liverpool now, I'd find myself a boardin' house," Flint grumbled as he followed him.

*****

The next morning dawned clear and fine, with memories of the storm all but forgotten by *Pandora's* men, apart from one unlucky member of the afterguard who had slipped while hauling on a brace, and now lay in the sickbay with a rupture the size of an apple protruding from his groin. Banks had joined Caulfield on the quarterdeck as the sun rose and was there to hear the cry that the first of Jervis's ships had been sighted.

"It's the *Fox*, Lieutenant Gibson, sir," Dorsey reported, when they had closed enough to exchange signals.

"Ask him of the fleet," Banks said. They waited for several minutes for the reply. *Fox* was a cutter and a small one at that. She would not carry a crew large enough to have a specialist signals department. Eventually the answer came, and Banks altered course by two points to intercept.

By noon *Pandora* was approaching the Mediterranean fleet as they cruised lazily under topsails alone, roughly twenty-five miles off Cape St Vincent. Dorsey was casually reading off the ships as they responded to *Pandora's* number and private signal.

"That's the *Excellent*, Captain Collingwood. Then *Diadem*, Captain Towry. *Culloden* and *Colossus* appear damaged, sir. *Culloden's* setting down her fore t'gallant, and her jib boom's all ahoo. I can see a fresh spar being moved on *Colossus*, though she seems straight enough, must have sprung a yard." Banks guessed that they had come to grief in the storm of last night, not an uncommon occurrence when ships sailed as a fleet, but regrettable all the same.

"*Barfleur*, sir Vice Admiral Waldergrave," Fraiser commented. "She was in the Channel fleet, Admiral Jervis must have received reinforcements." The master was right, Banks counted five more line of battle ships than they had encountered at Tagus.

"That about makes up for those Mann took when he made a run for it," Caulfield spoke to Fraiser under his breath, not wishing to cast aspersions on a flag officer, although the entire Royal Navy had been incensed by the admiral's actions.

"Byng was shot for less," Fraiser muttered.

"Flag's signalling for us," Dorsey continued. "Take station two cables to leeward of me, and receive boat."

"Very good, Mr Fraiser, if you please." Fraiser gave the orders that would bypass *Niger*, the first repeating frigate, and set *Pandora* next to *Victory* and under the eye of Jervis. Banks supposed that the admiral merely wanted his mail from Gibraltar, of which *Pandora* carried several sacks. Still it was galling to have to stay in such close station to the flagship.

"Flag's signalling to the rest of the fleet to send to us for mail," Dorsey continued, echoing his thoughts. That would mean upwards of twenty ships' boats would be bumping alongside; the mail would have to be sorted, and sealed before they arrived.

"On station, sir," Caulfield reported and, albeit that they were cruising the Atlantic, *Pandora* had now officially become part of the Mediterranean fleet.

"Very well, begin the salute, master gunner. And pass the word for the midshipmen to assemble aft."

Here he was in command of one of the newest frigates in the fleet, and they were staying tied to the flagship's apron strings while his midshipmen sorted out the niceties of postal distribution, and all the while an enemy fleet lay somewhere over the horizon. The first dull report of the salute rolled out, and Banks decided that the life of a naval officer was not all excitement.

*****

That evening King had the first watch, so Manning carried out the vigil alone. The previous night had brought no mysterious visitors, and as the bell rang six times, marking the third hour that Manning had been sitting in the lee of the knee, he wondered if he was wasting his time. Several men and one warrant officer had come up from the berth deck and passed by, but none, to his knowledge, had noticed him as he sat in the shadows. The last sentry had given the cry of "all's well", and Manning was just starting to steel himself for the final hour's wait when movement from the area about the galley attracted his attention.

He craned forward as much as he could and saw the well-remembered silhouette of an officer striding confidently towards him, his boots clumping eerily on the deck. Manning drew back for fear the apparition might spot him, controlling his breathing to a shallow sigh. The figure was opposite him now, and Manning had time to note the stature, which was well built, with just the hint of a paunch. It was Pigot to a fault; for the first time the surgeon's mate began to doubt the wisdom of his solitary watch. The man was peering over Sammy, watching him, as if with interest, while he slept. One of the animals stirred, but made no noise, then a sound from behind made them all start.

A second figure was coming, an ordinary hand; the sound of horny feet as they clambered up the companionway and stepped lightly on the deck was unmistakable. Instantly the mystery figure ducked down, and hid in the lee of the manger as Timothy, a ship's boy, made his way forward to the heads.

Manning stayed silent as the boy approached. From his position he could see the apparition more plainly as it squatted in wait for the lad. The timing was perfect; Timothy had all but passed the spot when the figure reared up, emitting a low but menacing growl.

"Get back to your berth, boy!"

The lad froze, aghast, as the spectre moved towards him.

"Get back I say!"

The second telling was sufficient to turn the boy and send him scurrying back down the companionway, desperate for the safety of sleeping men. Manning heard a small scream as he disappeared, followed by a good deal of commotion from below. The figure watched, then turned to make for the roundhouses. From that route he could escape by passing through and climbing up and over the forecastle; in a second he would be gone. Manning struggled to his feet, determined to catch him.

Sitting in an awkward position had sent his left leg to sleep, and as he staggered after the man he fell clumsily against a samson post. The apparition had almost disappeared into the darkness, and would soon be gone. In a desperate effort, Manning sprung after him, launching himself full length at the man and catching the heel of his boot as he fell headlong on the deck. A thump from forward told how the figure had fallen also, but Manning was still struggling to his own feet as it sprung up and headed off once more.

The hens were awake now as Manning clumsily chased the man, who dodged round the bitts and foremast. There was also something of a commotion from the berth deck below, but that could not be helped; the only thing to do was finish this here and now. Then they were at the bowsprit, and the figure was passing through to the larboard roundhouse. Again Manning sprang at him, but this time with more effect as, grasping the man round the waist, he pulled him to the deck, pinning him there.

Light flickered about as a marine arrived with a shaded lanthorn. "What's going on here?" the voice of Tanner, one of the ship's corporals, demanded.

"Hold him," Manning shouted, as the figure wriggled to be free.

"All right, all right, he ain't going nowhere." Tanner had stepped over Manning and reached down for the body that now seemed remarkably lifeless. The marine holding the glim moved in also, and stood over the figure. With a roar it rose up suddenly; there was a crash as the marine dropped the light, and for a second a slight scuffling sound, then several bleary-eyed seamen arrived from their sleep, filling the deck with their questions and complaints.

"Shine a light, shine a light, there damn you!" Tanner's voice boomed out amid the confusion and a few seconds later he was rewarded by the arrival of two more marines with lanthorns. Manning clambered to his feet, dazed by the sudden action. He looked about; everyone was speaking at once; and next to Tanner was a man dressed in a lieutenant's uniform. A man dressed in a lieutenant's uniform, but it wasn't Pigot, and it wasn't a lieutenant.

"What the devil do you think you're about, Cobb?" Manning asked.

The boy stared back at him defiantly. "'Tain't none of your business, I can go as I please. Besides, you're only surgeon's mate out of courtesy, whereas I am a senior petty officer."

The men shuffled uneasily, apart from the fact that he was a boy, and they had caught him causing mischief, there was little any of them could say. For all his faults, Cobb was indeed the highest-ranking officer present.

"You nearly woke the entire ship, and those you did were scared half to death." Croxley spoke with the authority of a father, although Cobb, it seemed, had been away from home for too long to take notice.

"You call me *Mr* Cobb, Croxley," he said. "And if the people are that frightened, maybe they should have chosen another calling."

"Belike you should have an' all." Croxley was not one to take the lip of the young lightly. Cobb pulled himself up to his full height.

"I will remind you one more time that you are talking to a superior officer," he said.

"Maybe so, but you ain't a lieutenant, which is how you're dressed. No doubt your divisional officer would care to know why you're about in that rig, or should we take this straight to the captain?"

Cobb's expression fell slightly. "It were a jape," he said, sticking his chin up a fraction. "There were not harm in it, and none done."

"I will be the judge of that." All heads turned to see Banks standing behind them. He was dressed in duck trousers and an open shirt, and had clearly been asleep barely minutes ago. Croxley and Manning drew back, glad that it would not be them who would face him. "Mr Cobb, you will attend me in my cabin. Mr

Croxley, Mr Manning, I would be grateful if you would also be present."

*****

An hour later the watch had changed and King and Manning were returning from their brief visit to the sick bay stores. The surgeon always kept the key about his neck, but it had been little trouble to remove it from Stuart, whose sleep was sound and unbreakable. On deck a heavy fog had fallen, and they were unnoticed by Fraiser, the officer of the watch. Manning was holding a heavy parcel in his arms and they went together in silence to the lee rail of the quarterdeck. The interview with Banks had been brief and decisive; Croxley and Manning had given their accounts and were then asked to leave, while Banks dealt with the youngster. This he did with exemplary speed; not for Mr Cobb the short humiliation of a beating or seizing, Bank's methods were different to Pigot's, although every bit as harsh. The lad had been sent back to the cockpit to collect his belongings, before being taken forward, allotted a mess and shown where to sling his hammock. *Pandora* now rated one less midshipman, and one more able seaman, and pity on him for those he had upset so far during the commission. Banks had intended punishing the other midshipmen, on the understanding that one does not rifle through a dead officer's belongings and set about scaring half the crew on a solitary impulse, but on consideration he decided against it. Cobb's punishment was public enough; no one could be in any doubt how that sort of tomfoolery would be dealt with in *Pandora*, and the captain was quietly confident that he had heard the last of the incident.

Resting the parcel on the lee rail, Manning paused. About him ships of the Mediterranean fleet were firing minute guns to warn of their presence in the fog, while in the distance similar sounds could just be heard from another, larger fleet not so many miles away. He shivered involuntarily and quickly released the parcel into the murky waters. It fell with a brief splash and then was no more. As if in final salute, one of *Pandora's* swivels was fired, answered by a series of faint echoes from the enemy just over the horizon. The two turned back from the rail and made for the main companionway. They kept their thoughts to themselves, although both were of a common mind; this was an end to it: tomorrow would be a new beginning, and one that may well find them at grips with the Spanish in a major fleet action. A few days from now could see them triumphant, in a Spanish gaol, or lying at the bottom of the ocean, but whatever the outcome *Pandora* was now a different ship: Lieutenant Pigot had finally departed.

CHAPTER FOURTEEN

The morning of the 13th brought bright sunshine, a slight shift of wind, and important news. At first light *Fox* signalled the arrival of a newcomer, and by the end of the morning watch, as the hands were being sent down for breakfast, *Minerve* was making her number, with the flag of Commodore Nelson flying from her masthead.

"One of the Navy's bright young things," Fraiser commented dryly to King as the sleek frigate drew closer to *Victory*. "Suckling's kin. Bit of a live wire in the Leewards; stirred up all sorts of trouble, but the Admiralty seems to like him almost as much as the men, though he's pulled a few duds in his time."

King nodded, there were few who had not heard of Nelson; post captain at twenty and now due for his flag before he was forty. Until then he was a commodore first class, with all the power and prestige of an admiral. "I'd heard he was blinded, wasn't there a shore action?"

"Aye, but only in one eye, and that's just messed about a bit. The other works fine, and the hands would respect him the same if it were in the middle of his head."

King gave the master a quizzical look.

"You see he goes with the men, none of your sending the lads in and watching from afar. It's a rare attribute in a senior officer, and the people appreciate it."

A boat had put out from *Minerve* and was making for *Victory*. Through the deck glass Fraiser could make out Nelson, along with several civilians and a couple of army officers.

A few feet away Banks was studying the boat through his own glass. He had also heard a lot about the commodore; his own time at the Leeward Isles station had not been made easier by the resentment stirred up by the young Captain Nelson and his officious manner when enforcing the local navigation laws. Nelson had quit the station some years before Banks arrived so they had not met, although the story was that he spent most of his latter time in his ship, ostracised and in fear of arrest. It hardly seemed the action of up and at 'em fighter. Still, Nelson had had right on his side and to make a stand when all were against him was a rare and useful ability in any officer; Banks decided he would wait until he met the man himself before passing judgement. Jervis had entrusted Nelson to the final evacuation of Elba, the last remaining base in the Mediterranean, before the British abandoned that inland sea. The extra men in the boat must be consular staff from there, or one of the other former holdings. Presumably Nelson had also called at Gibraltar and may be bringing up to date news of the Spanish; the entire fleet knew them to be close, but few, if any, could rightly guess their measure.

The squeal of pipes drifted over to *Pandora* as the men of *Victory* paid their respects to the commodore once he was safely through the entry port. A hush of anticlimax now greeted them as they all watched *Victory* for some sign of action. The hands returned from breakfast and the daily work continued, except all the officers stood waiting on the quarterdeck, passing the time by pacing, or talking in small groups, with each man keeping more than half an eye on the flagship.

They were rewarded some two hours later, when Nelson and his retinue quit the ship amid further screams of pipes and the clump of muskets. Almost immediately signals began to break out on the flagship, and Banks discovered that, besides the fact that the enemy was reported some seventeen leagues away, and that all ships should begin their preparations for action, he was invited to dine that afternoon.

*****

"Welcome aboard, Sir Richard," Calder said in a voice quite void of enthusiasm. "Grey here will show you to the admiral's quarters, I have to await the commodore."

Banks wondered slightly at the temerity of a commodore to be late for an admiral's invitation as he followed Grey, second captain of *Victory*, towards the great cabin. Little had changed since he had last been on board; she still shone with unashamed swank, yet there was also the unmistakable air of sleek efficiency about her people that said this was not just another bull ship.

"The commodore has brought Sir Gilbert Elliot with him," Grey told him as they walked along the spotless deck. "He was viceroy of Corsica, you know?"

"Yes, I had heard, I expect you'll have the honour of his company on board."

"No, I fear Sir John would not approve." Grey smiled. "Of course there's likely to be a battle on the morrow, and any number of excuses can be brought up, but the idea of a viceroy's party crowding our stern would not appeal to the admiral."

"Richard, is it not?" The Canadian accent was unmistakable as a beefy senior captain stepped into their path just outside the entrance to the admiral's quarters.

"Ben!" Banks had not expected to see Hallowell, an old shipmate from several commissions past. He winced at the well-remembered handshake and grinned eagerly into the open and honest face of the massive part man, part bear.

"Saw you had *Pandora*, lithe little thing, ain't she?"

Hallowell had lost his ship *Courageux* in a storm a few months back, and was serving in *Victory* as a volunteer. Banks was quick to change the subject.

"You're dining with us?"

"Indeed," he rubbed his abdomen with pride, "though I dare say this will be more in the nature of a scratch meal."

A commotion from behind signalled the arrival of the commodore's party, and Grey gratefully handed Banks over to Hallowell to show him into the admiral's presence.

Jervis was equally brisk; enquired of his fortune with the prize and congratulated him on his repairs, but a faraway look in his eye told Banks that there were others he wished to speak with.

He turned away and looked at the party that had entered behind him. A rotund man in a colonel's uniform, flanked by a far older gentleman, whom Banks took to be Elliot. There were two rather stiff lieutenants and a pompous civilian wearing a horsehair wig roughly ten years out of date. But it was the commodore that followed them who drew his attention.

The face was sharp, angular almost, with just a hint of sensitivity about the lower lip and he carried himself with the assurance of one who knows he has done well and expects praise. He wore a full dress uniform on which an unfamiliar and rather ostentatious award was pinned; something that gave the initial impression of a coxcomb. When he spoke it was with an unpleasant, high-pitched, nasal voice that sat on the very edge of being a whine. Banks was prepared to be unimpressed and had already written the commodore off as one to be tolerated until their eyes met, and he caught a flash of brilliance, one that could only come from a man born to be different from his fellows.

Jervis was greeting him now in a warm, yet reserved manner that betrayed the deep affection he held for the young officer. Turning to one side he naturally picked on Banks.

"Do you know Sir Richard?"

Nelson turned to Banks and again those eyes penetrated his.

"Only by reputation, but it is a fine one, sir, and I am proud to meet the man behind it."

Banks shook his hand, feeling a thrill that was very nearly electric. "You are too kind, Commodore."

"I mean every word." The voice was suddenly lower, and there was no taint of insincerity in the expression.

Banks nodded and mumbled something in reply. He felt quite overwhelmed and was almost relieved when the attention turned to Colonel Drinkwater, who seemed to be some kind of a celebrity.

"One of the Navy's finest," Hallowell whispered to him as they made for their seats. "The commodore is brilliant commander and an inspired leader; the people love him."

Banks nodded; it was easy to see why.

At just past two in the afternoon the spring sunshine flowed in through the stern windows and yet there were candles alight in heavy silver candlesticks that sat at precisely measured intervals along the great table. As junior captain present, Banks found himself seated between Hallowell and a tall but slightly blockish lieutenant who gave his name as Hardy. The meal was served with commendable speed, but was not one of the best Banks had eaten.

The few days he had spent on Gibraltar had robbed all novelty from the fresh vegetables and when it came to the pork, he found his to be tough, fat and hardly the ideal meat for a warm spring day. His opinion was not shared by the other guests, however, and the conversation all but died as the men delved into their heavily laden plates and ate with the relish and manners of lads. By the time the first of the desserts was served, and the port had begun to circulate, the talk became more general and Banks was interested to note how Nelson naturally became the centre of it.

"Sir Gilbert was telling me of your passage, Commodore. Quite eventful, by the sound?"

Nelson abandoned his full glass to the table and swept the room in one all embracing glance. "Yes, Sir John, we had a high time of it."

"Did you call on Mahon?"

"Indeed no, sir. The winds were contrary. We did take a look at Carthagena though, to no avail."

"The Dons had fled?" This was Calder, asking the question with a lack of enthusiasm. Presumably he and Jervis were well acquainted with the news Nelson brought and this little conversation was intended as an unofficial briefing for those present.

"Aye, fled they had; every one that could carry a sail. Though quite how they manned them, only the future will tell."

"Maybe they did not man them at all." This was Drinkwater who, despite his name, had clearly been indulging and was now in high spirits. "Belike we fight with women tomorrow!"

"Then no need to call for volunteers when boarding, what!" One of Elliot's staff had clearly been following Drinkwater in more than his train of thought. The laughter was general but light, as most of the naval officers present were well aware that many of the British ships were also carrying women.

"We called at Gibraltar to collect Culverhouse and Hardy." Bank's neighbour bowed slightly at the mention of his name. "Who had been carrying prizes..."

"Then damn me if we didn't try and hand them over to the Spanish!" Drinkwater again, clearly enjoying himself as only one in his state could.

"The colonel refers to an unhappy incident." Elliot was a little more controlled and spoke in a clear, authoritative voice. "As we left harbour we were followed by two Spanish line of battle ships and a frigate."

Drinkwater burst in. "I said to the commodore, shall we see action? And he replies, cool as you like, 'Very possible, but before the Dons get a hold of that...' an' he points to his flag, '...I'll have a struggle with them, and rather than give up the ship, will run her ashore!'"

The company beamed with pleasure at the words, although they struck Banks as being somewhat theatrical.

"Then the next we knows of it we're sitting down to dine, and they calls out 'Man overboard'." The viceroy had the bug now and was speaking with almost as much enthusiasm as Drinkwater. "Hardy here springs up and before you can say knife, he's in a cutter heading back for the man."

"Did you find him?" asked Hallowell.

"Sadly not, sir."

"No, but we damned nearly lost Hardy and the boat's crew into the bargain!" Drinkwater again. He finished his sentence by draining his glass to give him energy for the next.

"The commodore was good enough to back sails and pick the cutter up," the lieutenant said without enthusiasm. "Otherwise I would be in a Spanish gaol b'now."

"'By God, I'll not lose Hardy!' he says." Drinkwater had charged his glass from the circulating decanter and was ready to continue, but Miller spoke first.

"And what of the Dons, when they saw you turn back for them?"

"That is the strangest thing," Elliot shook his head in disbelief. "They only had to hold their course and we'd have been under their guns."

"And we'd *all* be in a Spanish gaol!" Drinkwater laughed, although this time no one joined him.

"But instead they luffed up and waited while we plucked Mr Hardy and his companions from the briny," Elliot finished with a puzzled smile.

Nelson moved slightly and instantly had the attention of the entire table. "I think they were under the impression we had joined with the fleet." His words were greeted with the wise nodding of heads.

"Well, I believe you will agree that it augurs well for the morrow." Jervis spoke with the air of one who wished to end the proceedings, and the company responded by clearing throats and wiping their mouths. "May I say that I have received two signals during the course of this pleasant meal. *Blenheim* and *Britannia* have both reported strange sail on the horizon, so let us raise our glasses. Gentlemen, the toast is victory over the Dons in the battle they cannot escape tomorrow!"

*****

The hands had eaten at twelve, but Cobb's meal had not been pleasant. In the early hours of the morning he had been allocated to the mess that numbered the least men, and little other attention had been given him. He awoke at four, the beginning of the morning watch, when the reason for his only having four messmates became obvious.

Each was a malcontent, each bore a grudge against the ship, and more principally, her officers, and each viewed the prospect of sharing their mess with a boy who had been an officer with appetite and hoarded spite. He endured two meals, four hours of drill and four hours of duty before cautiously approaching the first lieutenant and applying for a change of mess.

Caulfield eyed him gravely. News of the lad's adventures had circulated about the ship like any piece of gossip and it was quite clear by the look in his eye that Cobb's punishment had begun.

"Mess changes only come about at the end of a month," he said. "You've another two weeks to go, but take comfort that it's February."

Cobb's face dropped, and his head bowed slightly. "I'm sharing with Dickinson's lot, sir. They're spitting in my food, and..."

"All right, spare me the details. Maybe that wasn't the wisest move, considering their record, though you're not going to be popular wherever you go."

"I realise that, sir. And if it makes any difference, I'm sorry for what I did. It were only a prank."

"What you did disrupted the efficiency of this ship, that's a contradiction of the duty of any officer and I personally think you got off lightly." He paused to let his words sink in. "Still, let's see if we can't find a few more favourable messmates for you." He considered the watch bill for a second. "Flint's just taken one of the new men, Calver, so he's pretty well full. Mind, most of the others are also, we're uncommonly well set as far as people go."

"Flint would be fine, sir," Cobb said. He knew the men well, and trusted them to be fair. Caulfield had looked at the list again, and eventually agreed.

And so Cobb made his cautious approach as the men were sitting down to supper. Flint glanced up from the pease pudding he was eating and the easy atmosphere of friendly chat was suddenly suspended.

"Mr Cobb, what brings you to us?" The lad had his ditty bag slung over his shoulder, and all knew that he had been allocated a particularly hard mess, so the question was unnecessary.

"I come to join you, that's if you'll take me."

Despite Caulfield's words, the final decision lay with the men, who had the absolute right to bar any man from their mess, and expel those they found disagreeable. Flint looked about the faces of the other men, all of whom appeared as nonplussed as he felt.

"Well, what do you say? Anyone here fancy sharing with a failed reefer?"

Cobb stiffened slightly at the words, although the idea of returning to Dickenson's mess appalled him.

Wright shrugged. "I've no objection; the lad might even make a reasonable seaman, and I don't doubt he'll be back in the cockpit afore we knows it."

His words brought forward a series of nods and pursed lips, although no one seemed especially enthusiastic.

"Let's put it another way," Flint said. "Anyone not want Mr Cobb in?"

"I'll not call him mister," Dobson said defiantly.

"No, that you won't," Flint agreed. "I was awry. Cobb here wants to join us, any complaints?" The men seemed compliant enough and he turned to the lad. "All right, you're in for the month, but take it on trial, eh?"

Cobb nodded eagerly, and seated himself next to Bennet at the foot of the table. Wright slammed the pewter dish that held cold pease pudding in front of him, and the boy, Billy, knocked a square wooden platter clean, polished it on the seat of his trousers, and handed it across.

"You won't find no cockpit niceties in here, Cobb," Dobson told him, not unkindly. "Cold pease pudding, that's what the Man in the Moon burnt his mouth on."

"Yeah, but we got some fruit duff over from dinner," Billy reminded them.

"Dinner?" Bennet exclaimed. "He weren't in our mess at dinner!"

"Aye, but he is now," Wright said with certainty. "And we looks after each other, ain't that the case?"

*****

Later, when they were making their way back to the entry port, Banks and Hallowell found themselves next to Nelson once more. They stood waiting as Drinkwater and Elliot were saying their extended goodbyes to Jervis, while the latter tried to rid them of his ship. The viceroy, it appeared, was keen to remain on board *Victory* in order to witness the battle; Jervis was equally adamant that a frigate would serve as a far better and safer vantage point.

"Sir John is looking for a frigate," Hallowell whispered as they waited. "Sure your little *Pandora* would be ripe for the job."

Banks rolled his eyes; the last thing he wanted was a collection of stuffed shirts blocking his quarterdeck. Nelson smiled.

"I shall be shifting my flag back to *Captain* or, of course, I should volunteer." His expression was set, and his eyes appeared focused on the far distance. "Although I have benefited from the viceroy's company for some while now, and I would not have it said I was keeping him for myself."

Hallowell's laughter was loud enough to disturb Sir John as he was all but forcing Elliot out of the entry port. "Worry not, Dick, Jervie's made prior plans; Lord Garlies who has the *Lively* drew the short straw. See even now he's leading his merry men into her cutter."

"One simply hopes a cutter has been provided," Nelson added dryly, as the consular officials followed their master out of the entry port. The commodore turned to Banks. "By the way, I haven't wished you joy of your prize, sir. You seemed to have had an eventful voyage down here."

Nelson would have seen the *Aiguille* in the harbour at Gibraltar, but it was flattering that he should remember, not only the ship, but the circumstances in which she had been taken.

"Thank you, sir, but it seemed your trip was not without interest."

Nelson smiled. "What you have heard is only the half," he said.

"The commodore was in touch with the enemy only last evening," Hallowell added, his voice, for once, lowered.

Banks stared at him in disbelief; this was surely the wine speaking, although both Hallowell and Nelson seemed unusually sober.

"We met them in the fog, several leagues back and making for Cadiz," Nelson confided. "It were only providence and a good foremast lookout that saved us from running on board one of their liners."

"But you were sighted surely, did they not offer action?"

"Sailed right through the middle, didn't you, sir?"

Nelson nodded. "Aye, we managed to avoid any unpleasantness, and it did give us a chance to gauge their mettle. There should be few surprises on the morrow."

Such a feat was not unheard of, but Banks wondered slightly at the man. "Forgive me, sir but why did you say nothing of this just now?"

"As I have said, we learnt their strength, and Sir John was concerned that it may upset the people were they to know what they will be against."

"The fleet is large then?"

"Aye, upwards of twenty-five sail of the line, and a four-decker amongst them."

Banks swallowed dryly. At least ten more ships of the line than the British possessed. If there was action tomorrow, as seemed likely, they would be out-numbered by almost two to one.

"Never mind, friend." Nelson's voice had dropped and sounded almost confidential. "Spanish may build fine ships, but they cannot man them. When I was in Cadiz, during the peace, I was hardly impressed."

"Sure, but twenty-five to fifteen." Hallowell shook his head in wonder. "Those odds are mighty high to be reduced for want of men."

"The thicker the hay, the easier it is mown." Nelson's expression was intense. "Fear not, tomorrow will bring us a glorious victory, and I pray that we shall all be spared to see it."

*****

As soon as the guests had left *Victory*, Jervis signalled for the fleet to make their final preparations for battle. In each ship the various heads of department went through the prepared routine that would ensure they were as ready as they could be for the following day. In *Pandora* Manning, whose access to Stuart's medical equipment had been granted through laziness on his superior's part, rather than any confidence in his assistant's skills, set about sharpening knives, saws and scalpels; laying them out with the probes, retractors and tourniquets for Nairn and the other loblolly boys to wash down with vinegar, then polish with spit and brick dust. Later they would cut and roll fresh bandages, and unravel lengths of horsehair and gut for sutures. Nairn had applied to the cooper for an empty barrel for "legs and wings", the surgeon's off cuts that were as inevitable as death itself, while clean canvas was lying ready to spread over the decking of the cockpit.

Everit and the rest of his crew were busy stacking lead plates and wooden plugs into the wings of the ship, the narrow corridors that ran level with the waterline where the most important damage would be taken to the hull. It would be their job to block any holes as fast and efficiently as possible, in order that *Pandora* remained afloat and the wounded on the lower deck stayed dry.

The boatswain and his men were setting preventer stays to each mast and had already brought out the metal chain slings that would be rigged to the yards, while the cook emptied the steep bins, and roused out the several crates of oranges and lemons they had taken on board at Gibraltar. These would be handed out to anyone who needed them as soon as the battle began.

Boarding cutlasses, pikes and axes were sharpened. Powder, for the great guns and side arms, was mixed afresh, before being ladled into the new flannel cartridges that the gunner and his crew were now sewing, and the sand boxes between every other gun were filled.

The officers ate a light supper, with only Martin, the surgeon and the purser indulging in more than a single glass of wine. Caulfield retired early, and spent several hours in the cable tier, playing soft, meditative pieces on his 'cello, while in his mind he readied himself for action. King read his copy of *Norrie's Navigation*, his eyes running over the words without absorbing any meaning. Crowley had prepared a warm drink for him of goat's milk with rum in it, which now sat by his elbow, destined to grow cold and a skin. Stuart was deep in a laudanum-induced torpor, a card game ran for impossible stakes in the cockpit, and Fraiser was reading his well-thumbed bible.

In the great cabin, poorly lit by the single glim that still burned, Banks wrote a long, disjointed letter to his father, while his mind wandered over the possibilities of the next day. As a frigate *Pandora* would play only a minor part in the fighting. It was even possible that her guns would remain unfired, although her value was every bit as great as any of the more solid seventy-fours that would take the line. Accurate and fast communication would be called for from the flag, and it would be down to *Pandora* and her like to provide this. Should the British prove victorious, she may be despatched to secure a surrendered vessel, otherwise it would be the less glamorous but vital tasks of towing disabled ships, rescuing survivors and transferring flag officers. When heavy ships fought, frigates rarely distinguished themselves, but missing stays at the wrong time, or a signal relayed incorrectly could easily bring shame upon her, and defeat for the British.

And the men; those who would serve the guns and tend the sails: the lifeblood of the ship who may soon be shedding their own for her safety. A mess night had been called for the watch below and all sat yarning and drinking small beer, determinedly unconscious of the tension as it slowly grew about them.

Flint was cautious; despite being in action twice since the time he had all but lost his nerve, thoughts of the following morning brought images of terror and humiliation. He had never witnessed a fleet action, but could readily project the carnage and confusion of smaller engagements. Ever since first meeting the abject terror that could take a man in its grip and determinedly squeeze the fight from him, Flint had changed. Gone was the dashing young fellow who thought nothing of leaping aboard an enemy ship armed only with a cutlass and belief in himself; a slower, more careful man had emerged, one who considered the consequences and was silently terrified by them.

Jameson was less concerned. He too had known terror in the slaughterhouse that had been *Vigilant*'s 'tween decks but he was still young enough to require no absolution. The two times *Pandora* had been in action had been enough to whet the appetite of a young firebrand, and he looked forward to the coming conflict with all the unsound confidence of his youth. He had seen men die and knew that, in theory at least, it may happen to him, but just as the gambler tenders his stake, Jameson thought of the glory the next day was bound to bring, and nothing of what could be lost. Flint considered him as he threw the dice, immersed in the tenth game of Crown and Anchor, and roared as he triumphed; the older man envied this beautiful confidence, while wondering privately how long it could last.

Darkness came, and the fleet formed into its night-time cruising formation of two close formed columns. The British numbered fifteen line of battleships ranging from the mighty three-deckers, of which there were six, down to *Diadem*, built in 1782 and a mere sixty-four. In the great cabin of *Victory* Jervis was wide-awake, as he would be throughout the night. He had taken command of the Mediterranean fleet just over fourteen months ago, and since that time he had prepared for the battle that was about to begin. Strong willed, and highly opinionated, he ruled his charges with a rod of iron. But it was iron tempered with regard and foresight. Bad officers would evoke his extreme displeasure, and could be expected to be exchanged or recalled almost at once, whereas the good received his trust and no man would want or expect a greater compliment from this tough, but strangely understanding man. He had fifteen ships of the line to command, and they were the best he could make them. They carried his confidence and his hopes. Of all people, he was most aware how desperately a victory was needed. In those fifteen hulls the destiny of Britain itself was staked, while over the south-western horizon a force of no less than twenty-nine Spanish line of battle ships lay waiting for them.

CHAPTER FIFTEEN

The British fleet maintained close order throughout the night and as dawn broke, misty but fine, *Pandora* was at her correct station off *Victory's* beam, ready to repeat signals to the other frigates that ran to fore and aft of her. The wind, which had now come right round to the south-west, was hardly strong enough to disperse the early fog, which slowly revealed the British fleet to the expectant officers.

"*Culloden's* made smart work," Fraiser commented dryly, as the leading ship was finally unveiled.

Caulfield nodded. "Aye, and a fair job of that jib boom. I fancy Troubridge's had them at it double tides, wouldn't miss a day like this for want of a spar."

They watched as a line of signal flags broke out on the seventy-four.

"*Culloden's* signalling, strange sail in sight." This was Cobb's voice. Following his recent demotion he had been transferred to signals and was now facing the added ignominy of working under Dorsey, his friend and recent equal.

"Very good, repeat to the flag." Dorsey ordered the hoist while Cobb entered the time in the signal log. It was forty minutes past five.

Captain was next with a similar message then, at just gone seven, *Niger* and *Lively* in the van signalled a fleet, and the sloop *Bonne Citoyenne* was sent for a closer inspection.

The waiting was now getting positively painful. Officers began to pace the deck while the men grew restless and argumentative. Banks looked at his watch just as seven bells rang. It was half an hour before the end of the morning watch, but with the ship poised to clear for action at any second, and with every hand alert and waiting, there seemed little point in holding out the extra thirty minutes until breakfast. The signal finally came at eight-twenty, when the men were resting after wolfing down their bur-goo and small beer. The marine drummer began to beat out a rousing tattoo on the quarterdeck as the entire ship was raised to the final pitch of readiness. By nine-fifty *Bonne Citoyenne* returned with the news that eight strange sail had been sighted. Jervis had already ordered his leading ships, *Culloden*, *Blenheim* and *Prince George* to intercept and on receiving this news sent *Irresistible* and *Colossus* after them.

All this passed through *Pandora's* signal log, while the officers stood on the quarterdeck watching the young men work and silently envied them their employment.

"See there, *Orion's* breaking line!" This was Banks, stirred from his usual silence by the sight. "Dorsey, what orders for *Orion*?"

The lad looked at his signals crew and back at the flagship. "None sir, the admiral's not sent her."

Banks grinned at Caulfield. "It appears Captain Saumarez is spoiling for a fight." So typical of the feisty Channel Islander to want to get into the action and it was reassuring to note that others were finding the inactivity frustrating.

"*Minerve's* signalling, twenty sail, bearing sou-west." Dorsey's voice rang out in the silence. This was the first official indication that they had truly encountered the Spanish fleet and, to many, that the enemy force might be considerably larger than their own. King considered the men, still waiting to be called to quarters as they sat yarning in groups about the guns and on the forecastle. Occasionally a wandering boatswain's mate or corporal had to order silence when their conversation or laughter grew unacceptably loud. They had full bellies and the ship was cleared for action; all that they wanted now was a chance to close with the enemy and that, they were certain, would come in time. Gone were outward signs of uneasiness, and when *Bonne Citoyenne* reported 'strange sail are of the line' a cheer rose up that was all but impossible to quell. Amongst them Jameson grinned at Flint, who had just returned from one of his frequent visits to the heads.

"Reckon we're in for a bit of a scrape," he said breathlessly.

"Aye, Matthew," the older man's voice was heavy with sadness, "I reckons we are."

*****

In *Victory* the atmosphere was just as tense; Jervis, his face drawn from the sleepless night, hobbled painfully about the deck while Calder followed, his constant observations made in a thin, whining treble, grating as the admiral assessed the situation. On one occasion Hallowell had attempted to relieve Sir John of his Job's comforter, but Calder had rounded on him, pointedly reminding the captain that his position in the ship was merely as an onlooker.

"Not so, sir, not so!" Jervis raised his voice in a roar that caused all on the poop to turn to him, and then quickly away. "Captain Hallowell has more reason to be here than most, and I value his comment!" Calder blushed, and briskly withdrew as Jervis continued. "Walk with me, sir. A gentle piece of exercise before we start on the Dons, what?"

But Calder was not deterred for long. Further reports of the force that would confront them began to come through, although Jervis appeared not to notice. The captain of the fleet relayed the increasing number to his chief with every appearance of dire despondency. At the final count, when the enemy was reported as twenty-seven sail of the line, "near double our own", as Calder triumphantly declared, Jervis finally snapped.

"Enough of that, sir! If there are fifty sail I will go through them. England badly needs a victory at present."

Watching Jervis turn on Calder, rather as a bull might a particularly annoying terrier, Hallowell could contain himself no longer, and slapped his commander in chief heartily on the back.

"That's right, Sir John, that's right. And by God we shall give them a damned good licking!"

The Canadian's paw brought a cloud of dust from the surprised admiral's jacket: Calder looked on, speechless, although his expression was that of abject hatred.

*****

Rose stood at his action station towards the forecastle, in nominal command of guns one to seven. He was pacing the deck under the skids that held spars and larger ship's boats, with his hands set behind his back. He wore a round jacket and had a smart, but impractically ornate dirk at his waist and was trying very hard to remain calm in a world that was still relatively alien to him. Watching, King considered walking across for a brief word, but decided that even that small amount of stimulation might prove too much for the young man.

The waiting was probably the hardest part to bear; it would be all right once the action began. As soon as the guns started to speak and the ship was properly in the thick of it there would be no need to think. There would be no need to worry, to project the future in all of its myriad possibilities. To ponder on your own death, as well as the death of those about you. To wonder about the chances of survival, the thought calling forth visions of long distant friends and family; visions that must be put aside instantly if any show of composure is to be upheld. Images that determinedly repeated themselves in a different order, as soon as they had finally been cast out, until the mind became one continual spiral of jumbled yet recurring thoughts.

It would be all right, once the action began, it always was; the hardest part to bear was probably the waiting.

*****

"Flagship's signalling," Dorsey's voice cut through, edged with excitement. "Form line of battle, sou' sou-westerly heading, ahead and astern of the flagship as convenient."

Banks glanced at Fraiser, who bellowed out orders that set *Pandora* on the new course. The enemy fleet was still hidden from the men on the quarterdeck, although that did not stop every eye straining to make them out.

"Jervie must know something we don't," Fraiser muttered to Caulfield.

"Hardly surprising, her lookout's a mite higher than ours."

Still, in *Pandora*, the waiting went on, while the mighty battleships jockeyed for position. Their usual sailing order went completely by the board, and yet each was disciplined enough to sort out their own place with the minimal loss of time. Once set, and the line of battle established, they began to pile on more sail, wringing whatever they could from the light and fluky wind.

On the foretop Ford, Bennet and Lawlor were with the other topmen, sitting nonchalantly on the folded studding sails and waiting until they were needed again. Ford and Lawlor were quiet, although Bennet was still visibly excited, and was having to curb his almost insatiable need to chatter. Hunter, a former upperyard man who had been appointed acting master's mate, sat with them, but slightly apart. Hunter was a promising hand who had recently been rated to the top and was taking the responsibility very seriously indeed. He glanced across to the southeast, where enemy sails could be made out through the lifting mist. It appeared to him that the fleet had separated; only a few days ago, he would not have hesitated to give voice to his thoughts. Yet now, with the added weight his position gave him, he remained silent. Instead a flutter from the top of the main course caught his eye.

"Stuns'l boom's loose on the larboard arm," he said, almost to himself. The topmen looked across; Ford nodded.

"Aye, that'll run and catch the sail if we don't look to it. Want me to take a hand, Mr Hunter?"

"Do that, would you, Ford?" Two nights back he and Ford had tied the other's queue during the second dogwatch.

Ford hauled himself up, pleased to be given a job, but Bennet was too fast for him.

"Not to worry, I'll sort it. Settle that in a jiff." Bennet was still fresh to the tops, and keen for any opportunity to practice his new found skill. Ignoring Ford he skipped out on to the yard, his feet feeling for the footrope, and began to heave himself along the spar.

"That one's a mite too keen for my liking," Church grumbled. At thirty he was getting rather too old for his post and was inclined to resent younger men. Ford said nothing as he watched Bennet attend to the boom in a reasonably seaman-like manner. Once done the man stayed where he was for a moment, enjoying the novelty of his position to gaze at the enemy ships, now visibly closer.

"Come in Bennet," Hunter called. "Stay out there much longer and the Dons'll think we've got ourselves a monkey." The rest of the top laughed; Bennet turned and beamed at them, twisting his body around and scratching under his armpit while making appropriate noises. The laughter increased, joined by some on the maintop and the deck below. Bennet became proud of his performance and failed to anticipate the sudden gust of wind that sent him tumbling off the yard, down the face of the sail and into the surprisingly cold, surprisingly hard, waters of the Atlantic.

"Man overboard!" It was Ford who gave the alarm, almost as soon as Bennet had left the yard, but Cobb, standing by the larboard rail, was the first to act. Wrenching a tightly packed hammock from the netting, he hurled it towards the spluttering figure as *Pandora* shot past.

Banks looked back at Bennet in dismay; the ship was travelling fast, a good nine knots and to turn would take her right out of station, probably for good. "Launch the jolly." There was nothing else he could do; to leave Bennet to die would be a terrible blow to morale, yet he may well never see the boat and its crew again. "Volunteers, and mind you get a move on."

There was no shortage; Dickens, from the quarterdeck carronades led the rush, closely followed by Lawlor, whose descent via the fore backstays had only been marginally slower than Bennet's, Jameson was the third, quickly joined by Flint, Wright and finally Crowley.

"Who's to command?" Banks looked about the quarterdeck, his eyes naturally falling on Cobb. The lad appeared eager, hungry even, and as Banks nodded, he gratefully ran from his place at the signals, and jumped into the jolly-boat. By the time it hit the water Bennet was more than two cables off, and the men threw themselves back on their oars, heading directly away from the speeding frigate, while the might of the Mediterranean fleet lumbered passed them.

Bennet was afloat, but spluttering badly, and clinging desperately to the sodden hammock by the time they reached him. Hauling his sodden body over the stern, the men grumbled about the wetting he gave them as, for the first time, they realised the awkward position they were now in. The British line of battle was less than a cable's length away, yet their speed would make recovering a small boat dangerous. The alternative was to try to follow the fleet in the hope that they could at least stay close enough to be noticed and picked up after the battle.

"Make for the liners!" Cobb had lost nothing of his air of command in the few hours he had been a lower deck man, and the others obeyed him instantly.

The nearest ship would be gone before they reached her, Cobb set his sights on the one behind, a seventy-four that might be *Captain* or *Namur*. There were three ships beyond that, they could try for each and if they failed, the second option remained with them.

They grew closer and men could now be seen gathering at the mainchains, equipped with boathooks and falls to catch them.

"I'll take her straight in towards the forechains, then press the helm." Cobb was eyeing the distance as he spoke, and each man had every confidence in him. "As soon as we turn row for all you're worth, you'll have to keep us up with the liner so as we can hook on.

Closer, shouts of encouragement from the battleship's crew came to them, but every man in the boat was concentrating hard. Even Bennet, who had been shivering from a mixture of exhaustion, shock, and the effect of the ice-cold water, lay still as the small boat approached the lumbering giant that now towered above them. One wrong move on behalf of Cobb would see them smashed by the massive oak hull. Closer, the bow was pointing at a space just in front of her prow, then the ship was on them, and Cobb swung the tiller and the men dug deep into the ocean as the small boat surged forward.

"That's it, in oars!" Their momentum was good enough, and Cobb wrenched the tiller over, turning the slowing boat towards the hull of the battleship. The men threw down their oars and turned on the thwarts reaching up for the lines that had been dropped for them.

"I'm on!" Flint shouted, as he wound the rope about his wrist, and waited for another call. If no one else caught hold he could well be plucked from the boat.

"And here!" Lawlor yelled. The boat increased in speed and Jameson and Cobb also caught hold of a fall. A boathook snaked down and snagged their bow as the bare head of an officer peered out above them, the single epaulette on his shoulder marking him as a commander.

"We'll not take your boat. We can send a line down if your man's injured."

"Aye, sir," Cobb yelled back without reference to Bennet. "That would be welcome."

"I don't need no line," Bennet grumbled, although his face was still deathly white.

"You'll take one and be glad of it," Flint told him, as he tied a bowline with one hand. "It's on account of your lubberly ways that we're 'ere."

The rope was passed under his arms, and soon Bennet was soaring up the side of the two-decker. The boat lightened with his leaving, making the job of holding her against the side easier. It grew easier still as Jameson, Lawlor, Wright and Crowley took turns to clamber up to the entry port. Within three minutes of their being hooked onto the seventy-four, only Flint and Cobb remained, although now the boat was backing about in the wash from the liner.

"Lines for you two," the commander told them from above. "And make sure you both leave at my count of three."

The men were quickly secured and as the officer spoke they rose up from the boat, which was left to fall away in the wake of the ship.

Flint fell against a parbuckle strip, bruised his shoulder but righted himself. Soon he was struggling across the hammock netting and into the arms of the seamen who carried him over and onto the deck.

"Welcome to *Captain*," the commander told him. "Always glad of a few extra hands; there's likely to be a mite of work for you afore the day's out."

"All aboard, Mr Berry?" The commander turned to where Captain Miller was standing next to Commodore Nelson at the break of the quarterdeck.

"Aye, sir. Safe, and sound."

"Sir Richard will be deprived of your presence, I fear," the commodore told them. "Still, his loss is our gain, and I am sure you will have no objection to fighting with the *Captains*?"

Cobb shook his head and spoke for them all. "No sir, we're more than ready."

"Very good." Nelson flashed a smile at the men. "You will be issued with pistols and cutlasses, be'chance we'll get to grips with the enemy sooner than any of us think."

*****

Their rescue was witnessed by all in *Pandora*, although soon a fresh signal was breaking out on *Victory*, and in no time their thoughts had turned away from Bennet and the fate of the jolly-boat.

"The admiral means to pass through the enemy's line." Dorsey read out the signal in a monotone, before ordering the same hoist repeated to the rest of the fleet.

Fraiser walked to the break of the forecastle and peered forward. By now the enemy ships were in clear sight; they had broken into two distinct groups, and it was Jervis's intention to place the British fleet between them.

"It'll be a close one," Caulfield said, standing a few feet away. "If that line forms up before *Culloden* arrives we'll all be running into a solid wall."

"Aye, a solid wall that shoots thirty-two pound round shot," Fraiser added.

More canvas broke out on the line ships as the British raced for the gap. By now every battleship was carrying more sail than was wise in such fluky winds, causing Banks to order topgallants to enable *Pandora* to keep her station. The frigate surged forward as the wind bit into the new canvas and all on board were charged with fresh energy as the British line bore down upon the enemy. Caulfield and Fraiser said nothing as *Culloden* closed with the first of the Spanish. As time wore on a collision appeared inevitable, but Troubridge held his course until finally, in a blaze of fire, he despatched a double-shotted broadside directly into the hull of the Spanish ship.

The enemy battleship veered away and could be seen to be in irons as the noise of the first broadside reached *Pandora*. Caulfield drew a quick breath, and in what felt like the same second *Culloden* fired again, this time causing obvious damage. The men were cheering now, although the officers were too intent on what was happening to notice, or control them.

Fraiser's eyes flew back to the flagship. "He'll tack," he said aloud, but there came no signal in confirmation.

Caulfield shook his head. "Jervie's not one to make a point and walk away, he'll keep this course until the Dons are well and truly separated."

"Aye, that's as maybe," Fraiser turned to starboard where the main body of Spanish ships were already speeding for Cadiz and safety, "but if he takes too long that wee lot will be home in time for supper."

"*Blenheim's* opened fire!"

The two turned in time to see the last of the smoke wisp away from the second ship, as the British line cut deeper into the enemy formation.

"Watch for a signal, there!" Fraiser called to Dorsey, although the lad was dutifully keeping his eyes on the flagship.

"Dollar to a guinea he'll tack in succession." Caulfield's voice was light, knowing well his friend, a solid Presbyterian, would ignore the bet.

Fraiser treated him to a scowl. "I may not be a great believer in your fighting ways, but even I know the rudiments." They both looked again towards the flagship, but still *Victory* remained mute, and still the mighty battleships thundered on relentlessly.

The awaited signal came just after noon and Caulfield would have won. *Culloden* tacked almost as the flags were broken out, and soon was heading north-west, close hauled and so near to the wind that her bowlines were as taught as fiddle strings.

Blenheim tacked on the same spot as Culloden, and soon Rear Admiral Parker's flagship, *Prince George*, was putting her helm over. As she did ships from the Spanish lee division turned towards her.

"They've smoked us," Fraiser said. "We're tacking in succession, so they're gathering to meet each ship as they come down." The enemy force was large; one, a powerful first rate, far bigger than anything the British held. *Orion* the fourth ship tacked safely, but as the fifth, *Colossus*, approached the spot, she met the full force of Spanish broadsides. The shots rained about her, throwing up deep splashes around the ship as her foremast shook, and her foreyard fell, taking the foretopsail with it. Deprived of pressure from her headsails, the battleship missed stays and lay hopelessly in irons as the Spanish closed in about her.

"That's it, she's lost. One to the Dons." Fraiser's voice was low, but it echoed the thoughts of every man in *Pandora*. On board the Spanish flagship men could be seen cheering, whilst others prepared to take the British ship in tow.

Irresistible, the sixth ship in the British line was up with her now, and began to fire into the Spanish flagship as Saumarez, in *Orion,* backed topsails and covered the stricken ship with his own broadside. *Pandora*, sailing alongside *Victory*, was almost on them, and preparations were being made to tack as *Victory* bore towards the Spanish lee division. A roar of cheering came from the flagship's crew as she passed *Colossus*, her crew struggling to secure their ship, then a roll of thunder erupted and the heavy three-decker opened fire for the first time. The well-timed broadside seemed to stun the air for a second or two as the target, a Spanish two-decker, reeled under the shock. She veered away, almost colliding with another in her eagerness to avoid a second dose from the British first rate.

The Spanish flagship was less reluctant and led a second attack, centring on *Victory* as she prepared to tack. Clearly Jervis was expecting trouble and backed topsails, stopping his ship almost directly in the Spaniard's path and forcing the enemy to bear away. Her second broadside rolled out, sending up a cloud of splinters from the enemy flagship's bow, and for several seconds afterwards the crash and clatter of falling tophamper could be heard.

"And again lads!" Caulfield's voice was almost hoarse; he realised he had been screaming with excitement for several minutes. The third broadside was fired; now the Spanish lee division was in total disarray.

Victory and *Pandora* tacked almost simultaneously and it was then, with both ships on a north-westerly course, that realisation struck. The wind had backed and was now coming across their larboard quarter, giving the square rigged ships their optimum point of sailing, but the Spanish had the same advantage, and were a good distance ahead of them. Despite the fact that the British were faster, it would be a long chase, while the heavier enemy force would be able to take turns in veering to present their full broadsides to the oncoming British.

In *Captain*, five ships behind *Victory*, and only now preparing to tack, the situation appeared far worse. Ahead of them the Spanish lee division had backed away, and was working to windward, clearly intending to meet up with the main force without further attention from the British. Jervis, in *Victory*, was heading hell for leather in chase of the larger Spanish force, but the wind backing to west south-west meant that *Captain*, and the remaining ships still waiting to tack, had had to alter course to the south, taking them further from the enemy. Nelson, standing with Miller, his captain and Berry, formerly his first lieutenant, now promoted to commander, watched as the British fleet slowly broke into two divisions. There was a very real danger that either one could be overcome by the Spanish. The entire battle might be over in a matter of hours, with little chance of any British ship seeing a home port again. A signal broke out on *Victory*, instructing *Britannia*, flagship of Vice Admiral Thompson, to tack immediately with the remaining ships to follow in succession. They were to maintain a course that would take them to leeward of the Spanish force. Jervis then instructed the van division to alter course to windward, clearly attempting to benefit from having a divided force, and effectively trapping the Spanish between two fires. All well in theory, but the remaining ships waiting to tack were making slow progress; it would be some while before they were even heading in the correct direction for the manoeuvre.

All eyes switched to *Britannia*, where Thompson was taking his time, and had yet to tack. Miller and Berry watched in silent agony, not wishing to criticise a superior officer in the presence of the commodore, yet unable to contain their feelings as the British force was steadily led in the wrong direction.

"Has that fool, Thompson, no eyes in his head?" Nelson, less restrained and with more excuse than most to miss a signal, bellowed. The repeated signals were clear to read on *Pandora* but already the second ship, *Barfleur*, had reached the spot where *Britannia* had been ordered to tack. With an element of relief they watched as Waldergrave pushed his helm over, leading the remaining ships on the correct course, leaving *Britannia*, a powerful three-decker, and a significant part of the British fleet, to sail on to the original tacking point, and effectively out of the battle.

Nelson looked to the main Spanish division, where several ships were starting to push east, clearly to begin a concentrated attack on *Culloden*, and her fellows, currently exchanging rapid fire with the rearmost enemy ships. *Victory* was also in action and could be seen amid a haze of grey smoke as her broadsides rolled out with clinical efficiency.

"The admiral is mistaken," he said, with classic bluntness. "If we wait to tack in succession there will be no time to lend support." He shifted his weight from one foot to another, clearly undecided, then added, "Unless we can attack from another point, the Dons will centre on our van and all will be lost."

There was absolute truth in what he said, although Jervis, in the thick of action, and from a different viewpoint, would be unable to appreciate the situation.

"Do you wish to signal the admiral, sir?" Berry asked. The commodore shook his head.

"It might be of little consequence, and would waste what time we have." Certainly to accurately convey the complex situation to his commander in chief was well beyond the limitations of the signal book. Nelson shook his head, and thrust his hands behind his back. "No, if it is to be done, it is to be done now. Mr Miller, I require you to wear out of formation."

Miller jerked to attention; the command was in direct contradiction of the admiral's instuctions. "Wear sir?"

"If you please."

For a moment there was silence, all on the quarterdeck were aware of the situation, and the commodore's order, although no one seemed eager to act.

"Captain Miller, there is no time to waste, the Spanish must be stopped, and it is up to us to stop them."

"Sir, it will mean that we..."

"No, not we, it will mean I, sir. I am ordering this ship out of formation, and I will take any blame that is coming, is that perfectly clear?"

Miller opened his mouth to say more, then caught the look in the commodore's eyes. "Very good, sir," he said, and turned to the first lieutenant.

*****

"Strewth, we're pulling out of line," Flint muttered. Strangers in a ship at action stations, they were somewhat at a loss and the former crew of *Pandora's* jolly-boat had gathered at the break of the quarterdeck, awaiting employment. They watched as the ship was taken out of line, and turned with the wind. They passed in between *Excellent* and *Diadem*, noticed the surprised faces of the crew of both, and before long were heading at ninety degrees from the line of battle. The seas began to fly as *Captain* gathered speed, and soon they were entirely alone, the nearest British ship to windward being some three miles off, while directly ahead of them lay eighteen heavy battleships of the Spanish Navy.

CHAPTER SIXTEEN

In the very midst of a fleet action, with heavy battleships exchanging mighty broadsides all about her, *Pandora* sailed with impunity. Partly it was the universally agreed convention that a ship of the line shall not fire upon a frigate, unless the smaller vessel has been rash enough to fire first. And partly it was the more realistic notion that a broadside from a two or three-decker, one that might have taken four or five minutes and up to three hundred men to load, would be wasted on the frail hull of a ship that could do negligible damage to the sturdy frame of a liner. Still, amid the carnage, the crew stood to quarters. Both cutters swung from the quarterdeck davits, prepared to lower at a moment's notice and the launch and barge connected to their tackle, ready to swing out and manned for boarding or rescue.

Below, in the cockpit that was quickly becoming a mixture of dressing station, operating theatre and morgue, Stuart and Manning were already at work. *Pandora* had been hit by a stray thirty-two-pound round shot from a Spanish three-decker. She had suffered no material harm, but three members of the larboard forecastle carronade had been struck. One, Tunstill, a former weaver, was killed outright, and duly despatched over the side. The other two, the Morris brothers were now below, sharing their fate under the hands of the medical team, just as they had shared their lives. The older man by three years who was known as Pug, for reasons long forgotten, had been wounded on the shoulder, the shot passing on to hit his brother's right arm, which now hung by a thread as Manning prepared to finish the work. At the same time Stuart considered Pug's blistered and partly opened chest. The shoulder was shattered and most of his flesh across to the sternum was torn. Little could be done to save the left arm, but neither could he remove it without disturbing the already damaged muscles of the chest, and encouraging further blood loss. Pressing the flesh back as best he could, the surgeon wrapped the entire torso in a wide bandage, trapping the arm against the chest, and pulling the windings as tight as possible to restrict the blood letting. When he had finished the man looked almost presentable and, trusting Stuart far more than was his due, took his laudanum and rum, before falling into a deep and final sleep. Manning was fairing better with Michael; the arm was strong, without fat, and came away cleanly. He tied off the arteries efficiently enough, even though it was a relatively novel procedure for him. The stump was also stitched neatly, and the wound sealed with turpentine and the pledget set before the leather tourniquet was released. Throughout the operation he spoke in a soft, but often distracted tone to the man who, wide-awake though shivering horribly, listened with an air of hope and wonder.

"You finished with your mutterings?" Stuart asked sharply, as Michael was laid next to his brother, and the two left to ride out their own personal battles. "'Cause if your prattle don't kill half the people, it's knocking seven bells out of me."

Manning watched as the surgeon turned from wiping his hands on his already soiled apron, to swig from the obligatory bottle of Hollands. He decided that no reply was called for and, as a topman was brought down with a bruised head and a broken arm, he attended to him with no further thought of Stuart.

*****

For some while Fraiser and Caulfield had been watching as *Captain* carved her lonely course towards the enemy. The seventy-four was almost level with them now, and must be obvious to *Victory*, currently in the thick of action with two Spanish ships, the signal 'engage the enemy more closely' seemingly nailed to her yard. *Captain* should be in action within minutes and some support would be needed if she were not to be lost within the hour. Directly ahead of both *Victory* and *Pandora*, Collingwood, in *Excellent,* had joined the admiral's line to the windward side of the enemy, while *Diadem* and *Irresistible* were equally engaged to leeward, their shots occasionally hulling, or passing over the Spanish, to fall perilously close to *Victory*.

"Hot work," Caulfield commented briskly, then looking across at *Captain*, whose first broadside had just been released, "and hotter soon for some." *Culloden* had come across and was now in a position to support the commodore, although they were woefully ill matched compared with the heavy warships they would engage.

"Flag's signalling!" Dorsey sang out, before writing down the numbers on his pad. "To *Diadem* and *Irresistible*, sir. Restrict fire."

Sensible words, clearly the two British ships were oblivious to the risk they were running to their own flagship, and had not ordered first reduction on their powder.

"Parker's coming to support Nelson." Caulfield spun round to look where Fraiser was pointing, and sure enough *Prince George*, along with two other liners, was creeping up behind *Captain* and *Culloden*. Their presence might well persuade the Spaniards to back off, but even with this assistance the British would be heavily outnumbered. At that moment *Captain* disappeared amid the double smoke of exchanged broadsides and it looked highly unlikely that any help could arrive in time to save her.

*****

On board *Captain* at least some of the crew of the jolly-boat had found employment. Four men had fallen at one of the quarterdeck carronades, and a lieutenant had ordered them in to assist. Jameson had taken over the lambs wool sponge, and was washing the barrel free of embers after each discharge, in time for Flint to ram a fresh charge into the still warm metal. Lawlor and Wright acted as tackle-men; within two broadsides the four were working with the others of the gun crew as if they had been born together.

A master's mate spotted Crowley, Cobb, Bennet and Dickens standing useless on the gangway.

"There'll be close hand work afore long," he said, pointing his thumb back over his shoulder. "You men prepare yourselves as boarders; pistols and cutlasses by the main."

They walked across as another broadside rolled out behind them. Bennet reached in and picked up two cutlasses in each hand and held two out to Dickens and Cobb. One he placed in his own waistband, and the last was offered to Crowley. The Irishman hesitated, and actually drew back; this was not what he had volunteered for, following a man you respected was one thing, as was rescuing a fellow from certain death, but to fight for King George, that was quite another matter.

"What you worried about?" Bennet asked him artlessly. It was well known amongst the men that Crowley had come over from the French, but he was an Irishman after all; a neutral almost, and could be forgiven most things. Besides he spoke their language: didn't he know what side he should be on?

"If you're not willing to fight you may report to the surgeon," Cobb said. The voice was firm, his words reasonable and belied both his age and reduced status. Crowley considered for a second; then a scream of enemy bar shot came about them, forcing all to the deck and sending a rain of blocks and shrouds down.

"Axe men, axe men, there!" A midshipman was screaming from forward where the foretopmast had fallen onto the deck. A rush of men came forward to assist, and in the confusion Crowley collected the cutlass from where it had dropped, and placed it in his waistband.

*****

In *Pandora*, action seemed to be taking place on every quarter while time sped past at an ever-increasing rate.

"Flagship's signalling," Dorsey shouted yet again, his voice growing hoarse. Banks made a note to commend him later; the lad had carried out his duties in an exemplary manner, and might even warrant promotion.

"*Excellent's* number, sir. Pass through the enemy line." It seemed that Jervis had finally recognised Nelson's position to leeward and was sending him further reinforcement. Such had the battle moved that *Captain* and *Excellent* were barely half a mile apart now, although there were several enemy ships between them. Even assuming Collingwood could bring his ship into a position to be of help, it would not be a speedy deliverance. One of the Spanish, a massive four-decker, opened up as she moved away. The seventy-four looked almost insignificant against the mighty warhorse that loomed over her.

"There's over a hundred and ten guns in that beast if there's a dozen," Lewis muttered to Conroy as they watched from the forecastle.

"Aye, but it don't seem to cause them trouble."

Sure enough Collingwood was replying in brisk, and definite style, sending two carefully aimed broadsides back for every one he received. In no time the damage was starting to show on the larger ship, and soon her broadside rate had dropped, eventually breaking down to individual guns being fired as they were loaded. *Excellent* continued its previous crack rate of fire, with every round digging deep into the very heart of the first rate.

"They've struck!" The cry came from Lewis, but it was universally accepted by all on board. The colours had come down, and *Excellent* had broached to, and was hailing her capture.

"Larboard the helm," Banks ordered suddenly. "Lay her alongside; *Excellent* has her orders; we can take over here."

The frigate moved in slowly, the wind was all but dispersed by the broadsides that were raging about her, but soon she was creeping up behind *Excellent*, who was moving on, gratefully leaving the job of securing the prize to *Pandora*.

"*Salvador del Mundo,*" Conroy said, reading out the name on the big ship's counter. "There's a mouthful an' half."

"Cutter's away, marines and boarders." Banks took a pace or two towards the fife rail, "Mr King, you have experience of these matters, I collect?"

King glanced back and smiled ruefully, remembering so well the shattered remains of *Aiguille*. He exchanged nods with Rose, who moved to the centre of the deck, and made his way aft to the quarterdeck. Lieutenant Martin was preparing his marines to board the larboard cutter as *Pandora* drew level with the silent Spanish battleship, now wallowing with the swell less than half a cable away. There was little movement on board and all thoughts in *Pandora* were for how they should deal with securing her.

Banks was on the quarterdeck; next to him stood Caulfield and Fraiser. King turned and caught the eye of Dorsey, at his signal station. "Don't feel like coming along this time, then?" he asked. The lad grinned and shook his head. Then there came the unexpected crash of nearby thunder. The noise continued, growing in intensity and volume, gathering power with every fraction of a second until the world went black as the Spanish ship released a full and deadly broadside directly into the British frigate.

*****

HMS *Captain*, a seventy-four, was now engaged with the *San Nicolas*, who mounted more than eighty-four guns and the *San Josef*, a first rate of over one hundred and twelve. On the quarterdeck carronade Flint, Jameson and Wright had been joined by Cobb and Bennet, who replaced two further casualties. Lawlor was one; in the midst of a broadside a twenty-four-pound shot had accounted for him. It had been horrific in its simplicity; one moment the Welshman was there, hauling on the train and grumbling about the work, and the girls that would be missing him in Gibraltar, the next he lay dead, barely recognisable as human, let alone a friend. And now he was gone, swabbed over the side like so much waste. Bennet had taken his place, and to the men who worked the carronade it was almost as if he had never been.

They moved with the regularity of machines and in total silence, albeit the roar of battle was all about them. *Captain* had been severely mauled, and was now little more than a wreck, although she had caused serious damage to both ships, and her broadsides still rolled out with parade ground regularity.

"*Excellent's* coming to larboard!" the dry voice of a lieutenant croaked, and sure enough the bulk of Collingwood's ship could be seen as she squeezed between *Captain* and the *San Nicolas*.

"Cease firing, Check, Check, Check!" the lieutenant yelled again. His words appeared to have no effect as all crews continued to load their weapons. Bennet heaved the carronade forward in its slide into the firing position, before slumping down on the deck with his fellows. *Excellent* was now level with them and pouring fresh broadsides into the enemy, giving the crew of *Captain* a chance to rest and secure their ship.

On the quarterdeck the commodore exchanged salutes with Collingwood, captain of *Excellent*, and a friend of many years, before turning to assess the situation. Miller was deep in conversation with the first lieutenant; only Berry had time to talk.

"I could make a signal for a frigate to take you off, sir?" he suggested.

Nelson looked back to where a heavy pall of smoke covered the last sighting of HMS *Pandora* and shook his head. "No, Edward, there is fight in the *Captain* left. And when she is finished we'll raise some more for boarders."

Excellent's broadsides continued to pound into the Spanish ships, and it was difficult to note any returning fire. The officers peered through the dense grey smoke.

"Stand by your pieces, there!" Collingwood's ship was still moving, indeed, would be clear of *Captain* in no time and they would have to start work again.

"I believe the enemy have run aboard each other, sir." Berry said in a tone that was almost conversational. Nelson peered through the smoke, but what sight he had in his undamaged left eye was not good and he could make out nothing definite. Then a gust of wind cleared the air for a second, and the two ships were revealed. It was just as Berry had said, the *San Nicolas* must have luffed away from *Excellent's* relentless fire, and now stood almost broadside on to the flagship, their yardarms deeply enmeshed.

"Captain Miller. The enemy is disabled. Chance that you could take us alongside?"

Miller looked at the two ships, then up at the tangle of rags that was all *Captain* now possessed in the way of sails.

"Aye, sir. We can luff up and broach her starboard quarter, if that would suffice."

Nelson nodded. "Make it so, and call for boarders."

The men from *Pandora's* jolly-boat heard the cry, and fired off the last charge from their carronade before abandoning the piece. Two men were handing out further small arms; Bennet collected a wicked looking tomahawk, while Cobb took a boarding pistol, and two charges. Crowley also helped himself to a pistol, and loaded it with care. He would go with the boarders because that was what everyone else was doing. All about him men were fighting and dying, for whatever reason he had placed himself on one side and this was not the time to change coat, or turn neutral. He loaded the pistol carefully, over filling the priming pan and closing the frizzen, before throwing the second charge away. There was no room in his mind for any other thoughts.

"On the forecastle, form up." Two infantry lieutenants were organising the boarding parties; the *Pandora's* picked their way along the battered gangway. On the quarterdeck Captain Miller removed his coat and went to follow. The commodore stepped forward, and placed his arm on the officer's shoulder.

"No, Miller, I must have that honour. Look to your ship."

Nelson had already thrown off his coat and now wound the lanyard of his plain but functional fighting sword about his wrist. The forecastle was filled with men, but a path cleared as he approached and there was a murmur of approval as the commodore made his way to the very front. For a captain to lead a boarding party was rare enough, for a commodore of the first class, one due to be gazetted admiral any day, was quite unheard of. The ships were drawing closer and the dull thud of small arms fire could be heard as the Spanish attempted to pick off the British before they attacked. Dickens fell, struck in the thigh by a musket ball that knocked him off balance and sent him into the dark waters beneath. Without a conscious thought those behind took one pace forward and filled his space.

"Take the poop, Berry," Nelson shouted to the commander, who was standing farther forward on the trunk of the bowsprit. "My party will move through the stern. Berry nodded, and *Captain's* sprit yard passed over the Spanish ship. Then the two met with a slight jolt and the crash and grind of splintering timbers.

The first across were soldiers of the 69th regiment, led by a lieutenant who bellowed orders even as he leapt. Bennet found himself next to the rail and jumped the short distance to the shattered stern windows of the battleship. He half fell, half tumbled over the ledge, only to be trodden on by Cobb, who came immediately behind him. Wright was next, taking a more sedate route over the larboard bower anchor, which was wedged tightly against the enemy's starboard quarter-gallery. He gripped hold of a piece of timber, and swung himself though the shattered window, landing inside the quarter-gallery itself, right next to the captain's privy. Crowley followed him, and the two pushed the small sliding door to one side, and moved out into the cabin that now seemed to be filled with shouting men.

Watching from behind, Flint felt his bowels turn to water. The sudden urge to bolt was all but quelled by the knowledge that there was nowhere to run; on either side men were pushing him forward, the only option was to drop down between the two ships, and that would mean certain death. A scream gathered in his throat, and as he made the leap with Jameson, it came out in a horrible blood-curdling cry.

Then they were in the Spanish captain's cabin. Jameson turned to grin at him, but Flint did not respond. The only thought in his head was to move, to quit the room as fast as possible. Behind him more men were pouring in through the opened windows, his only escape lay in the doors at the end of the cabin.

Nelson was standing in the centre talking to one of the infantry lieutenants. A shot came in through the shattered skylight and struck a soldier next to him. Crowley looked up to see several men on the deck above pointing muskets at the intruders below. Without further thought he raised his own pistol and shot one of them dead. Then the crowd dispersed, presumably by the arrival of Berry's men as they attacked the poop. Crowley considered the pistol for a moment; the shot had been instinctive, one of self defence almost, but now that it had been fired there seemed no going back, and he pressed on with the crowd towards the doors that would lead them out onto the quarterdeck.

"Forward, forward and on!" Nelson's voice roared out, and they made their way as one body towards the double doors.

Bennet, near to the front, was horrified to see dark jagged holes appear in the panelling. "They're firing through!" he yelled, ducking down. An officer bellowed an order, and musket shots began to rain down on the doors as the British soldiers responded.

The commodore was there again, moving forward, leading from the front. "Axe men, take out those doors!"

Bennet looked stupidly at his hand that still held the tomahawk, before stepping forward. There were three other men with far larger axes, and between them they hacked out the hinges, pressing the ornately panelled doors down in front of them. The shout to secure themselves came just in time for Bennet's party to drop to the deck, as a second volley of musket fire bit into the crowd of Spanish that were waiting for them. Bennet stayed where he was and the boarders charged over him. Flint, Cobb and Jameson went next to Commodore Nelson as they barged through to the quarterdeck. Wright was midway in the throng, while Crowley, who had tripped in the crowd, arrived with the last of them.

A Spanish officer, brilliant in his crimson and blue uniform, stood in front of Cobb. Without a thought the lad brought up his pistol. He squeezed the trigger; the pan flashed impotently and there was no shot. Flinging the useless weapon away he went to raise his cutlass, but the man had already disappeared.

"Deck clear, sir!" Nelson turned to see Berry standing by the poop ladder, a grin on his blackened face. Forward the Spanish crew were retreating from the guns on the upper deck, taking refuge in the forecastle. More men were coming across from *Captain*, and it would take little effort now to secure the entire ship.

"Very good, Edward. Take down the colours, if you please." Berry raised his hand to touch the hat that had fallen off some while ago, and grinned foolishly.

A Spanish officer stepped forward and offered his sword to the commodore. Two more followed, one of whom looked no older than a boy. The deck shuddered as the Spanish thirty-two-pounders opened fire on the lower deck. Forward the *Prince George* could be seen off the starboard bow. Nelson turned to one of the infantry lieutenants. "Take a party and one of these officers below and inform the people their ship has surrendered." The lieutenant unceremoniously dragged an officer away, and thrust him down the nearest companionway.

After the brutality of the battle there came an uncertain pause; then shots started to rain down from above, and men began to fall.

"The flagship!" Berry yelled from the poop, pointing up to the tangle of spars and rigging that had caused the ship to be taken. Sure enough Spanish marksmen on the tops of the first rate were firing down on the British. The *San Josef* towered above them, and was perfectly placed to send boarders across to retake the prize.

Nelson brought his hands up and bellowed across to *Captain*. "Mr Miller, more boarders, if you please!" Then raising his sword once more, he turned towards the Spanish flagship.

Crowley and Wright, their blood up from the fighting, followed Nelson's lead without hesitation. The commodore was one of the first across, accompanied by his coxswain, John Sykes, who parried a cutlass swipe that would have ended his commander's career in decapitation. A short climb, then up and over the rail; the men clambered, cursing and screaming, while shots from the British soldiers flew up above their heads, knocking down the marksmen in the tops.

Cobb made his way across without difficulty, and soon stood on the deck of the Spanish first rate, a blooded cutlass in his hand. He looked about, somewhat bewildered. Rather than the rush of fighting men he was expecting, the ship appeared deserted; presumably the crew had taken refuge below once they had considered boarding to be inevitable.

Above them, on the quarterdeck, a Spanish officer brought his sword up high into the air, only to toss it down, hilt first, at the feet of the British. Cobb picked the weapon up; it was jewelled and heavily ornate; a splendid exhibition piece, but not a fighting weapon. He looked back to where Nelson was collecting more swords from the vanquished officers, passing each back to a seaman who stuffed them under his arm like so much firewood. One of the officers was speaking in broken English. The admiral, Don Francisco Winthuyen, was wounded below. It was considered that he would die, and he sent his compliments to the victors, together with his sword, to be surrendered with the rest. Cobb heard the words as if in a dream. He turned to see Jameson and Flint, squatting down on the deck. The younger man was bleeding from a wound in his left forearm, and Flint was tying his own shirt about it. Men of the 69th had assembled the Spanish crew next to the larboard rail and were standing guard while two corporals searched them. Bennet was nowhere to be seen, neither was Wright, but more men were coming across from the *San Nicolas* now, and the *Prince George* was athwart their bow, her guns still pointing at the vanquished ships, and her decks teeming with men eager to help secure the prizes. About them the battle continued. He had not seen *Pandora* for some while, and there would be a lot more fighting before the sun came down to put an end to the action. But this particular episode had drawn to a close, and the lad was not sorry.

CHAPTER SEVENTEEN

King heaved himself up from the deck where he had fallen. His head hurt; something had struck him just above the left temple: he felt dizzy and sick. He rested on all fours, waiting for the spinning to stop. There was a loud, pitchless buzzing in his head and his tongue felt dry and too large for his mouth. To one side there was movement; he turned suddenly, the sound increased, and he had to fight to control the wave of nausea that threatened to envelop him. He pushed himself further upright, and sat back on the deck. Apart from the buzzing, there was no sound. *Pandora* had ceased to fight; the broadside had all but accounted for her.

"Are you sound, Thomas?" It was the captain, very much alive, and even smiling.

"Aye, sir. Just a bit shaken."

Caulfield was next to him, extending a plump hand. King took it and felt himself being heaved upwards with unexpected strength.

"Passed you by, it seems," he said. "You were lucky. Can't say the same for our friend Martin, though."

King followed his glance to where two marines were dealing with Martin's body.

"What of the ship, are we bad?" King mumbled. Caulfield's face was white with shock, but other than that he seemed unhurt. He shook his head.

227

"No, like most Don broadsides, all wind and roar. Took a nasty to the mainchains; Fraiser's seeing to that now with the bosun. The foretopmast was hit in two places but holding for now, apart from that most of the top hamper's rather a mash; carpenter's due to make a report on the hull presently."

"How long was I out for?"

Caulfield shrugged. "Couldn't rightly say; a fair while. Seemed better to leave you to sleep as you were judged to be breathing. We've had to fall back, of course, but I reckons we can let the battle wagons sort it out from here on. We've done sufficient for a tiddler."

Sure enough the frigate had fallen off the wind, and now wallowed on the swell. What sails she had left were mostly holed or torn, and flapped impudently in the breeze. At a glance her damage did not seem bad, she might even be expected to take sail right away, although the fore topmast could withstand very little strain and, without the support of the chains, the main would be almost as unstable.

"I see." The wind was suddenly very cold, and for the first time since they were hit the sounds of the battle came to them. King rubbed his arms with his hands. A trickle of blood came down from his forehead, and when he reached up he found an open cut that was bleeding steadily. Having fallen back, *Pandora* was effectively left behind, the battle continuing ahead of them. They could see *Victory* along with other British ships as they continued the fight. Over the starboard bow a small huddle of ships were lying in silence. Two appeared to have struck while in the distance ahead and to larboard, the rest of the Spanish were stoically making for Cadiz.

Britannia, with Thompson's flag flying proudly, was the nearest British ship. Delayed by her late tack, she had all plain sail set, and was heading for the enemy with the obvious haste of a latecomer. As they watched a flurry of bunting broke out at her yard; presumably she was enquiring after *Pandora*, or the state of the battle. Dorsey rushed forward, but he had lost his signal book, along with most of the flags. Five men from the afterguard turned up and began clearing away the debris that still crowded the quarterdeck. Lewis appeared in a torn jacket and began to organise the waisters into working parties. A nine-pounder that had been blown free of its tackle was being secured by a group from the forecastle, while two men who had been knocked unconscious by falling tophamper were carried down to the cockpit. Below, the

carpenter and his team had already started work on the three jagged holes that had pierced the hull just above the waterline and
the sail maker was rousting out fresh canvas ready for the time
when they could set sail once more.

The petty officers did what they could to allocate the work,
bearing in mind the relative urgency and each man's individual
skills, while the men pulled together in such a way that any short-
falls or omissions in one was more than made up by his fellows. A
ragged cheer came from the British ships ahead, followed by several cracking broadsides; clearly the action was still raging, although the men in *Pandora* were fighting their own private battle.
Whatever Caulfield might have said, no frigate faces the broadside
of a first rate without sustaining serious damage, and it was with
care, skill and not a little love that they nursed their ship back to
life.

King had done his best to ignore his wound and had been helping to remount one of the quarterdeck carronades. He turned to
Fraiser who had returned from securing the main chains and now
stood watching the battle with the air of a dispassionate spectator
while one of Stuart's loblolly boys who had been sent up for the
purpose, strapped a bandage about his injured forearm. "Surely
the Spaniard had struck?" he said, feeling not a little foolish as he
did; so much had happened in such a short time that he was starting to doubt his sanity.

"Aye, she'd struck all right, but then she took a change of
heart."

King was puzzled. "No, but that's wrong, she can't do that."

Fraiser gave a sudden and bitter smile. "Some might say she
could, and some might say she could'ne; fact is she did." He
winced suddenly as the bandage was pulled tight. "And as to the
rights or wrongs of the matter, war's a barbaric act however you
look at it, and certainly not something to be governed by rules or
honour."

They could both see the four-decker now, *Victory*, and a
seventy-four were close to her, and from the look of the punishment they were handing out, she would be striking for the second
time before very long. King supposed Fraiser was right, there was
little point in looking for reason when men choose to kill one another as a means to an end.

"Hey, laddie, you're shivering." Fraiser turned to him. "Reckon
you'd better get below and let the doctor take you in hand."

King shook his head, the dizziness returned and he felt the world grow slightly hazy. The loblolly boy caught him as he was about to fall and, as if in a dream, he found himself being helped below by two unknown bodies. They left him lying on a patch of canvas roughly three feet away from where he usually berthed. After lying still for a moment he felt his strength return, and pulled himself up to lean against the spirketing. To one side, Dupont, the captain's servant, was waiting patiently, one hand clapped about a wound on his left thigh; opposite there were several seaman and two marines who were also supporting minor wounds, while further on less distinct shapes lay prone and unconscious. To his right he could see the surgeon's mate silhouetted against the swinging lamps as he worked. There was a sudden shout from his patient, instantly stifled by Soames, the purser, who appeared to be assisting. As he watched, Manning straightened himself up and said something to Soames as the patient was carried away. Their eyes met as he looked back to see the number waiting and Manning gave him a tired smile. Cleaning the worst from his hands on some tow, he walked away from the makeshift operating table and over to where King lay.

"Done for you at last, have they, Thomas?" he asked.

"Not yet, belike that job's been left to you and Mr Stuart."

There was a flash in Manning's eye, and he indicated behind him with a shake of his head. "The latter I would certainly not recommend."

King looked at the line of waiting wounded, and was horrified to see the surgeon amongst them. Apparently comatose, he lay in a foetal position, his arms gripping something tight to his belly.

"I took him for a stomach wound," King said, the surprise evident in his voice.

"Brain more like. Our friend has allowed two bottles of spirit into a belly already filled with the dear knows how much laudanum."

"But that will kill him, surely?"

Manning snorted. "In a normal person, doubtless. A lot will depend on what he's made himself accustomed to," he sighed. "But we live in hope." King was struck by the strain that was evident on his face; it was a look that even the poor light could not hide. "At least most of the dangerously wounded have been attended to, so there's no real trouble." As he talked he wiped his hands unconsciously on his apron. "A couple of hours will put this little lot back on their feet, and by then Stuart should either be sober or dead. Either way I wouldn't expect him to hold his warrant for much longer."

"Does the captain know?"

"Doubtless the captain has more important things on his mind at present, but I dare say he will get word."

King nodded, and the pain and dizziness returned. Manning noticed this and placed a restraining hand on his shoulder. "Hey, I won't be tiring you." He brought his hand up and felt about King's scalp, exploring it with his fingers before standing back, and smiling once more. "It's not a bad one, a bit of stitching should sort you. Take your place with the others; I'll give you a proper eye afore long."

"I'm fine, just a bit shaken."

"There's a few down here like that, but it's best to be safe." A loud crash from above told how the foretopmast had finally fallen. A rumble of feet, followed by several shouts followed. Manning raised his eyes. "'Sides, there's no telling what's going on up there. Best keep out of it."

*****

By twenty-past four Jervis decided he had exposed his fleet for long enough and ordered all ships who were capable of it to come onto the starboard tack. Enemy reinforcements could be seen to the north, while eight ships of the Spanish lee division were now approaching from the south. Nine minutes later a second order to form line ahead in close order came, frustrating Saumarez in *Orion* who, along with Collingwood in *Excellent* and Frederick's *Blenheim* had been battering the Spanish flagship *Santissima Trinidad* for the best part of half an hour. To them it seemed they were being called away just at the point of victory, yet Jervis was conscious that, however well the British fleet had fared, they still faced a force considerably larger than their own. Most of his ships were now weakened by several hours of action, action that had also severely depleted their store of powder and shot. To continue would be foolhardy; now was the time to close ranks and protect their prizes.

As dusk fell Commodore Nelson finally quit the battered *Captain*, temporarily transferring his pendant back to the frigate *Minerve*, that brought him to meet with Jervis in *Victory*. Despite taking two prizes, one of which being a first rate, Nelson was very well aware that he could not expect to be in favour. At best he had acted on initiative; at worse, by wearing out of line, he had weakened the British force at a time when it was already separated. Worse, he had wantonly exposed his ship and men to devastating odds; it might easily be said that luck alone had kept both from being taken by the Spanish.

They met on the quarterdeck, the commodore dressed in the torn jacket he had worn before boarding the *San Nicolas*. In turn, Jervis' face was blackened by smoke, his uniform bore the record of a marine who had fallen next to him, and his red rimmed eyes betrayed the lie that an elderly admiral could stay awake for over forty hours, then fight a battle, without it affecting him. Nelson removed his hat in salute to his commander in chief, who promptly encased the younger man in his arms, hugging him as if he were a much loved son.

"Tremendous work, Horace, tremendous." The admiral's tone was almost tender, and he used Nelson's familiar name like a father. Hallowell joined them, adding his own congratulations, along with a bear hug that caused the commodore to wince and pull away.

"Are you hurt, sir?"

Nelson straightened up and shook his head, but his hand went down to his belly and he was clearly in pain. "A strain, no more, it will pass directly."

"What of *Captain*," Jervis, once more the admiral, demanded. "Can she be made fit for port?"

"Yes, oh yes, with care she will see England, although her people are fagged at present."

The admiral glanced about the darkening horizon. "Martin's *Irresistible* is relatively unhurt; transfer to her directly, we will make for Tagus as soon as the last close up."

Never one who sought delay, Nelson made to go at once, pausing only to take the cold hand of Calder who wished him joy of his captures in a voice innocent of emotion. Jervis watched him leave, a fond, paternal smile upon his face. Calder turned to him.

"The commodore holds luck close to his chest." He gave one weak, condescending, smile. "Belike he should be more careful when exhibiting initiative in future. Certainly when that initiative is so contrary to fighting instructions."

Jervis eyed him with ill concealed contempt. "It certainly was so, and if you ever commit such a breach of orders, I will forgive you also."

*****

As the following morning broke the Spanish fleet was still in sight. Hull up to the north-west, they lay in an untidy group. Several had lost masts, and one, the *Santissima Trinidad*, was little more than a hulk. King took over the forenoon watch at eight and stood looking back at them, fascinated by the sight of so powerful an enemy lying close by. His head was bare, the bandage Manning had used being too large to accommodate his hat, and he wore a heavy watch coat that almost covered the fact he was otherwise dressed in purser's slops. The ship was still cleared for action, and he could see little chance of reaching his chest for fresh clothes until they raised Portugal. As the watch ran on Lewis came to join him; he too was dressed very much as a scarecrow, the effect being heightened by his face, which was dark with grime. All on board had spent the night securing the ship; as a result she now appeared in remarkably good order, with a brand new spar to take the place of the foretopmast. The fleet was still at their night stations, with *Pandora* lying two cables off *Victory*, once more ready to relay any signals. Ahead their four prizes; prime Spanish ships, one a first rate, were being taken under tow. The fire that had threatened to claim the *San Nicolas* had been successfully dealt with, although there would still be much to do before any of them were able to sail unassisted. From where he stood King could see the lines of British infantry, men of the 69th who had stood in place of marines so handsomely, as they organised the prisoners. He remembered, only too well, the scene on board the *Aiguille*, and was not sorry to be watching from afar.

At five bells a commotion from the waist caught his attention. The men were peering over at something in the water close by. King followed their gaze, and saw a ship's cutter drawing in her sails as she came alongside. Dorsey hailed the boat, then stood back; both watches were on deck and a mixture of cheers and cat-calls erupted from them as the cutter's crew began to disembark. Flint was first, followed by Jameson, who had a bandaged arm. Then Crowley. Their eyes met and the Irishman gave King a grin and an offhand salute as he clambered up the side. Bennet came next, the cause of the trouble in the first place. Hoots of mock derision greeted him, along with a half-eaten orange that someone had thrown for good measure. Then Wright, who looked tired, and smiled weakly at his reception. Cobb was the last; the lad also appeared weary and almost shy as he boarded *Pandora*. His reception was different, no one was quite sure of his status and what had been a roar was suddenly muted, before dying away to nothing at all. The lad stood upright on the gangway looking down uncertainly at the people. He appeared to be about to say something, when Wright turned back, reached for the lad's arm, and held it aloft. The men from the boat cheered and clapped, followed, after the shortest of pauses, by the entire ship's company. Lewis turned to smile at King as the chaos finally died away and the ship returned to normality.

"Appears the lad done well," he said. "Captain'll make him back to midshipman, sure as a gun."

King nodded. He held no personal animosity for the boy; a prank was a prank after all. To take Pigot's clothes and play the fool was really quite enterprising; it was only his timing that hadn't been quite up to the mark.

The diversion over, all eyes went back to the Spanish fleet.

"Think they'll give us trouble?" Lewis asked.

King sighed. "Who can tell with the Dons? We have one of their admirals, though doubtless there will be others to take his place."

"He died in the night."

"In truth? I had heard him wounded."

"Maybe they're after revenge, an' and maybe they aren't. The next few hours will tell."

*****

The bell rang six times, it was eleven o'clock, an hour before the end of the forenoon watch, an hour until up spirits and dinner, though little could be expected of the latter with the ship cleared for action and no meat in the steep tubs. The sentries called out their statutory "all's well" and when the last cry had died away, the masthead lookout reported a change in the Spanish fleet.

"Enemy appears to be forming line of battle."

At the words the tired men looked to one another. To fight again, to repeat all that had gone on the day before, seemed totally impossible, and yet as the lookout reported the Spanish ships advancing, every man automatically took up his action station without comment.

"*Victory's* signalling, sir," Dorsey's voice rang out just as Banks appeared on deck. "Close about flag and form line of battle."

Banks nodded, and watched as the hoist was repeated to the fleet. They had fought well, and given the Spanish a terrible drubbing, but the British were in poor shape for a second bout. Slowly they took up their positions in the line, some under jury rigs, and more than a few sending clean jets of water from the dales as their people desperately fought against the shot holes that were threatening to take their ship from under them. The Spanish had certainly received reinforcements yesterday evening. More may well have joined them in the night; fresh ships, manned with men eager to avenge the day before; the more he thought about it the more an uncomfortable feeling inside told him that the battle would finally be seen as a British defeat.

Banks began to pace the quarterdeck, his hands clasped behind his back. Fraiser and Caulfield were standing in front of the taffrail looking forward, while King still officially had the conn, and was with Lewis and Parry, the senior quartermaster, by the wheel. All were tired, and all were waiting for the orders that would send them into battle once more. Then Banks stopped in his pacing and looked to the masthead.

"What of the enemy?"

Although clearly in sight from the deck, the height of the main mast would give a better perception of the fleet's movements.

"No change, sir. Still heading towards us; wait, no, they're coming around."

All eyes on deck turned towards the far-off ships; sure enough the leading Spanish first rate was visibly altering course, her braces swinging round until her hull was almost parallel with the British line. Banks looked doubtfully at Caulfield, who shrugged and shook his head. They might be intending to form a line, then wear once more in succession, although that would be foolish tactics, as each ship would mask her neighbour's broadside. The men on the quarterdeck watched in puzzled silence, as the line was seen to alter course once more.

"They're pulling out," Frasier said softly, although his words carried across the silent deck.

"Aye," Caulfield nodded. "Belikes they've had enough of us for one season."

The ships were clearly heading away now, and throughout the British line men drew breath and thanked whatever they held dear. A loud retort rang out; the *Barfleur* had fired a gun, either by accident or in salute it was hard to say; there was no chance of doing damage, the enemy were now considerably out of range.

"*Victory's* making another hoist." Dorsey's voice held the tone of wonder. "Not a signal though, she's raising the Spanish flag."

Once more all turned to look; sure enough the Spanish ensign could be seen boldly flying from the British flagship's jack.

"*Culloden's* hoisted one too!" a voice from the lower deck shouted, "and *Orion*."

Caulfield looked to Banks and received a nod in reply. The first lieutenant bellowed an order, and soon *Pandora* had joined the rest of the British ships, who now all flew the Spanish ensign.

King walked over to Fraiser and smiled. "A nice compliment," he said.

The master nodded. "Aye, it's always good to show respect."

"Hardly the act of barbarians, though."

Fraiser smiled and placed a hand on King's shoulder. "I said war was barbaric, and it is; there's few who could be doubting that." His eyes twinkled. "Mind, there's nothing to say that it cannot be fought by gentlemen."

CPSIA information can be obtained
at www.ICGtesting.com
Printed in the USA
LVOW03s1756050118
561978LV00001B/90/P